RECLAIMING LOVE

Praise for Amanda

Under Her Influence

"Light, sweet, and remarkably chaste, this sapphic love story will make as enjoyable a vacation pick as it is an armchair getaway."—*Publishers Weekly*

"My heart is just…filled with love and warmth! Finally, I have found an author who does not rely on sex to make a book interesting!! I'm probably going to go on an Amanda Radley read-a-thon."—*Periwinkle Pens*

"*Under Her Influence* by Amanda Radley is a sweet love story and leaves the reader feeling happy and contented. And that's exactly what I want from a romance these days. Ms Radley keeps angst to a minimum and lets her readers enjoy the blossoming of love between her characters."—*Kitty Kat's Book Review Blog*

Detour to Love

"If you're on the lookout for well-written sapphic romance with stellar characters, wonderful pairings, and outstanding plots, I wholeheartedly recommend any of Amanda's books!!"—*EloiseReads*

Flight SQA016

"I'm so glad I picked this book up because I think I've found my new favourite series!…The love brewing between these two is beautifully written and I was onboard from the beginning. I had some laugh out loud moments because this is British rom-com at its best. The secondary characters really added to the novel and the rollercoaster ride that is this book. The writing is tight and pace is perfect."—*Les Rêveur*

Lost at Sea

"A.E. Radley knows how to write great characters. And it's not just the main characters she puts so much effort into. I loved them, but I was astounded at how well drawn the minor characters were…The writing was beautiful—descriptive, real and very funny at times."
—*Lesbian Review*

"This book was pure excitement. The character development was probably my favourite overall aspect of the book…A.E. Radley really knows how to keep her readers engaged, and she writes age-gap romance books beautifully. In fact, she probably writes some of my favourite age-gap romance tropes to date. A very intriguing book that I really enjoyed. More Captain West, please!"—*Les Rêveur*

"Absolutely amazing, easy to read, perfect romance with mystery and drama story. There were so many wonderful elements that gave twists and turns to this adventure on the sea. I absolutely loved this story and can't rave about it enough."—*LesbiReviewed*

Going Up

"I can always count on this superb author when it comes to creating unforgettable and endearing characters that I can totally relate to and fall in love with. A.E. Radley has given me beautiful descriptions of Parbrook and the quirky individuals who work at Addington's." —*Lesbian Review*

"It was an A.E. Radley story, so naturally, I loved it! Selina is A.E. Radley's iciest Ice Queen yet! She was so cold and closed off, but as the story progresses and we get a good understanding of her, you realise that just as with any other Ice Queen—she can be thawed. I loved how they interacted, with a wit and banter that only A.E. Radley can really deliver for characters like these."—*LesbiReviewed*

"This story is a refreshing light in the lesfic world. Or should I say in the romance lesfic world? Why do you ask me? Well, while there is a lot of crushy feeling between wlw characters and all, but, honestly that's the sub-plot and I've adored that fact. *Going Up* is a lesson in life."—*Kam's Queerfic Pantry*

"The author takes an improbable twosome and writes such a splendid romance that you actually think it is possible…this is a great romance and a lovely read."—*Best Lesfic Reviews*

Mergers and Acquisitions

"This book is fun, witty, and adorable. I had no idea which way this book was going to take me, and I loved it. Each character is interesting and loveable in their own right. You don't want to miss this one—heck, if you have read any of A.E. Radley's books you know it's quality stuff."—*Romantic Reader Blog*

"Radley writes with a deceptively simple style, meaning the narrative flows naturally and quickly, yet takes readers effortlessly over rocky terrain. The pacing is unrushed and unforced, yet always leaves readers wanting to rush ahead to see what happens next."—*Lesbian Review*

The Startling Inaccuracy of the First Impression

"We absolutely loved the way the relationship between the two ladies developed. There is nothing hurried about the relationship that develops perfectly organically. This is a lovely, easy to read romance."—*Best Lesfic Reviews*

Huntress

"The writing style was fun and enjoyable. The story really gathered steam to the point of me shirking responsibilities to finish it. The humor in the story was very well done."—*Lesbian Review*

"A.E. Radley always writes fantastic books. *Huntress* is a little different than most of her books, but just as wonderful. The humor was fantastic, the story was absolutely adorable, and the writing was superb. This is truly one of those books where the characters really stick with you long after the book has ended. I wish I'd read it sooner. 5 Stars."—*Les Rêveur*

Bring Holly Home

"*Bring Holly Home* is a fantastic novel and probably one of my favourite books by A.E. Radley...Such a brilliant story and one I know I will read time and time again. This book has two ingredients that I love in novels, Ice Queens melting and age-gap romance. It's definitely a slow burn but one I'd gladly enjoy rereading again."—*Les Rêveur*

Keep Holly Close

"It was great to go back into the world of the Remember Me series. The first book in the series, *Bring Holly Home*, is one of my favourite A.E. Radley books. I love Holly and Victoria; they tick all the boxes for me when it comes to my favourite tropes. Plus, Victoria's kids are adorable, especially little Alexia. She melts my heart."—*Les Rêveur*

"So much drama...loved it!!! I already loved Holly and Victoria from the first book in the series, *Bring Holly Home*, so it was brilliant to be back with them. Victoria hasn't changed and I adore her as much as before. She was utterly brilliant at every moment of this follow-up story and she even managed to surprise me from time to time. The Remember Me series is so beautiful and one of my all time favourites. 5 of 5 stars."—*LesbiReviewed*

Climbing the Ladder

"What a great introduction to what will undoubtedly be another fantastic series from A.E. Radley. After I finished it I just kept thinking that this book is amazing and it's just the start...enough said!"—*Les Rêveur*

"Radley has a talent for giving us memorable characters to love, women you wish you knew, and locations you wish you could experience firsthand."—*Late Night Lesbian Reads*

Second Chances

"This is an absolute delight to read. Likeable characters, well-written, easy flow and sweet romance. Definitely recommended."—*Best Lesfic Reviews*

"I always know when I get a new A.E. Radley book I'm in for a treat. They make me feel so good after reading them that most of the time I'm just plain sad that they have finished...The chemistry between Alice and Hannah is lovely and sweet...All in all, *Second Chances* has landed on my favourites shelf. Honestly, this book is worth every second of your time. 5 Stars."—*Les Rêveur*

The Road Ahead

"I really enjoyed this age-gap, opposites attract road trip romance. This is a romance where the characters actually acknowledge their differences and joy of joy, listen to each other. I love it when a book makes me feel all the feels and root for both women to find their HEA. Hilarious one minute, heart-tugging the next. A pleasure to read." —*Late Night Lesbian Reads*

Fitting In

"Writing convincing love stories with non-typical characters is tricky. Radley more than measures up to the challenge with this truly heart-warming romance."—*Best Lesfic Reviews*

By the Author

Romances

Mergers & Acquisitions

Climbing the Ladder

A Swedish Christmas Fairy Tale

Second Chances

Going Up

Lost at Sea

The Startling Inaccuracy of the First Impression

Fitting In

Detour to Love

Under Her Influence

Protecting the Lady

Humbug

Reading Her

Reclaiming Love

The Flight Series

Flight SQA016

Grounded

Journey's End

The Remember Me Series

Bring Holly Home

Keep Holly Close

The Around the World Series

The Road Ahead

The Big Uneasy

Mystery Novels

Huntress

Death Before Dessert

Visit us at www.boldstrokesbooks.com

RECLAIMING LOVE

by
Amanda Radley

2022

RECLAIMING LOVE

ISBN 13: 978-1-63679-144-9

This Trade Paperback Original Is Published By
Bold Strokes Books, Inc.
P.O. Box 249
Valley Falls, NY 12185

First Edition: June 2022

CREDITS
EDITOR: RUTH STERNGLANTZ
PRODUCTION DESIGN: STACIA SEAMAN
COVER DESIGN BY TAMMY SEIDICK

For the readers.

CHAPTER ONE

S arah Campbell leaned on the handrail and let out a soft, contented sigh. Wisps of ocean mist touched her face as the ferry made its way from the Scottish mainland towards the island of Celfare, her new home.

It was a beautiful spring day. The sun shone brightly but wasn't blinding, and a gentle breeze kept temperatures pleasant. If Sarah could have picked a perfect day to move to her new home, then it would have been this one. She imagined that the secluded island just off the western tip of Scotland could have been a dreary and inhospitable place at certain times of the year. She definitely wouldn't have wanted to visit in the dead of winter.

There was something special about making her way to Celfare during such perfect conditions. It added to the sense of excitement and anticipation of what she was about to do. Remembering the experiment and her assignment, she took a step back and looked around the deck at her fellow passengers. She shared her journey with eight other passengers and four crew members. Four of the passengers appeared to be related to deliveries, while the other four were residents or tourists. They had probably picked Celfare for a variety of reasons, and she was sure that one was the lack of tourism compared to nearby Scottish islands that had more to offer travellers. She hoped that she was doing a good job of blending in.

There was a fine balance to be found. On one hand, fewer tourists were preferable, but on the other Sarah didn't want to stand out as the only person who didn't belong. Celfare had just over two thousand permanent residents, and Sarah was about to add to that number. She'd need to walk a line between fitting in and not attracting too much attention if her work was to remain out of the news.

Her mobile phone rang. The name of her boss, Gail Young, appeared on the screen. Sarah made her way from the front of the ferry to a quiet area at the rear.

"Hi, Gail," she said.

"Sarah! How's it going?"

"It's good. We left Oban half an hour ago. Just another three hours to go, and I'll be there."

"Great! Excellent job."

Gail was typical of every manager Sarah had worked under since starting at Swype Technologies. She was enthusiastic, demanding, and didn't take no for an answer. Being on the right side of Gail was wonderful and meant being bathed in praise and held up as a glowing example to the rest of the business. Being on the wrong side of Gail was something Sarah desperately hoped she would never have to experience. Disappointing a normal person was hard, but disappointing a passionate optimist was horrible.

"I'm hoping to get settled in pretty quickly, and then I'll be in touch with the first update this evening," Sarah said.

"Fantastic," Gail said. "Seems you have everything under control. One quick thing, did I tell you about the cottage?"

Sarah hesitated. Gail hadn't said a thing about the place that was going to be her home for the short-term. It seemed a little late to be mentioning something now. "Um. No, I don't think so. What about it?"

"Nothing to worry about. I just wanted to say that it's a little… old. I didn't want you to think you were walking into an immaculate modern apartment or anything. It's a little tired, wonky, that kind of thing. Obviously, you can get someone in to tidy up and decorate to your liking as you'll be there for a while with any luck."

Sarah's assignment was scheduled to run for six months. If things went well, then she'd be there for longer. Everyone hoped things would go well, but they all knew the risks.

"Oh, right," Sarah said. "Yeah, I expected it to be a little dated. It is an old property, after all. I'm sure I'll be fine."

Sarah hadn't seen her new home, but Gail had stayed there briefly during the installation of the data centre. Sarah knew it was a quaint three-bedroom cottage that had been purchased by Swype a couple of years ago at the start of the project. It was one of eleven properties they had purchased over a course of four years while they researched the best place to base their experiment.

In the end, they had chosen Celfare as the best location for weather conditions, connectivity, and secrecy. Secrecy was key. Submerged data centres were controversial and not universally loved. In fact, many people hated the very idea of them. It wasn't unheard of for militant environmental activists to find data centres and destroy them for fear of what they might be doing to the sea life and wider environment.

"I hate to ask, but what have you told your mother?" Gail asked.

Sarah sucked in a quick breath to brace herself. Her mother was a frequent topic of conversation at Swype. Being the daughter of an opinionated climate change protestor wasn't easy. It was even harder when that protestor was a respected physicist and former head of the Climate Change Research Centre before joining—and ultimately leading—a movement using civil disobedience tactics to disrupt governments and companies around the world. Some called them ecoterrorists—some called them heroes fighting against climate change. Sarah called her Mum and told her as little about her day job as possible. Professor Angela Campbell put saving the planet well above nurturing her relationship with her only child. If she learned what Sarah was doing, then the entire project would be at risk.

"I told her where I'm moving to. I had to," Sarah admitted. She couldn't have kept moving six hundred miles away a complete secret from her only living relative. "But I told her that I met someone and am moving in with them. She'll ask fewer questions this way. A half-truth is better than a full lie."

"And she'll buy that?" Gail asked.

"Yeah. We don't talk much. She doesn't really know what's going on in my life," Sarah explained.

When Sarah got her dream job working at Swype Technologies, it had devastated her mother. Angela considered Swype to be digital terrorists holding the world to ransom in their quest for profits, and she wasn't afraid to tell Sarah just that. Not a week went by without Angela sending Sarah a news article from some questionable source about how Swype was treating employees poorly, not paying fair taxes, or killing the planet in some manner. Sarah had long ago stopped defending them because trying to win an argument with her mother was like trying to stop the tide coming in.

Swype wasn't perfect, Sarah knew that. But she also knew that working with rather than against large tech companies was the best way to ensure genuine change. Boycotts and protests were one thing, but Sarah wanted to work from the inside to push through positive change. Even if that meant giving up her life in London for a while to live on a quiet island.

"I don't need to tell you that she can't know a thing about this, Sarah," Gail said. "Not even a hint of a suspicion. We'll be sunk if she finds out."

"I know. Don't worry," Sarah reassured her boss.

Angela Campbell knowing about the data centre would spell the end of the experiment. Any chance of collecting data to prove that submerged data centres were far more economically and environmentally efficient than data centres on land would vanish the moment Sarah's mother told her colleagues.

The experiment on Celfare wasn't the first time Swype had attempted to sink a data centre. In fact, it was the fifth time. Each previous attempt had been quickly thwarted by activists.

"Okay, that's great, Sarah. Keep up the good work. I have to go—I have a thing with Damian shortly, but I'll be in touch. I think Abbie wants to check in with you. Give her a call, will you? Oh, and enjoy your new home!"

Gail hung up before Sarah could reply.

Abbie was Sarah's new assistant. Completely new to the company and the department, keen but ultimately clueless, Abbie had been hired through a Swype graduate scheme the previous month. The human resources department at Swype seemed to enjoy gathering up university graduates and peppering them throughout the building. The only issue was that these eager newbies had never worked in an office and had no idea how anything worked.

It made Sarah feel a little old to be explaining to the influx of youngsters how photocopiers worked and why meeting minutes existed. But Abbie brought an air of enthusiasm and drive to the office that Sarah hadn't realised was missing. The team had been so entrenched in their secretive work that they sometimes forgot how exciting it was and the potential they were sitting on.

Sarah called her office.

"Sarah Campbell's office, Abbie speaking, how may I help you?"

"It's Sarah."

"Oh! Hi! How are you?" Abbie's tone changed from professional to casual like the flick of a switch. "I was going to call you. I didn't know if you'd have a signal on the ferry."

"I do. Better than in Covent Garden, weirdly enough. Gail said you needed to talk to me? Everything okay?"

"The people organising the expo in June wanted to know if you could present something. Obviously I know that you won't be around, but I wasn't sure if you wanted me to suggest Gary in your place."

Sarah chewed her lip as she thought. One of the many little issues with uprooting her entire life was missing out on opportunities like speaking at Swype's yearly expo. It was a chance to tell departments what was happening and to speak with like-minded colleagues about collaboration. She'd miss out this year, but if all went well, then the next year she would have some very exciting news to share.

Vanishing from the office was an easy thing to do. Swype was a hive of frenetic activity with homeworking and worldwide travel built in as standard. No one really noticed when someone from outside their immediate team wasn't around. But her entire team missing the expo would raise a few eyebrows.

"Yeah, ask Gary if he wants to talk about the new chips. That should generate some interest," Sarah said.

"Will do. Are you excited? I'd be excited. I went to Scotland once, but we only went to a zoo and a castle. An actual island will be so amazing. Is it small?"

"Smallish. Two thousand people live there, but they are quite spread out."

"And no one knows?" Abbie asked.

"No. Well, I hope not, or all of this is for nothing."

Sarah ran a hand through her hair. The main thing keeping her up at night was the worry that someone had discovered what they were doing. They'd been extra careful, but there was always a risk. It was very hard to drop a submerged data centre without anyone noticing. Thankfully, Celfare had an inhospitable and rocky side, which allowed them some cover when the ship had dropped it off in the middle of the night.

"I don't get it," Abbie said.

"Get what?"

"Why are we putting this thing into the ocean? Isn't that really bad? It's full of hard drives and wires and stuff, isn't it?"

Sarah chuckled. "It's complicated. Do you know what a data centre is?"

"Not exactly," Abbie confessed in a whisper.

"It's okay, most people don't. A data centre stores all the data the world needs to work. It's like the nervous system of the electronic world. There's more than eight million of them around the planet. Without them, the world as we know it stops. Banks. Hospitals. Communications. Everything will stop. So we need them. The problem is they get hot, and when they get hot, they break. So we need to keep them cool. With me so far?"

"Eight million hot data centres need to be kept cool. Got it." Abbie's eagerness to learn was infectious.

"Data centres are so delicate that they break all the time. And then we have to go in and fix them. And us going in to fix them disturbs the environment and causes more things to break. So we have to power it, cool it, and then replenish parts all the time. All of that takes a huge amount of energy, and that mainly comes from electricity generated by fossil fuels."

A member of the crew started to walk along the deck to where Sarah was standing. She smiled at him and ducked into another quiet corner to continue her conversation.

"About twenty percent of that energy is dedicated solely to cooling the data centre. So if we can keep them cool without using any energy then that is a huge amount of energy and fossil fuel saved."

"So...you put them in the water," Abbie said, a chink of understanding emerging. "But wait, if they are so delicate, doesn't being in water make them more likely to break?"

"No, this is the genius bit, they are completely sealed in a way that land data centres aren't. It's a steel cylinder, about the size of a small train carriage, and it is completely sealed and packed with dry nitrogen. Inhospitable for humans but perfect for equipment. Which means, better still, that the failure rate is a lot lower. The amount of energy and resources it takes to replace parts is staggering. We think that submerged data centres will be at least eight times more reliable than land ones."

"That's so clever," Abbie said. "But how do you, you know, plug it in?"

"This is another great thing about this location. The data centre is served by the wind farms in the sea. Which means it's more stable than being plugged into a service on land. And it means, if this works, that there will be big incentives for more wind farms to be built because they will have a dedicated customer right there in the water with them." Sarah couldn't contain her enthusiasm. She'd lived for this project for years since she'd first heard about the strange idea of submerged data centres. Her small team had approached Swype's Future Technology department and been given immediate funding. They were up against some of the biggest names in tech, but they had the edge.

"But wait," Abbie said, suddenly sounding concerned. "What about the fish?"

Sarah grinned. "Well, that's yet another positive. When you

put anything in the sea, it quickly gets covered in these bacteria. Then organisms grow, and then fish use them for habitat. Let me tell you, Abbie, I have become a fish expert since starting this project. Apparently, fish love solid structures near to land and anything with any nooks and crannies. They will live near it, use it for shelter, that kind of thing."

"So the fish like them?" Abbie sounded happy again.

"Love them."

"Okay, but what about global warming? Isn't filling the ocean with data centres going to make the water hot?"

Sarah chuckled. "No. It's negligible warming. About the same as undersea power cables."

"Even if there are lots of them?"

"Yep. They are packed with dry nitrogen, and any heat is quickly balanced by the cold ocean. They don't have a chance to get hot."

Abbie blew out a breath. "Well, it sounds perfect. Why all the secrecy? How could anyone argue with this?"

Sarah faltered. Her mother's disapproving face came into her mind. She wished that she could convince her mother as easily as she had convinced Abbie. But misinformation and competing theories just meant that every discussion turned into an argument.

"Because it's intangible," Sarah said. "Some of it is the result of research and still only theoretical. It's complicated and technical. You must understand, in detail, a lot of different things. And it's new. And new is scary."

"But it sounds like such an easy win for the environment," Abbie said.

"I know. And I wish I could explain it to everyone like that, but some people think that Swype is evil and just out to make money. No matter what you say, they don't believe you. And when people are looking for conspiracies, then they'll find them. The thing is, we're doing the tests now to prove our theory works. We're sure we're right. But some people think we're wrong and will do anything to stop us. Which means we can't prove it works. We're in a cycle. Hence all the secrecy."

"Yeah, I can see that. Wow, it's complicated."

"It is."

"How did you even get it out there without anyone seeing?"

"Luckily there are a few wind farms around, and so maintenance boats are frequently around the island, and nobody takes much notice of them. And we did it in the middle of the night."

"I hope it works, Sarah," Abbie said, her tone suddenly serious. "Really. It sounds like an amazing thing, and I know I'm just holding down the fort while you're gone, but I'm super excited to be a tiny part of it."

"Thanks, Abbie. I appreciate that. Teamwork is what it's all about."

"Okay. Thanks for explaining. Sorry for the stupid questions."

"No such thing as a stupid question," Sarah said.

Abbie hummed as if she disagreed. "Anyway, I'll get Gary booked in for the expo. Thanks, Sarah. Enjoy your new island life."

Sarah hung up and pocketed her phone. She turned to look out at the sea. Land could be seen in all directions as the ferry navigated its way through the narrow waterway passages between the mainland and the many islands scattered along the Scottish coast. Lighthouses, old stone buildings, and even castles could clearly be seen looking down at the ocean. It was breathtakingly beautiful and a long way from the concrete jungle of London that she was used to. She tasted the salt in the air and closed her eyes to appreciate the breeze upon her face.

Idyllic didn't even begin to describe it. Hopefully she'd be able to enjoy it despite the enormous secret she was carrying.

CHAPTER TWO

Pippa Kent turned upon hearing the horn of the arriving ferry echo through the quiet dock. She'd been reading the community noticeboard and wondering whether anyone knew that the council meeting minutes hanging inside were now over three years old.

She trudged down the footpath towards the ferry terminal building and hoped that this time her delivery would be on board as she had been promised for the last three days in a row.

Life on Celfare was very different to her previous life in Bournemouth. Bournemouth, a town on the southern coast of England, was by no means a busy city, but it felt like New York compared to Celfare. Pippa had gotten used to it over the years, but even now she sometimes missed the convenience of being able to drive to get whatever she wanted, whenever she wanted it.

The ferry service operated once a day—twice a day during some busy periods, and sometimes not at all when the weather turned. Celfare wasn't cut off from the real world, but there was a reliance on the ferry and the deliveries it brought.

She stopped outside the terminal area, leaned on the metal railings, and watched the ship slowly make its way into the narrow dock.

"Afternoon, Pippa," Tom Muir said. He stood beside her and leaned on the railing, mirroring her position as he also waited for the ferry to arrive.

"Hello, Tom, how's the new shower?"

"I don't know, it's for Marie. And the dog. I like a bath, personally. Nothing better than a good soak in some hot water," Tom replied.

"I'll ask Magnus the next time I see him," Pippa said, referring to Tom and Marie's Great Dane.

"We're thinking about getting them spotlights in the kitchen," Tom continued. "Is that something you can help with?"

"Sure. Would you like me to pop over?"

"Aye, whenever you have time. No hurry."

Pippa made a mental note to drop by sooner rather than later. If Tom was only just concluding that they wanted to upgrade the lighting in the kitchen, then Marie had almost certainly been aware of it for several weeks.

When she'd started up a handywoman service to keep herself occupied, she'd had no idea how busy she would be. She'd expected to fit the occasional electrical outlet or mend a leaky tap, but before long people had swamped her with work of all sorts.

Not that she minded. She enjoyed working with her hands. The joy of fixing things was something she'd learned from her father, who had taught her everything she knew and encouraged her into a career in structural engineering.

Since she left her old job and only consulted occasionally, the handywoman work filled her spare time nicely.

"Are you waiting for a delivery?" she asked.

"Aye. Hooks."

"Hooks?"

"Big hooks."

"Big hooks?"

"For the garden. Planters. Hanging ones." Tom let out a sigh and looked at his dirty hands. "We ordered them two weeks ago. They said they'd be here today, but you never know."

Pippa nodded. "Very true."

"Is your internet playing up?"

"Always." She sighed. Internet connectivity was a huge topic of conversation on Celfare. With more and more residents wanting to use the internet, the little bandwidth they had seemed to be constantly fizzling out. Pippa didn't understand the technical aspects of it. All she knew was that whenever she needed to use it, it seemed to stop working.

"I got a new…what's it called?" He looked up at the sky and thought for a moment. "Booter?"

"Router?" Pippa asked.

"That's him. Rubbish."

"Didn't help?"

"Nah."

"I called the service provider, but they said they couldn't help," Pippa said. "Apparently, the problem is at our end. Whatever that means."

"It means they don't know, and they want you to stop asking," Tom guessed. "Are you waiting for a delivery?"

"Yes, some bits and pieces. Hinges, glue, sealant, drill bits."

"Doesn't Harrow's have all of that?"

Harrow's was the general store on the island with a reasonable homeware and DIY department. While they had an approximation of everything that Pippa could want, she didn't feel that the quality stacked up.

Pippa couldn't stand paint that was too thin, brushes that lost their bristles, switches with a poor design, or hinges that were too flimsy. If a job was going to be done, then it deserved to be done well.

Pippa rarely shopped for supplies at Harrow's, much preferring to order from competent suppliers on the mainland. She'd been called fussy in the past, and she wore the description like a badge of honour.

"They do. But not quite what I want," Pippa replied.

They stood in companionable silence as the ferry docked. The foot passenger bridge was the first to be connected, and a couple of people strolled off the ship and quickly disappeared into the town. The car ramp lowered, and the automatic gates beeped loudly as they opened.

Pippa was scanning the vehicles to see if she could see her delivery on board when her eyes caught on a young woman who was excitedly watching the ramp lower. Often people looked fed up with any delay after a tiresome journey across the water, but this woman seemed thrilled. Pippa had never seen her before—not that she knew everyone who ever stepped foot on the island—but she was sure that she would have remembered this particular individual.

She wasn't laden down with a heavy rucksack and wasn't taking pictures of everything in sight, so Pippa assumed she wasn't a tourist.

"Who's that?"

Tom cupped a hand above his brow to block out the sun and looked towards the mysterious newcomer.

"No idea. Might be the new one."

"New one?"

"Aye. Marie said someone's bought Hillcrest Cottage. She noticed a redirect on the post. Londoner."

Pippa wasn't surprised that someone as curious as Marie would notice a redirect on the mail she handled daily. Pippa sometimes wondered if Marie had taken the job in the sorting office just so she could know what was going on around Celfare before anyone else.

Pippa returned her gaze to the woman. She didn't look like the usual sort of person who came to the island on a whim. They'd had their fair share of people from English cities wanting to settle into rural Scottish life. Most hardly lasted six months. Pippa knew she had little right to judge, having arrived from an English town herself. But her grandfather had grown up on Celfare, and she'd visited frequently until his death. It felt like a home to her, even though she'd spent most of her life living elsewhere.

With the ramp finally down, vehicles disembarked the ferry. Pippa watched as the woman slowly drove a battered old car off the ferry, filled to the brim with what looked like personal effects.

Pippa didn't know why she was so curious to know who this newcomer was. She tried to convince herself that something about the woman snagged on her curiosity. She also tried to tell herself that it would pass.

She's attractive, that's all, Pippa thought. *Of course you'll notice an attractive woman on this island.*

She glanced at Tom, who was now licking the palm of his hand in order to clean the muck off. A newcomer was going to make a welcome change.

CHAPTER THREE

Sarah found the Hillcrest Cottage easily, which wasn't much of a surprise considering Celfare only had three roads outside of the principal town by the port. She parked her car on the drive and let out a relieved sigh.

It had been a long journey—a nine-hour drive followed by an overnight stay in a bed-and-breakfast just outside of Oban, which hadn't left her refreshed at all. Then the ferry and a fifteen-minute drive to the very end of the island and her new home.

She felt as if she'd travelled to the North Pole or somewhere equally remote. Sarah had always known that coming to Celfare would be a culture shock, but she hadn't realised just how different things would be. She couldn't put her finger on why she felt so different, but she did.

She got out of her car and stretched her hands above her head. The cottage sat on a clifftop, the back garden leading right out onto the rocky edge of the island that faced the ocean. She listened to the pleasant sound of waves crashing nearby. Aside from that, everything was quiet. No distant sound of cars rumbling, no planes flying overhead, no murmur of other people going about their everyday life. Just…waves.

Sarah shivered at the sudden complete absence of background noise. She knew many people would find it relaxing, but she just found it disconcerting. Having lived in the city her whole life, peace wasn't a concept that she was familiar with.

She put her hands on her hips and looked around her new abode. The cottage was compact, made of stone, and definitely needed a little love. Paint on the window frames was peeling away and some splintered wood was on display. The entire building looked like it was leaning ever so slightly to the left.

Sarah tried to ignore that worrying detail. If the cottage had stood for the last hundred and fifty years, then it would surely stand for another year, wouldn't it?

She tore her gaze from the cottage itself and looked at the garden instead. There was a paved driveway where she had parked and a footpath to the door, with the rest of the garden being covered in overgrown grass.

She'd never owned a garden before and wondered if there was a lawnmower somewhere on the property. Swype had provided some furniture for her, but she didn't know if it ran to gardening equipment. If there was anything, she supposed they would store it in the shed.

Suddenly remembering why she was there, she set off in search of the shed. They had submerged the data centre just off the inhospitable coastline, and cables ran towards the cottage, buried under the earth and coming up in the base of a shed that sat in the garden.

Sarah walked around the cottage and down to the very bottom of the garden, and she found what she was looking for. To anyone else, it would look like a normal garden shed. Most would expect to find garden tools, some compost, and a few spiders within.

She pulled the keys out of her pocket and selected the padlock key Gail had given her a few days earlier. She looked around the area to check that she was alone before unlocking the padlock and stepping into the shed.

A smile touched her lips.

The shed was fitted with a small generator and all the monitoring and analysis equipment she would need to keep an eye on the data centre. She realised that this was the closest she had ever been to her beloved project. The data centre was officially called B.1004.51, but Sarah called it Billy. Her colleagues joked that she talked about

Billy like it was her baby, which in a way it was. She'd been there from the idea on a drawing board, to construction, to deployment. Now she'd be watching over Billy's vitals for at least the next six months.

Sarah knew few people could ever understand how important Billy was. To them it was just a gigantic mass of wires, switches, servers, and circuit boards enclosed in a steel capsule and sunk to the bottom of the ocean. To Sarah, it was the start of the change of everything.

More efficient data centres meant less energy used, and that meant less global warming. There was a real possibility that Billy could contribute to saving the world. At least, that was what she and her colleagues had surmised during their early experiments. Now she needed to find the real data to prove it. The data centre could transmit its vital statistics wirelessly to anywhere in the world, but if it did that, then it risked being discovered. The only way to get the data and to protect the secrecy of the location was via a wired connection.

Sarah turned on the monitoring equipment screens and made a note of temperatures, both inside and out, and the health of each of the nine hundred and ten servers on the thirteen racks within Billy's core. Already a power blip had caused a few of the servers to be performing at less than peak efficiency. Sarah bit her lip as she wondered if she should change the set-up now or get herself settled in the house first.

Knowing that it could wait, she reluctantly left and locked the shed to go and check out her new home. As she walked back around the cottage, she plucked the front door key from her bunch of keys. The excitement caused at seeing the shed was short-lived when Sarah saw the inside of the house.

The carpet looked like it was from the 1960s, and most of it was curling up at the corners, probably to escape the walls where wallpaper was coming away from the surface. Upon closer inspection, she noticed some *walls* were coming away from the walls, too. The paint on the steel radiators was peeling away, and everything was covered in a film of dust.

And that was just the front room, which Sarah could see from the doorstep. She took a hesitant step inside. She turned on the ceiling light and blinked when the dimmest bulb in existence flickered to life on the seventh attempt.

In some ways she was pleased that the light wasn't doing a stellar job of illuminating the horrors. Curtains from the previous tenant hung in all their chintz glory, an explosion of giant flowers, shades of beige, and years of dust.

The furniture was new and seemed completely at odds with the house. It was as if someone had placed a brand-new sofa in the middle of a landfill site.

"Eww."

She entered the bathroom and winced. It was clean in the sense that some brave soul had wiped a cloth over it, but it was filthy from being at least seventy years old. Cleaning would be pointless against many years of ingrained dirt, dust, and even mould.

She checked out the kitchen and then the upstairs bedrooms. Every room was the same. Spiderwebs filled every ceiling corner, a variety of old and dirty curtains hung from windows, and paint and wallpaper practically wilted from the walls.

She shivered. She'd known the house was old, but she'd not expected it to be filthy. Without any doubt she knew that her bare feet would not touch a surface in the house, and she made a mental note to order some more slippers.

She looked out of the window in the upstairs bedroom and let out a sigh. The Hillcrest Cottage was in a beautiful location and had the bones of being something really special. Sadly, it had been allowed to age with no renovations or maintenance. She glanced down and saw a large cluster of spiderwebs wedged between the wall and the radiator.

She took a step back and winced. She didn't like spiders, and she logically knew she was sharing a house with hundreds of them.

Sarah wasn't a neat freak by anyone's standards. She routinely left clothes on the floor, cups on her desk, and vacuumed when the dirt was visible and not a moment before. But this house was giving her palpitations.

There were signs that the house had been loved and well-lived in for years. Nothing was cheap or make-do with the property. There were solid, original doors, and she'd spotted earlier that the roof looked reasonably new. Even the built-in oven was a very expensive brand. Whoever had lived there hadn't been able to keep up with basic maintenance, upkeep, and deep cleaning. Which meant that some parts of the house had gone feral.

She went downstairs, noting as she progressed that each stair leaned slightly more dramatically into the wall than the one above. She wondered about her earlier prognosis, that the house must be stable simply because it had been there for so many years. It seemed there wasn't a flat surface or straight edge in the house. Everything fell down eventually, didn't it?

Eyeing the door frame to the living room, she attempted to close the door. As she suspected, it didn't close. It wasn't even close.

"Are you subsiding, old girl?" Sarah asked the house. "Give me some warning before you go, please."

She got her phone out of her pocket and called her boss. The last thing she wanted was to spend a night in the wonky, dirty cottage that was supposedly her new home.

"Gail Young speaking."

"Gail, it's Sarah."

"Oh! You've arrived! Is everything in order? How's Billy?"

"Yeah, Billy's fine. Um…this cottage is a lot older than I expected. And, like, really grubby."

"It is a little tired," Gail agreed. "There's a budget for you to modernise, if you want to get rid of that carpet or do some painting. But I know you'll sort it out. You're pretty handy, aren't you?" Her tone was light and breezy, attempting to keep Sarah calm and deflect from the fact that she'd knowingly sent Sarah to live in an old, gross cottage that was probably about to fall down.

Sarah realised then that Gail knew full well that the cottage was in a state that most people wouldn't wish to live in and hadn't wanted to mention it for fear of Sarah refusing to go.

Handy wasn't a word anyone used to describe Sarah. She was technically minded and could program an Excel macro or reroute power to the right server switch in a matter or moments. Household maintenance was lost on her. She lived in a rented, serviced apartment for that very reason. Changing a light bulb was the extent of her skill set. Sometimes doing even that took her a few days if she could manage without that particular light.

"I'm not that handy, no," Sarah admitted.

"Oh, well, I'm sure you'll find someone on Celfare who can help you. As long as they stay away from the shed, it'll be fine." Gail spoke in her usual carefree and blasé tone that she used when she encountered a problem that she wanted to go away. "Go online. Or ask in town—they do that kind of thing in the country, right? Anyway, I must go. Great work, Sarah. Really excellent!"

The line went dead before Sarah replied.

She looked around the room and exhaled. She didn't know where to start. Cleaning was essential, but she didn't know how much good it would do. Or what it would uncover.

Perched on the edge of the sofa, she unlocked her phone and searched for *handyman*. Logically, she knew there must be someone on Celfare to help people with the odd leaking tap. It wasn't as if they expected everyone on the island to be hardy, can-do types who could fix any issue.

She hoped.

Two results came up: Kent Handy Service and Robin the Handyman. Sarah clicked on the website for Robin the Handyman and winced at the bright colours and jumping images that assaulted her eyes. The design was straight from the nineties, and while Sarah knew she shouldn't judge a business by their website, she did.

Kent Handy Services was better. Not great, but a definite improvement. It was a simple and clean website that clearly listed the services offered. Plumbing, electrics, decorating, gardening. Kent seemed to do the works, and Sarah knew the cottage needed it.

She used the contact form to compose a quick message that explained that she had recently moved to Celfare, and the property needed a lot of odd jobs done. She left her phone number and email address and hoped that someone would come and save her from the dust, spiders, and any other hidden horrors.

It wasn't how she had expected her arrival to go. She'd never considered the genuine possibility that the cottage would be a run-down disaster, despite Gail's extremely veiled warnings.

Looking at her watch, she wondered if she had time to unload her things from the car and then go into town and find a shop that could sell her a mountain of cleaning supplies. There'd be no sleep until she at least tried to make the house liveable.

CHAPTER FOUR

Pippa entered the house and hung her keys on the key hook by the door. She put her shoes on the shoe rack and took the mail out of the letterbox. It was beyond Pete's ability to actually push the post all the way through the door, always leaving it precariously hanging in between the draft-excluding bristles. She'd spoken with him about the matter in the past, but nothing had changed. He was young and did the bare minimum in what was essentially a relatively undemanding job.

The letters were the usual collection of bills, statements, and sales literature. Having recently turned forty-eight, they had now put her on some kind of list for helpful tools around the house, woolly cardigans, and soft food meal boxes. The last one stung a little, especially when she found herself musing how good the cottage pie looked before throwing the leaflet into the recycling bin.

Pippa's phone rumbled, and she removed it from the holder she had attached to her belt. She read the email from her website contact form and quickly surmised that this was the newcomer she had seen arriving by ferry that morning.

Marie's snooping had been right. A Sarah Campbell was the new occupant of Hillcrest Cottage down by Baycliff. Pippa wasn't surprised that she needed help. The cottage hadn't been occupied since Linda Cunningham had died three years ago. There had been rumours that someone had bought it as a holiday rental, but nothing much emerged from that.

She walked into the dining room that doubled as a home

office and looked at the clipboard that hung on the wall. Electronic calendars had never worked for her. A piece of paper attached to a clipboard that she always kept with her when working was a much more efficient schedule, as far as she was concerned.

Not a lot was in the schedule for the rest of the week, and Pippa tapped out a quick message to Sarah that she could come over and discuss the work and quote, either that afternoon or the following day.

Picking up a pencil, she faintly added in Sarah's name for that afternoon and the following morning with a question mark next to each entry. The moment she put the pencil back into the pot, her phone rumbled again.

Sarah had already replied, saying that any time was fine. The sooner, the better. She included her address and phone number. Pippa raised an eyebrow and wondered just what kind of state the cottage was in. Clearly bad enough for Sarah to need help as soon as possible.

The thing Pippa enjoyed most about her work was that she could help people out of sticky situations. While she'd always been what was considered *handy*, it was only as an adult that she discovered she was in the minority in that regard. Apparently, most people couldn't wire a plug or fix a tap.

Pippa found herself constantly bemused and sometimes even shocked by people's lack of knowledge when it came to their own home. The first thing Pippa did when she moved into a new house was seek out where the water stopcock and electrical consumer unit were located. She'd discovered that many people did not know *what* these necessities were, never mind *where* they were.

She tried to balance her pleasure in helping people with her curiosity and sometimes frustration at people's lack of home maintenance knowledge. Not always successfully.

She knew that she'd always had something of a saviour complex. Helping others was an important part of her personality, even if it sometimes came from a place of exasperation. She'd nearly cried the eighth time she'd needed to explain a new front door lock to Mrs. McEwan.

Pippa walked a fine line between wanting to help others and being stunned that others couldn't help themselves. At first she had assumed that most people who hired a handyperson to do something relatively simple were just too busy to perform the task themselves. She was quickly corrected that most people couldn't do the jobs that she thought were simple.

Deciding that there was no time like the present, Pippa gathered her things and prepared to head up to Hillcrest Cottage to see what the situation was.

❖

Pippa rang the doorbell and waited. And waited. She pushed the button again and listened out for the sound of the bell inside the house. When nothing seemed to happen, she knocked.

A few moments passed and then the door opened to reveal the woman Pippa recognised from the ferry earlier that day. She was in her thirties, wore glasses, and had an unmistakable air of someone whose mind occupied a hundred places simultaneously. Her hair was piled into a loose bun and looked like it could fall at any moment. Pippa couldn't help but notice that she was effortlessly attractive.

Confusion graced her pretty, soft features. "Yes?"

Pippa blinked before finding herself enough to reply. "I'm Pippa Kent. You wanted me to come over and look at some work you need doing?"

Realisation appeared to hit. "Oh! *Pippa* Kent. I expected a man named Kent. Come in. I'm Sarah." She backed away from the door and gestured for Pippa to enter.

"Hi, Sarah, nice to meet you. Do I need to take my shoes off?" Pippa asked, gesturing to her boots.

Sarah snorted. "No. In fact, you'll probably want to keep them on when you see this gross carpet."

Pippa entered the hallway and looked around the run-down property with interest. The painted over wallpaper was so old that some of it had come away from the wall with the weight of years of paint. The carpet was hideous, both in terms of pattern and the fact that it was curling away from the walls. A couple of black spots in the corners of the ceiling alerted Pippa to the presence of mould.

Pippa had long ago learned to shut her mouth when attempting to guess what work a client wanted completed. She'd once asked if someone had called her in to remove a bathroom suite she'd thought was dreadful, only to find that it was newly installed and simply retro in design.

She'd never been blessed with the ability to easily read or converse with people. If there was a way to put her foot in it, she did. Usually up to the neck. Not that she'd ever let that hold her back. She wasn't one to be quiet when something needed to be said.

"So, what can I help you with?"

"Everything," Sarah said. "I've just moved in. I need to make this place habitable."

Pippa smirked to herself. The cottage was dirty and needed updating, but it certainly wasn't that terrible. She wondered what Sarah would have been like if the house had truly been uninhabitable. Pippa had seen plenty of properties that had lost a window, had the gas shut off, or developed a serious leak from the roof. "I see. What are you thinking of starting with?"

Sarah gestured for Pippa to follow her into the kitchen and pointed as she spoke. "For starters, this tap is leaking. I worry it might not stop soon. And the light doesn't seem to work. That plug socket is making a really loud humming noise, which worries me."

Pippa looked up at the kitchen light. She pressed the light switch on and off twice. Nothing happened.

"Also, this back door is really hard to open. I worry that if I get it open, I might not close it again," Sarah continued. "And then there's that."

Sarah was pointing up. Pippa looked up at the long crack in the middle of the ceiling that ran the length of the room.

"Do you think it's falling down?" Sarah asked.

"The ceiling?"

"The cottage," Sarah said.

Pippa laughed but paused when she saw Sarah was deadly serious.

"No. I think it's okay for a good few years yet."

"But that's a really terrible crack."

"It's stepped cracking on the outside that would be something to worry about," Pippa explained. "This cottage was built to last. How else do you think it has survived harsh winters, storms, and the corrosive sea air coming in from the Atlantic for all these years? This is just a plasterboard crack. Ugly but nothing serious behind it."

Sarah chewed her lip and looked at the crack in the ceiling.

"I'm sure this cottage will outlive many of the newer builds they're throwing up on the mainland," Pippa said. "Anyone who lives in a new build these days is an idiot."

Sarah looked away. Pippa wondered if she'd maybe said the wrong thing. Rather than waiting to find out, she opened some of the kitchen cupboards and found a few maintenance supplies under the sink. She dug through them and found a spare light bulb. It was old, but it looked like it was still in working order. She stood on her tiptoes and unscrewed the old bulb from the existing light fitting and replaced it with the new one. She flipped the switch, and the light sprang to life.

A light blush touched Sarah's cheeks. "Oh, I…didn't think of that."

"I bet you didn't," Pippa said. "What was the next thi—" She paused and gaped at the kitchen tap. For reasons she couldn't quite understand, a rubber glove was tied around the spout. "Did you do that?"

"It was dripping," Sarah said in a tone that felt like it should explain all. It didn't explain anything as far as Pippa was concerned.

Pippa untied the glove. A large splash of water hit the sink.

"And this helped in what way?" She didn't wait for a response as she looked at the nozzle of the tap and then slowly turned it on. She could feel resistance and realised that the rubber washer had gone. Not surprising considering the age of the tap.

"The washer has disintegrated," she explained. "I can replace it, but the tap itself is old and there may be other problems. Personally, I'd recommend a new tap."

"Yes, I'd like a new tap." Sarah bit her lip and looked around the room. "I'd like a new…everything."

Pippa couldn't fathom why the woman in front of her had bought the house. She didn't seem like an island sort, and she certainly wasn't very handy. Why anyone would buy a run-down fixer-upper when they clearly had none of the required skill sets was beyond Pippa.

"Did you buy with the intention to flip the property?" Pippa asked.

"No."

"Good, because I doubt that you'd make much money if you did," Pippa said. "Which socket is the one making a noise?"

Sarah pointed to a socket next to the kettle.

Pippa leaned her head closer to it and could hear a slight buzzing sound. She knew that a lot of the older properties on Celfare needed new sockets at least, and completely rewiring at best.

"I think there could be a loose wire," Pippa said. "I should look at that now, as it could be a fire risk. I charge forty pounds an hour for my time—consider the light bulb a freebie. Should take around half an hour to either fix it or make it safe. If you're okay with that, I can get my tools from the car."

Sarah nodded her head quickly. "Yes, please."

Pippa went and got her toolbox. While she was outside, she had a look at the external wall of the property to see if there were any indicators of subsidence. The last thing she wanted was to tell Sarah that the property was safe and then find out that it wasn't. She noted a few cracks here and there, but nothing that showed any risk of movement. Cracks were to be expected in a property of that age. In fact, the absence of cracks would worry her more in a property as old as Hillcrest Cottage.

She took her equipment into the house and noticed a blinking modem in the hallway. It seemed odd to Pippa that someone would prioritise the installation of broadband over things like running water, electrics, and cleaning.

Sarah appeared in the hallway. Her gaze seemed fixed on Pippa, and she wondered if she'd managed to get dirt on her face again. She'd lost count of how many times she'd gone to a client's home with a smudge of something across her cheek. It was all part of the job.

"I'm going to have to turn the power off," Pippa said.

"Oh. Okay. I don't know where the off thing—"

"It's in the cupboard under the stairs." Pippa opened the cupboard and lowered the flap on the fuse board. It was old and definitely needed replacing in the future. She decided she would broach that subject with Sarah later. She imagined Sarah was already adding up the expense and disruption that all the works would mean to her.

Pippa felt Sarah stand behind her as she looked at the board and switched off the mains. The lights went off, and the familiar buzz of electrical current running through a home faded to nothing. Pippa opened her toolbox, took out a piece of red electrical tape, and placed it over the switch.

"What's that for?" Sarah asked.

"So people know that I'm working on the power and to keep it switched off."

"But I'm the only other person here," Sarah said.

"Safety first." Pippa stood up and went into the kitchen.

Sarah followed her. Pippa was used to clients standing over her shoulder and watching every move she made. It was natural—she was a stranger the first time she came to work in someone's house. But Sarah's presence was more than a little distracting. Probably something to do with the fact she was by far the most beautiful woman on the island as far as Pippa was concerned.

Pippa hadn't thought that way about another woman since Kim, and the fact that she was now was more than a little disorientating. She'd thought that part of her was gone. Hoped that it was, too. She didn't want to notice how good Sarah's perfume smelt or how cute it was when she used her finger to poke her glasses back onto the bridge of her nose. Being alone was part of the reason Pippa came to Celfare, and she'd been very happy with that choice.

"So, what made you choose Celfare?" Pippa asked conversationally to move her thoughts to a safer topic.

"Work," Sarah said.

"What do you do?"

"I work for Swype."

Swype needed no introduction. It was as big as Amazon, Google, or Apple. Pippa didn't entirely know what they did, but she knew that without Swype she'd have no email, no website, and no telephone. The little green logo was pretty much everywhere she looked.

The company was enormous and had divisions in nearly every sector that she could name. She knew also from news articles that Swype had dabbled in self-driving cars and even medicine.

All of which meant that Sarah had provided precisely zero information about what she actually did. Saying that she worked for Swype was like saying she worked on a laptop. Which she no doubt did, as Swype had no office on Celfare.

What Swype had to do with Sarah living on Celfare was a mystery, but Pippa suspected it would remain one if Sarah's brief answers and tense posture were anything to go by.

She removed the screws and took the front plate off the socket. She laid each item down on the worktop in a neat row so she wouldn't lose anything. The cabling was old and presumably installed by a madman, judging by the state of it.

She tutted.

"What?" Sarah asked. She sounded on edge.

"Just the workmanship," Pippa replied.

"Is it dangerous?"

"It certainly could be." Pippa pulled the cables through as much as she could and snipped off the frayed ends of the wire. "Plug sockets buzz when the cables aren't tightly secured. These were becoming loose. I can fix it for now, but to be honest you probably need to rewire the house. This hasn't been touched since they built it, and technically the fuse board should be upgraded."

"Sounds expensive."

"It isn't cheap," Pippa admitted. "And you're welcome to get a second opinion. In fact, I suggest you do. It's about eight to ten days' work. Plus cabling and sockets, including a new consumer unit. I'd have to see what you have in the property, but I'd say that you're looking at at least three thousand pounds."

Pippa kept working, not wanting to make eye contact with Sarah after giving her such bad news.

"Okay. If you can send me a quote, that would be great. I have some other things I'd like you to quote for as well."

It surprised Pippa how Sarah had taken that information in her stride. She wondered if perhaps Sarah had been aware of the state of the property after all. But then why would Sarah be so worried about a meaningless crack in the ceiling? And why was she fixing a leaking tap with a rubber glove tourniquet?

"I bet," Pippa agreed. "It seems like there's a lot to do. May I ask why you bought such a run-down house?"

"I like the view," Sarah said.

"What view?"

"You know…the quiet."

Pippa paused what she was doing and looked at Sarah. "I'm sure there are plenty of better maintained houses you could have bought with a view of quiet. Which, by the way, isn't something you can see."

"Do you know who can replace bathrooms?" Sarah changed the subject.

"Yes, I do."

"Who?"

"Me." Pippa smiled. She knew she was being cocky, and she didn't mind showing it. She prided herself on being able to do it all. It hadn't taken long for her to go from being a basic handyperson service to being able to fit kitchens and bathrooms. Her education in structural engineering had taught her everything she needed to know about the inner workings of any house, and from there it was relatively simple to learn the rest. Especially with an island population calling out for help.

"So you do everything?" Sarah asked.

"I do," Pippa said. "And I think you might need a bit of help around here. Especially if that glove around the tap is anything to go by. I'm happy to quote for whatever work you need doing."

"I have a few jobs in mind. Maybe you can quote for them when you're done with the socket?"

Pippa could detect an edge to Sarah's tone and wondered if she'd gone a little far with her words, but she was genuinely shocked that Sarah had taken on a project that she clearly wasn't equipped to deal with.

Sarah's mobile phone rang. She slid it out of her back pocket and looked at the screen. "Excuse me, I need to take this."

Pippa waved her away. "No problem. I'll get this squared away."

Sarah answered the call and walked into the other room. Pippa tried to focus on the task at hand, but her mind was swimming with questions. Sarah seemed like the last person who would take on an extensive renovation project. In fact, the cottage seemed to scare her. It was as if she'd never seen it before, and that seemed more than a little strange. Who bought a house without seeing it? And if Sarah wasn't the owner but was renting, then who'd rent the property in such a poor state of repair? They were breaking several rental laws, for starters.

It was clear that no answers would be forthcoming from Sarah, but no one could keep a secret on Celfare for long.

❖

Sarah tried to focus on the work call, but the incredibly attractive woman who was currently in her kitchen was a distraction to her. When she'd accepted her assignment, she did not know that Celfare would be hiding such a gorgeous woman. Sarah had lived in the bustle of central London her entire life and dreamed of maybe one day meeting someone like Pippa Kent, but no one had even come close. Now she was on a speck of land hundreds of miles away from civilisation, and here she was—her ideal woman.

Sarah had a type, a very specific type. She liked women who appeared as though they had been everywhere and seen everything and nothing could possibly faze them. They walked with a confidence that Sarah attempted but ultimately failed to emulate. Exuding calm, dignified confidence, they were often a little older than Sarah, and that suited her just perfectly.

A friend had once commented that Sarah was simply seeking a sugar daddy type, but that wasn't true. Sarah was independent and enjoyed her career. She had no need for anyone to take care of her in that way. She sought the gratification that came from dating someone who didn't get hung up on the little things but also let nothing stand in their way. They had enough life experience to know when to let things pass them by and when to stand up and fight. There was something incredibly attractive about someone who just had their life in order. In her short time with Pippa Kent, Sarah suspected Pippa was exactly that kind of woman.

It had taken Sarah a couple of moments to recalibrate when she had opened the front door and seen a hot, older woman looking expectantly at her. Never did Sarah expect a female handyperson. And she certainly didn't expect one as eye-catching as Pippa. Dark, questioning eyes had bored into her, and Sarah had nearly forgotten how to speak. She'd done her best to stay calm and play it cool.

Pippa had gradually made that a whole lot easier to do, as she'd shown herself to be a little cocky and even a tad condescending, both of which were traits that Sarah found insufferable in a person, no matter how striking their appearance.

Sarah hated being made to feel stupid for her lack of knowledge on a topic. It wasn't a feeling that she could simply brush off like some people did. It cut her to the core and made her feel weak and foolish. Doubts lingered at the back of her mind, and she disliked feeling so unsettled because of someone's judgement of her abilities, or lack thereof. She knew she wasn't the most practical person in the world, but that didn't mean that she needed to be told that by other people. She certainly didn't need to be made to feel like a lesser person just because she didn't know where a fuse board was or because she had an interesting strategy for stopping a dripping tap.

"Sarah?" Gail asked. "Are you still there?"

"I'm still here. Sorry, the line dropped for a moment."

It was a lie. The connection was fine—it was her mind that kept dropping out. Seeing Pippa had done something to Sarah's concentration. Ordinarily, she wasn't the kind of person to get flustered or to gape at a tradesperson, but Pippa had somehow caused her to do both in just a matter of minutes despite the patronising comments that had put her back up.

Sarah crossed to the window and looked out at the terribly overgrown garden to push thoughts of Pippa from her mind and focus her attention back on the work call. Gail repeated her question regarding some data from the scientific studies that Swype had recently funded, and Sarah gave an update of the findings.

It was nothing too confidential, so she could speak freely despite Pippa being in the next room. Even so, she kept her tone low and said only what needed to be said. Pippa seemed observant and perceptive, two traits that she typically would have thought were wonderful qualities in a person, but also two things that Sarah absolutely didn't need when she was trying to run a secret experiment from a base at the end of the garden.

Her well-defined sense of gaydar had pinged loud and clear on Pippa, and that had definitely been a factor in Sarah's inability to focus. She'd been certain that she'd be the only lesbian on the island, and now she found she wasn't, and that intrigued her.

But are we the only two lesbians on the island? Sarah mused. *Or is Pippa attached?*

There had been no ring on Pippa's finger—she'd checked—but she knew that meant little.

Why are you even thinking about this? she asked herself. *You're supposed to be undercover, not lusting over the first potentially eligible woman you see. Not to mention she's arrogant and nosy. In just a few minutes she belittled you and poked about, asking you questions you couldn't answer. You need to avoid her, not wonder if she's single.*

Sarah made a few noises of agreement so Gail didn't think she'd gone again. Her mind was no longer on the work call—it was planning her next move. Pippa was appealing, but she was also snooty, and Sarah didn't need that in her life. If she wanted to be told how foolish she was and how she was ruled by her heart and not her head, she would never have left home. Her mother would do a far better job than Pippa ever could in crushing Sarah's self-confidence and making her feel useless.

She decided that she'd be polite and ask Pippa to quote for the work as she'd agreed to do, but then she'd seek out the other handyman on the island. And then she would just try to avoid Pippa for the rest of the time. It was for the best.

CHAPTER FIVE

Sarah strolled around the tiny market and gently swung the metal basket as she browsed the aisles. This was her third visit to the small grocery store. The first time had been the day she arrived, when she bought water, a pre-packaged sandwich, and cleaning products as if her life depended on it. She thought it had at the time, but that was three days ago, and she felt like a completely different person now.

If someone had told her three days before that she would somehow manage to settle into her new life, she never would have believed them. She'd set aside most of the first day to deep clean the cottage. She'd seen things she never wanted to think about ever again, but she'd also removed about twenty-five years of grime, and that had made her feel somewhat better about her situation.

The cottage was by no means clean, but it was cleaner. And now she had a plan. She'd spoken with Gail and agreed on a renovation plan, which included gutting most of the cottage and replacing everything, starting with the dangerous wiring and the creaking plumbing. Gail had agreed to Sarah's requests so quickly that Sarah suspected Gail knew the cottage was a deathtrap and had been expecting Sarah's pushback once she'd seen it for herself. Gail agreed to finance the renovations, as long as Sarah was prepared to live in the property while work was being undertaken. They couldn't risk the shed being stumbled upon by a tradesperson looking for a spanner.

Sarah had decided not to ask Pippa Kent to come back to the

cottage. Pippa had been a little arrogant and smirked unattractively at Sarah's obvious lack of home repair knowledge. After Pippa had fixed the socket, Sarah had shown her around the rest of the house and asked her to quote for work. Pippa didn't seem to be able to stop herself from chuckling to herself.

Sarah didn't need someone so opinionated and self-righteous in her house for weeks and weeks on end. Not to mention the fact that Pippa's attractiveness was a terrible distraction for her. That coupled with the fact that she clearly thought Sarah was an idiot made it a straightforward decision to get someone else in to do the work.

She'd called Robin the Handyman and asked him to come out and fix the light in the upstairs hallway that afternoon. She'd read online that it was always best to get someone to do a minor job to see if you liked them before you invited them into your home for a longer time. And Sarah would love to get the broken upstairs light fixed.

"Hello, dear, have you moved into Hillcrest Cottage?"

Sarah looked up to see an elderly lady with kind eyes and a genuine smile looking at her.

"I have. I'm Sarah."

"I'm Louise. I work at the library. Welcome to Celfare."

"Thank you." Sarah noticed a small group of women doing a terrible job of hiding a few aisles away and assumed that Louise had been sent to welcome the stranger and get the gossip.

"If you need anything, don't you hesitate to ask. Everyone is very friendly," Louise said.

"Thank you, that's really kind."

"And lots of us meet at the Ram's Head on a Friday night—you'd be more than welcome to join us."

Sarah held no desire to ever visit the island pub, but nodded her head regardless. She wasn't really a pub person, much preferring to curl up on the sofa and watch television or read a book. Attending a local pub on a small island where she was trying to keep a secret was a recipe for disaster.

"If you need anything fetched from the mainland, then you can speak to Daphne at the terminal or Marie in the post office. But I think we have nearly everything anyone could want right here on Celfare."

Sarah resisted the urge to glance around the market with its two choices of each basic essential and nothing more. It had only been a couple of days, and she already missed fibre broadband, the cinema, a choice of restaurants, and the sight of skyscrapers in the distance.

Celfare might be idyllic to some, but Sarah wasn't the sort of person who would be happy on a rural island. She loved city life. Or at least the option to get involved in city life. While she rarely went out to pubs and bars, knowing that she could was a great comfort to her.

"I suspect you'll be wanting to tidy that garden," Louise continued, "what with the nice weather on the way."

Sarah chuckled. "I will. But I think I'll be focusing on the inside of the house for a while."

"Then you'll be wanting some paint and things. Harrow's is the place for that."

"Great. I'll check it out, thank you," Sarah said.

"No problem. If you need anything, then you let us know. Everyone is very approachable, and we're like a little family here. We stick together."

Sarah suspected that some of that was curiosity about the newcomer and why she was on the island. Pippa had been interested to know what had brought her to Celfare, and Sarah knew her answer had been flimsy at best. Pippa's confused expression had said it all.

She needed to work on her story. She'd thought that she would have a few more days to get herself sorted before she needed to come up with a reasonable excuse as to why she had chosen Celfare, of all places, to work from remotely.

The state of the cottage had thrown her. Her detailed game plan had been ruined. She'd not even unpacked, fearful that her belongings would end up covered in dust and grime. And spiders.

"Can you recommend a handyperson?" Sarah asked.

"There's Pippa Kent," Louise said immediately. "Very thorough. Good price."

"I have someone called Robin coming this afternoon to fix a light," Sarah said, hoping for a little information on the man.

Louise shifted on her feet and tried, but failed, to maintain a neutral expression. "Nice man, Robin," she finally said. "Anyway, I'd best be off."

Sarah watched the older woman rush away. It seemed like a bad omen, but there was nothing to be done now. Robin was booked in and on his way. Sarah would have to see for herself what Louise's panicked expression was all about.

❖

An hour later, Sarah had bought some supplies and then cleaned the kitchen cupboards to be worthy of holding them. Thankfully, Swype had invested in a new refrigerator. She tentatively leaned closer to listen to the plug socket that Pippa had fixed the other day. It made a small noise, one that every other plug socket in the house made. Sarah had been left wondering if all sockets made a noise. She'd never needed to check before. In her ultra-modern apartment in the city, plugs buzzing would have been the last thing on her mind. Now she was obsessed.

A knock on the door caused her to jump. She looked at her watch and wondered who it could be, as Robin wasn't due for another hour and a half.

She made a mental note to do an online search about the acceptable amount of buzzing to expect from a plug socket and then headed through the hallway to open the front door.

"Where's this light, then?" The man held a toolkit in one hand and had a stepladder balanced on his shoulder. He wore a dark navy ribbed woollen jumper, which put Sarah in mind of the Air Force. Tiredness and boredom framed his expression.

"Oh, I thought we said three?" She assumed this was Robin, although he hadn't bothered to introduce himself.

"I had a gap in my schedule." He sighed and adjusted the stepladder on his shoulder. He looked at Sarah as if he was doing her a favour and her ingratitude was blinding him.

"Okay. Um. It's just through here." She climbed the stairs and pointed to the light. "I tried a new bulb, but it wasn't that."

Robin flicked the light switch on and off several times. "Nah, it wouldn't be the bulb. It's a loose connection. Never mind. I'll get this fixed up for you, love."

Sarah winced at the term. She knew that some men enjoyed sprinkling supposed terms of endearment over women they worked for, but it made her skin crawl.

Robin set up his ladder and climbed the steps to look at the light. He tutted and then sighed. "Ah, it's going to be one of them, is it?"

"One of what?" Sarah asked.

Robin ignored her question and unscrewed the bulb, and then the ceiling rose to reveal the wires. Sarah wondered if maybe the power should have been turned off before he started. She glanced at the light switch and realised she didn't know if it was on or off anymore.

"Would you like to me to turn the power off?" Sarah asked.

"We'll get to that in good time." He put his face close to the exposed cables.

Sarah wondered what he could find out with no tools. Whatever it was, he wasn't telling her and clearly had no intention of involving her in whatever was going on with his process.

"I'll leave you to it," Sarah said.

He grunted in reply. She slowly walked back down the stairs, casting a glance over her shoulder to wonder about his strange attitude. So far, Robin wasn't winning any tradesperson of the year award. She knew she shouldn't care as long as he did a good job, but she couldn't help but feel uncomfortable with someone so aggressively miserable poking live wires in her ceiling.

She'd set up her laptop, iPad, phone, and other work equipment at the dining table to make a temporary office. She had intended to use one of the bedrooms but had quickly realised that all the bedrooms needed to be fully redecorated as a matter of urgency. Cracks had appeared in the ceilings, wallpaper curled away from walls, ominous black spots showed she wasn't the only life form in the house, and the carpets were vile. She was sleeping in the main bedroom, but only because Swype had provided a brand-new double bed and fresh bedding. Otherwise, she would have been tempted to sleep on the sofa.

She got to work and started logging all the data from Billy from the overnight data packet she had collected from the shed. Upstairs she could hear quiet cursing, banging, and huffing. Robin came downstairs a few times and went to his vehicle to get something before thudding his way back up the stairs. At one point, he turned the power off without telling Sarah what he was doing. Thankfully, she'd recently saved her work and wasn't in the middle of anything important.

Sarah mused that maybe Pippa was the better option. Her eyes drifted to the paperwork on the desk, paperwork that she knew she'd have to hide if Pippa was around. Robin wasn't interested in Sarah or what she was doing, but Pippa seemed the curious sort. And then there was the fact that Pippa was damned distracting. Sarah couldn't put her finger on what it was about Pippa that she found so enticing, probably a blend of confidence, attractiveness, and intelligence. Robin had none of those things. He distracted Sarah, but only because of the noise he made and the fact that she worried he might break something or himself.

Ninety minutes of cursing and stomping around passed before Robin finally appeared in the dining room.

"All done. It was a bugger, but I sorted it out." He puffed his chest out as if he'd single-handedly wrestled a lion into submission. Sarah knew she wouldn't have been able to fix the problem, but she didn't think it warranted the cockiness he displayed, considering that he was supposed to be an expert at these matters.

"Great. Thanks. Are the electrics okay? I know this is an older house…"

Robin laughed. "You'll be fine. Nothing wrong with this place." He banged the palm of his hand against the wall. "Built to last."

Sarah was no expert, but she was happy to side with Pippa in this case. The wiring in the house hadn't been updated since it was installed at a time long before any of them had been born. Some things were built to last, but even Sarah knew that cabling was not one of those things.

"Let me show you what I've done," he said.

She stood and Robin gestured for her to lead the way. When she arrived upstairs, she saw that the light was now working and everything seemed to be in good order. Robin flipped the switch, and the light went off. He turned it back on and looked smugly at the illuminated bulb.

"All done. Was a pain but I got there."

"Brilliant. Thanks so much."

"Not a problem. If you need any help with anything else, drop me a bell."

Sarah nodded silently. She wasn't sure she wanted Robin back in her house. He was loud, couldn't keep time, and seemed to make a mountain out of a molehill. He'd ignored her at the start and at the end seemed to want her to cover him in praise for completing a supposedly arduous task.

They went downstairs and settled the bill, and she waved him goodbye.

Deciding what to do next would be difficult. Pippa was clearly more qualified, but then she also spoke down to Sarah in a way that made her feel small and uncomfortable in her own home.

Robin had ultimately fixed the problem, even if it had taken an extraordinary amount of time and grumbling. And Robin wouldn't be curious about what was lurking in the garden shed. In fact, he'd barely looked Sarah in the eye, such was his lack of interest in anything to do with her.

The need to keep her work secret and the desire to be treated like an adult were enough to make Sarah decide there and then that Robin was the person to help with renovations. He wasn't perfect, but he'd do.

She turned the kettle on to make a hot drink, realising that she'd been getting a little cold in the draughty dining room. The small gaps between the window frame and the wall that let the outside air flow freely through the house were something else that needed to be fixed.

She headed upstairs to get a sweater. In her previous life in the city, she'd never had to dress differently throughout the day. The climate-controlled heating system kept her apartment exactly how she liked it all day long. Now she was waking up sweating because the morning sun streamed through her bedroom window and made the room like an oven. By midday the sun had moved enough to cause the side of the house where the dining room was located to feel like a fridge.

She entered the bedroom and turned on the light but stopped dead when nothing happened. She flipped the switch back and forth a few times and still nothing happened. It had worked the day before, which meant only one thing. Robin had fixed one light but broken another in the process.

Sarah closed her eyes and took a deep breath. "I hate this damn house."

Chapter Six

Pippa looked at the data printout and shook her head. She glanced up at her laptop screen and shook her head again at the face of her former boss, Lawrence Mason.

"This isn't going to work," Pippa said.

"I know. The load bearing is all wrong. Can you help?" Lawrence asked.

Pippa sat back in her office chair and mulled over the problem. They hadn't allowed extra supports for the new roof frame. And the size of the steel was all wrong. She sighed.

"I don't work for you any more," she reminded him.

"Which is a shame because I no longer get to see your smiling face in the office and have to make do with the laptop camera you have, which must be at least ten years old." Lawrence grinned. "At least the internet is working today."

"For now," Pippa added.

"Can you do the calculations?"

"Of course I can do the calculations."

"*Will* you do them?"

She tossed the pages of data onto her desk and removed the clipboard from the wall and looked at her schedule. When she'd left Mason Architects, she'd never expected to still be working for them six years later. She'd barely been on Celfare a week when Lawrence had called and asked her about an old project she'd worked on. Despite no longer working for him, she'd felt duty-bound to assist.

Then Margaret had gone off to have a baby, and he needed someone capable of calculating load bearing on a party wall. Then he had a new project and needed someone who knew something about drainage conditions near a riverbed. Every other week, he was calling her with an additional request and pleading for her help.

In the end, she'd taken him up on his offer to be a self-employed consultant. It had come at a time when she needed the distraction. Moving away from her old life had helped heal some wounds but torn open others. She'd been right that getting away from everything had been cathartic, but she hadn't expected to feel every single unfilled minute so keenly. Time passed slowly when she was alone and unoccupied.

A purpose was what she needed, and the consultancy work fit the bill perfectly around her handyperson service. Sometimes she spoke to him every day, sometimes once a month. The work was engaging and complicated, allowing her to block out the outside world for a while and get lost in the maths.

"I can get it back to you by next Wednesday."

Lawrence beamed. "Excellent, I knew I could rely on you."

"Did you get that contract for the new drainage system?"

He shrugged. "No idea. They keep rescheduling the meeting because people in town are complaining about the route, or the noise, or the traffic restrictions, or whatever."

"The usual, then," she said.

"Exactly. We'll probably know by the end of the month." He leaned back in his seat. "I'm going to Pico's for lunch."

Pippa rolled her eyes. "Don't."

"I'm going to have the shaved steak sandwich with that Dijon mustard special sauce they have." He grinned playfully. "I'll opt for the melted cheese today because I went for a run this morning and decided I can treat myself."

Talk of her favourite lunchtime location caused her stomach to quietly rumble. She'd spent many a long lunch in Pico's, talking to clients or having team meetings. The owner had gotten to know her well, and they frequently offered her a free takeaway coffee in the morning.

Celfare didn't have a Pico's. It had nothing much. If you didn't feel like cooking for yourself, then there was a fish and chip shop, which seemed to specialise in squeezing as much cooking oil into food as possible. Pippa had only eaten there once and had felt so sick afterwards that she never returned. There were coffee shops and cafes for the few tourists that visited, but nothing that matched up to Pico's.

"Always a space for you here, Pippa," Lawrence said. His expression had turned serious. He'd made no secret of disagreeing with Pippa's plan to move as far away from her old life as possible.

"I appreciate that, but I'm happy here. Really."

"You may be, but I miss my friend," he said. "No one to play squash with. No one to talk about rugby with."

Pippa laughed. "Oh, come on, it's not like you don't have any friends. I mean, I know you're a massive pain in the arse, but some people seem to like you for some reason."

The seriousness of the mood was broken, and they both chuckled.

"Sod off," he said. "I'm going to really enjoy that sandwich now."

"Do. I'll enjoy not having to listen to you eat it." She winked.

"I'm going!" He waved at the camera before disconnecting the video chat.

Pippa watched his image flicker away and let out a small sigh. It wasn't that she didn't miss him or her old life. At times, she missed it terribly. But it wasn't as if she could just slip back into it as if nothing had ever happened. She could return to her old job, even move back into her old house, but that wouldn't change the fact that Kim was gone.

Her gaze fell to the framed wedding photo on her desk. They looked so young and so happy. Pippa could scarcely believe the time and heartache that had passed since that photo had been taken.

Her phone rumbled and displayed a new text message. She was surprised to see it was from Sarah, up at Hillcrest Cottage. It had been a few days since she'd been to the property and quoted for a vast amount of work that Sarah wanted to be done.

Sarah's attitude had changed from when she'd first arrived to when she left. Pippa hadn't been able to figure out why, but she could tell that Sarah hadn't been particularly happy. She guessed it was something to do with the enormous amounts of work that the property required and the equally eye-watering sums of money it would require to put it all right.

Sarah's text was about a broken light, and Pippa quickly replied to say she was available to fix it that afternoon, if that was convenient. Sarah replied a few moments after to say it was, and Pippa arranged a time.

She couldn't remember a broken light being on the list of repairs that needed to be done, but she wasn't surprised, considering the state of the property. She picked up a pen and added Sarah to her afternoon's schedule. Truth be told, she was happy to be seeing Sarah again. She was a breath of fresh air on Celfare, even if Pippa really didn't understand why someone like Sarah had moved from London to Hillcrest Cottage of all places. She hoped she'd find out more that afternoon.

❖

Sarah leaned against the doorframe with her hands in her pockets. There was a shiftiness to her that led Pippa to wonder what she was hiding. Pippa had turned off the power and unscrewed the light fitting in the bedroom but couldn't see anything that would cause the light to suddenly stop working.

"Maybe it's something to do with this light?" Sarah asked, gesturing to the hallway light.

Pippa glanced at the other light and frowned. It wasn't unusual for lights to operate on a ring with power coming into a light and then travelling to the next on the circuit. A broken connection in one light could definitely stop another from working. The question was, how would Sarah know that? And even if she had an understanding of ring circuits, how would she know which order the lights were in?

"It could be," Pippa agreed. She lifted the stepladder and put it beneath the hallway light. She climbed up and unscrewed the light fitting and then let out a sigh. The jumble of wires and electrical tape could only mean one thing.

"You've had Robin here," she said.

"How could you possibly know that? Did he tell you?" Sarah demanded.

Pippa chuckled. "Do you think this is the first time I've had to fix Robin's mess? It accounts for about a quarter of my work. I should pay him commission." She leaned against the top of the ladder and looked down at Sarah. "Why on earth did you get him in? He's an idiot."

"Well, I know that *now*," Sarah said, her cheeks flushing a little.

"You could have called me," Pippa said. "It would have been a lot easier. Now I have to figure out what he's done. What possessed you to call him?"

Sarah folded her arms across her chest. "Because you were mean."

Pippa blinked several times. "Mean?" The thought dazed her, and she felt a small shiver of discomfort run up her back. Of course, she knew she was direct, but *mean* was a line she hoped never to cross. Especially with someone she hardly knew.

"Yes." Sarah jutted her chin in the air. She was trying to look confident, but Pippa could easily see that she was hurt and nervous. She hated that she might have inadvertently been the cause.

"I…when was I mean?"

"You laughed at me. You were, I don't know, you were just condescending. I'm not going to list what you did. I felt you were mean. So I called Robin. But, apparently, he's an idiot. And I got sick of stumbling around the bedroom in the dark at night for the last few nights, so I had to suck it up and call you."

Pippa opened her mouth to issue a quick denial that she had been mean but stopped herself. Kim's voice echoed in her ears, reminding her that sometimes she was a little quick to speak and late to think. It wouldn't have been the first time that Pippa's harsh tongue had offended someone.

Not to mention that it wasn't up to Pippa to confirm or deny if

Sarah had been hurt by her words. That was out of Pippa's hands. If Sarah felt bad, then Pippa was to blame and had to take responsibility for that. Especially as she knew she had form for being a little sharp.

"I'm sorry," Pippa said. "It's no excuse, but it's been a while since I've spoken to someone I haven't known for many years. I'm naturally a little…"

"Rude?" Sarah asked, a twinkle in her eyes.

"Let's say *honest*." Pippa smiled.

"Maybe a touch condescending?" A small smile appeared on Sarah's lips.

"Possibly," Pippa conceded. She smiled in return at the gentle joking. "Either way, I'm very sorry that I hurt you. I didn't mean to. I'm just bad with people."

Sarah looked surprised at the honesty.

"May we start over?" Pippa held out her hand. "I'm Pippa Kent, your new and non-patronising handyperson."

Sarah's cheerful grin sent fireworks through Pippa. Her pulse raced, and she hoped Sarah couldn't tell that her hand was quivering slightly.

Sarah took hold of Pippa's hand. "Nice to meet you."

"Likewise. Honestly, I'm sorry if I came across as harsh. It's not my intention. I'll try harder."

"You could start now by not chastising me for getting useless Robin in," Sarah said, a lopsided grin on her face.

"I think having Robin work in your home is probably punishment enough." Pippa looked up at the mess of cables. "He hasn't even thought to see if this was on a ring. He's just taped this up. What a mess." Pippa paused and looked down at Sarah. "I can still criticise *him*, yes?"

"Absolutely. He's an idiot."

"He is." Pippa returned her attention to the light. "But there are only the two of us on the island, so I'm afraid you have to choose him or me. Or teach yourself."

Sarah laughed. "Yeah, it's going to be you. I don't want him back in my house, and I'm useless with all this stuff."

"It's quite simple when you know how." Pippa picked off the

electrical tape from the wires and attached each piece to the top handle of the ladder so she could throw them away later.

"I've never been very good at house things. Neither was my mum. We always got someone in. Which was a lot easier in London."

"You came here from London?" Pippa asked. While she'd heard that through the local rumour mill, she knew it was always best to get information from the source.

"Yeah. Swype are testing their new remote working technology. I'm here to check everything works."

Pippa could detect a slight hesitation in Sarah's voice and wondered what it meant.

"So…who owns this house?" Pippa asked.

"Swype."

"Seems odd that a technology company would own a cottage on a Scottish island," Pippa said.

"They own a lot of weird stuff. Schools, houses, a mine somewhere in Tanzania, a protected forest in Norway. Swype work on a lot of projects, and so they have a lot of divisions doing all kinds of things."

"And you work in the remote working division?"

"I work with new technologies," Sarah explained.

Pippa didn't really have a clue what new technologies might be. She supposed it was inventing stuff, but Sarah didn't seem the type to don a white jacket and head to the lab to whip up a new device. But then, who was she to judge? Technology bamboozled her. She rarely replaced anything because the new features took so long to learn.

"So Swype own this cottage, and you're going to live in it and, presumably, renovate it?" Pippa clarified.

"That's right."

Pippa was sure that there was a piece of the puzzle she was missing, but she was on thin ice with Sarah already and decided not to push too far. She didn't want to upset Sarah again—it irritated her that she had done so once before.

She wondered, not for the first time, what Kim would have said. Kim had been the one to bring balance and harmony to Pippa's life. When Pippa started ranting about an idiot client, a foolish politician, or even a postman who couldn't put letters fully through the letterbox, Kim would calmly smile at her. Nothing more. Just a smile. It was all Pippa needed to know that she was overreacting and to pause and think.

She wasn't an angry person by nature, but she found some people's behaviour so astounding that she couldn't help but rant about them. It was a feature of her personality that had grown over the years and had only been tempered when she'd met Kim. Over dinner on one of their early dates, Pippa had told the story of a pernickety client who was causing mayhem in the office. Kim had simply shrugged. In a soft voice, she asked if Pippa might not be happier if she didn't let it bother her as much.

It had seemed simple, even nonsensical, advice at first. Pippa had even ignored it for the first couple of weeks, but one day she tried not to let anything bother her, just to see if she could get through a day without rolling her eyes so much that she developed a headache. Positive thinking, Kim had told her. It had worked, and it had opened Pippa's eyes to how negative she had become. It had been a slow slip, and one she hadn't noticed. When she did finally notice, she was surprised at how much she grumbled about things throughout the average day.

The behaviour never went away fully. It was a part of who Pippa was. But it faded into the background throughout the course of their romance and into their marriage. Pippa had felt lighter and happier as a result. A small smile from Kim or a muttered *Does it really matter?* was all it took to reset Pippa's negative mindset.

It had been six years since Kim died, and Pippa was realising that she'd slipped back into old patterns.

"What do you think?" Sarah said in a tone that suggested she'd been speaking for a while.

"I'm sorry, I didn't catch all of that," Pippa said. She took a few steps down the stepladder to give Sarah her full attention.

"I said that I thought we could start with lifting the carpet out. It's gross and I feel like a thousand things are living in it. Then I can paint, and you can do the electrics, so the house doesn't melt while I sleep. Does that sound like a good plan? Unless the carpet just walks out by itself one night, which I think is a real possibility."

Pippa pinched her lips together to stop herself from laughing at Sarah's words. Clearly, the carpet was a genuine issue for Sarah.

"Don't laugh," Sarah warned, a smile still gracing her lips.

"Wouldn't dream of it. I can definitely get the carpet out for you. But that would mean old, probably splintered wooden floorboards everywhere. And it might get cold."

"I'll wear more clothes. As long as the carpet is gone."

"I can start on that tomorrow, if you'd like."

Sarah's eyes lit up with excitement. "Really?"

"Absolutely. I'll cut it into strips, roll it up, and take it out. Any underlay as well."

Sarah looked positively giddy, and Pippa's heart warmed at being able to elicit such a response.

"That would be amazing! Thank you." Sarah looked down at the patterned carpet beneath her feet and shivered slightly. "It's really gross."

"So I gather," Pippa said. "Let me fix this light, and then maybe we should draw up a plan. Building works are best done in the right order, but you'll have your own priorities as well. We can figure something out."

"So the house doesn't kill me," Sarah said in a joking tone.

Pippa's stomach lurched. She swallowed and told herself that it was just an innocent joke and Sarah did not know what extra meaning it held for Pippa.

She tried to smile and nod. "Exactly," she managed to force out. "I'll fix this light and we'll talk."

She climbed the ladder quickly, eager to hide her face from Sarah, as she was certain she could not hide her grief. She felt relief flood through her when she heard Sarah walking away.

"I'll put the kettle on!" Sarah said.

Pippa took a few deep breaths and focused her attention on what she was doing. She needed to get herself together, fast.

❖

Sarah walked down the stairs, casting a worried glance over her shoulder to Pippa, who was picking electrical tape from the wires in the light fitting. Something had changed while they were talking. In a moment they had gone from light chatter to a shadow passing over Pippa's face. Sarah hadn't pushed—it had been very clear that Pippa didn't want to talk or even show that she was upset.

Instead, Sarah walked away with a promise of making Pippa a hot drink when she was done.

She hadn't intended on admitting that Pippa had hurt her feelings when she'd previously visited, but the exasperated sigh and the scolding were enough for Sarah to want to justify her actions. If Pippa had been a little nicer, then Sarah would never have asked Robin to fix the light, and then Pippa wouldn't have to repair it. As far as Sarah was concerned, it was all Pippa's fault. Or perhaps Sarah's fault for being overly sensitive, but that wasn't an easy fix.

Overall, she was glad that she did speak up. Pippa had seemed genuinely surprised and had apologised, which made Sarah feel a lot better about the idea of getting Pippa to help her with the renovation work. She'd pretty much already decided that she'd need to get Pippa in, as Robin appeared to be the sort of man who would break more than he would fix and take four times as long to do so.

Sarah thought about Pippa's words. She didn't think she'd met anyone before who actively admitted to being bad with people. Plenty of people had crossed her path who actually were terrible at interacting with others, but never had anyone admitted to it. It was an awareness that Sarah found charming and curious.

The lie about Sarah's presence on Celfare was something that had been dreamt up in a boardroom in London a number of months ago. She'd never been fully happy with the lie, as it made little sense to her technical mind. But she was assured by her teammates that the average person would have no idea that it sounded so unlikely. Pippa had seemed happy enough with the explanation or was at least willing to pretend she was to maintain the peace and move on to helping Sarah with a project plan for the renovation.

Sarah got a couple of mugs out of the kitchen cupboard and

filled up the kettle. At the very back of the garden she could see a little gravel path that led to the wooden shed that she visited at least six times a day to monitor Billy. She'd somehow have to keep it a secret from Pippa, and she wasn't entirely sure how to do that yet.

How would she declare an innocent-looking shed out of bounds? Especially when she herself kept going down there. Sarah suspected that she'd find that out in due course. She wasn't all that good at lying, except when it came to her mother, where she excelled at it. If she wanted to survive in her mother's sphere, then she needed to tell her exactly what she wanted to hear. Anything else led to enormous arguments and painful silent treatment. For an educated woman, her mother could certainly have a childish streak.

She felt Pippa's presence behind her and looked over her shoulder in surprise.

"Are you done?"

"Yes, all finished."

Sarah let out a relieved breath. She'd felt for sure that Robin had caused a massive issue that would take a while to fix. How one light being fixed could stop another from working was beyond her.

"Your garden will need cutting back soon," Pippa said. "Or you'll not see the cottage from the road anymore."

"I know—I'm trying to get some tools. The lady at the hardware store said I'd have to order it from the mainland, and it could take up to a week." Sarah wasn't sure when she'd get used to the idea of being so cut off from everything. Back home she could order a packet of instant mash, and it could be at her door within half an hour. Some enterprising youngster on a bicycle was more than happy to get her anything at any time, as long as she paid them the right amount and tipped accordingly. And Sarah was happy to do so. She loved convenience. Everything about Celfare seemed inconvenient.

"I could do it for you," Pippa offered.

"You do gardening?"

"I do. I have a scythe that I could use."

Sarah narrowed her eyes. "Tell me you're joking."

A smile crept across Pippa's features. "I'm joking. I have an industrial strength grass trimmer that will take care of that lawn in no time."

"I can see I'm going to be asking you to do quite a lot to get this place fixed up." Sarah gestured to the kettle. "How about a down payment of a cup of tea?"

"Sounds wonderful." Pippa took a seat at the kitchen table and got a small notepad and a pen out of one of the pockets of her cargo trousers.

Sarah made some tea for them both while listing all the things she wanted to be fixed. Pippa dutifully jotted them all down. Eventually, Sarah ran out of steam.

"I think that's everything," she said. She frowned, sure that there was probably more that she had forgotten.

Pippa looked at her notes, flipping through page after page with a smirk. "Maybe you could just move?"

"Har-har," Sarah said. She sat opposite Pippa. "I'm here now. Better make it habitable."

"It *is* habitable," Pippa argued.

Sarah laughed. "Would you live here with it in this condition?"

Pippa looked around the kitchen thoughtfully. "I think I would, yes. There's a lot of potential with the house. It could be lovely. You just have to see through the dirt and think about how it will look when it's fixed up."

"I'm sure the roof will collapse," Sarah said. "It creaks."

"I'm sure the roof isn't going to collapse. What creaks?"

"The roof."

"But what? Is it the ceiling of the bedroom? The joists?"

Sarah blinked. "I don't know. It creaks." She made a noise imitating the sound she heard when in bed at night.

Pippa bit back a laugh.

Sarah smiled. "I'm not great with roof impressions, okay?"

"Oh, you did very well." Pippa hid her smile behind her mug of tea. "I'd say it was joists based on your first-class roof impression. I can pop up and have a look."

"Thank you." Sarah grasped the warm mug in her hands as Pippa added a note to the list.

"What worries you most?" Pippa asked. "About the house, I mean?"

Sarah looked around the kitchen as she gathered her thoughts. Everything worried her about the house. The way the taps leaked, some sockets buzzed, the roof creaked, and the doors didn't fit in their frames. She'd always lived in modern homes, and suddenly finding herself in an older property was a shock. Of course she'd been in old houses before. Whenever she visited her grandmother as a child, she was almost comforted by the sound of hot water pipes gently thumping in the morning to indicate her grandmother was awake and had turned on the heating. The quirks of that house had seemed reassuring. The quirks of Hillcrest Cottage were just frightening.

Sarah was aware of Pippa's gaze on her. She swallowed. She wasn't used to feeling frightened and certainly not because of her home.

"I'm not usually like this," Sarah confessed.

"Like what?"

"On edge." Sarah rubbed her face and sighed. "This place has shaken me, and I'm not sure why."

"It's home," Pippa said. "And you're not relaxed in it. It's bound to make you feel unsettled. But we're going to fix that. Do you mind if I have a look around?"

Sarah nodded. "Of course."

Pippa walked slowly around the kitchen. She opened the cupboard under the sink and looked at the pipes. Then she looked at the boiler affixed to the wall. Her gaze followed the line of the ceiling and she sucked in a cheek as she prodded the black seal around the back door with her pen.

Sarah could easily tell that Pippa had a good eye for detail and knew what she was doing. There was a certainty about her that hadn't existed with Robin. A quiet power emanated from her, and Sarah couldn't help but be impressed.

And turned on.

"Excuse me, I just need to…" She allowed her sentence to drift to nothing as she exited the room. She didn't know what she needed to do, other than escape. Finding herself on the upstairs landing, she paused and took a couple of breaths. The house needed to be fixed, and Pippa had to be the one to do it. That much was clear.

The only issue with that was that Sarah was already struggling to keep her interest in Pippa under wraps. If Pippa was going to help her make the house liveable, they'd be spending a lot of time together.

Sarah needed to get her attraction to Pippa under control. Yes, she was her type of woman. Yes, there was a chance that Pippa was single. And, yes, they'd be spending a lot of time together. But Sarah couldn't start a relationship now even if Pippa was interested, which was incredibly unlikely. Pippa wouldn't be interested in someone who didn't have her life together, who lied to her mother, who lived for her work, who owned a new build in the city.

And Sarah had a secret to keep.

The idea of Pippa being a good match for her was nothing more than fiction, probably brought on by the fact that Sarah had spent the last few years so desperately lonely and sitting through more than her fair share of disastrous first dates.

Thoughts of a perfect partner had obviously been brought to the forefront of her mind because of her lie to her mother. Sarah had created the perfect girlfriend and told her mum that they were blissfully happy on Celfare. For the first time in memory, Angela Campbell had sounded genuinely happy for and proud of her daughter. It stung bitterly that her mother would only be truly proud of Sarah for finding someone to love her, which Sarah was finding impossible to achieve.

She sucked in a quick breath, jutted her chin high, and promised herself not to cry. She was emotional because of the move, the project, and the state of the house. Her mother's disappointment in her and her woeful social life needed to take a back seat for a while.

"Sarah?" Pippa called.

"Coming," Sarah replied. She took a couple of cleansing breaths before plastering a smile on her face.

Chapter Seven

Pippa knocked on the front door to Hillcrest Cottage and took a step back as she waited for Sarah to answer. They'd agreed on a seven thirty start, as Pippa was keen to get as much done as possible on the first day. The first jobs she'd planned were the messiest ones, and the amount of dust that she was about to send flying was considerable. It was due to be a warm day, and so it would be perfect weather to open the windows and allow at least some of the mess to float away on the wind.

The door opened to reveal Sarah in a white T-shirt with denim dungarees, tan boots, and safety glasses, which were far too big for her face.

Pippa bit back a smile. "Good morning."

"I started!" Sarah said. She excitedly waved Pippa into the house.

Pippa followed her into the living room, where she saw the corner of the carpet had been lifted and folded over.

"It wouldn't let go, but I used my ruler and got underneath it and then it gave up the fight."

Pippa noticed a nail in the floorboard and assumed some enterprising individual had, at some point, nailed the carpet into place. It wasn't usual practice, but she imagined there would be a lot of that in Hillcrest Cottage.

"What do we do now?" Sarah asked eagerly.

Pippa looked at her young employer and couldn't help but smile at the adorable outfit and the determined look on her face.

Strands of hair had fallen from a loose ponytail and framed her face. Red cheeks showed that she'd been working for a while, despite the lack of progress.

"You hired me to do this," Pippa pointed out gently. "There's no need for you to get yourself messy if you have work to be getting on with."

"I couldn't sleep," Sarah confessed. "So I got up early to move some of the furniture out of the way. And then I just carried on. I'm a bit stuck now, not sure how to get the rest of it up."

Pippa wondered why Sarah couldn't sleep and only just stopped herself from asking. It wasn't any of her business, but she found she wanted to know what kept Sarah awake at night.

"I only have one face mask," Pippa said. "Unless you have one, a proper one, then I'd prefer it if you stayed out of the way. For your own safety. I don't want you breathing in all the dust and fibres that will come up when I move this lot out."

Sarah's face scrunched up in mild disappointment. "Oh. Yes, that makes sense. Sorry, I just really want to see the back of this carpet."

Pippa chuckled. "I can tell. What is it with you and carpet?"

"My mum." Sarah removed her safety glasses and removed her spectacles from where they hung from her dungarees pocket and put them back on. "She's obsessed with the environment. She didn't used to be, but then she got involved with a few organisations, and she became really militant about saving the planet. Which is great, and I love her for it, but her methods weren't always the best."

"I'm really interested to hear the connection between your mum and carpets," Pippa said to lighten a darkening mood.

Sarah smiled, but a heaviness remained. "We had carpet throughout the house when I was younger, and it needed replacing. My mum wanted to get bamboo flooring—it looks like normal wooden flooring, but it's much more sustainable."

Pippa nodded. She knew the virtues of bamboo flooring well. It had changed the wooden flooring industry forever when people had started to use the fast-growing grass over other hardwoods.

Sarah sat on the arm of the sofa and sighed. "I wanted carpet because it's warm and soft under your toes, and things don't break when you drop them on carpet. So my mum told me a few things about carpet. I was eight when she explained that the average carpet has more germs than a toilet seat. She's a scientist, and she explained to me, in great detail, how a carpet can easily become really gross and how the fibres trap air pollutants until it gets full of them and then it releases them into the air that we breathe."

Pippa winced. She knew carpets were unhygienic unless regularly cleaned and replaced, but thinking about how disgusting they could become made her a little queasy. And she wasn't eight years old.

"Ever since then I've had a bit of an aversion to carpets," Sarah explained. "And really gross carpets like this freak me out. I know there are tons of bacteria living in it, I know that it's full of harmful toxins that are being spread every time I walk on it. It makes my skin crawl to think about."

Pippa had never been a mother but was fairly certain that if she ever cared for a child, she'd have enough common sense to not gift them a life of distress through oversharing information that no child really needed to hear.

"That makes perfect sense." Pippa looked through the window at the morning sun. "It's a beautiful day. What do you say we move a table and chair outside for you to sit and work while I get on with getting the carpet out of the house?"

Sarah looked keen on the idea, but uncertain. "Are you sure? I feel like I should do something."

"You're paying me," Pippa reminded her. "I appreciate you wanting to help, but I think you'd probably prefer to just never see this carpet again. Work outside for the day, and by the middle of the afternoon the carpet will be a distant memory."

"That soon?"

Pippa looked around the room and thought of the house layout. She intended to take a knife to the carpet to roll it into tubes to easily remove it. She'd allocated three and a half hours for the task, and that was an overestimate.

"Sooner," she said.

Sarah smiled as if she'd won the lottery. "That would really make me happy, thank you."

Pippa felt a rush of pride. She enjoyed helping people—it was her main reason for being a handywoman. But there was something special about helping Sarah. Being the reason for the smile was like the sun shining just for you. She swallowed and turned away, hoping that Sarah wouldn't notice.

She wasn't sure when making Sarah happy had become such an important thing to her. It had gone beyond just wanting to make sure that the client was satisfied with her work. When Sarah smiled, Pippa's heart beat a little faster, and she wasn't sure she knew what to do with that information.

It had been a long time since she'd felt that way. Escaping to Celfare was supposed to keep her away from the possibility of ever feeling that way again. But when she'd left her old life all those years ago, she hadn't expected someone like Sarah to pop up in the middle of nowhere and need her help.

She pushed the feelings down and discussed with Sarah where she would like to be set up in the garden, and between them they carried the small kitchen table out onto the back patio. Sarah brought out her laptop and some papers and thanked Pippa yet again for all her help.

When she was satisfied that Sarah was out of harm's way, she got to work ripping up, cutting, rolling, and removing the carpet. Decades of dust flew into the air, and Pippa was glad for her protective clothing and equipment. It was a messy job, but even more worthwhile now that she knew why Sarah hated the floor covering so.

❖

Sarah closed her eyes and enjoyed the sun on her face for a few moments. She'd rarely worked outside in the past, always thinking it would be too hot, too cold, or too bright. She supposed that made her sound like Goldilocks, but she really wasn't used to roughing it.

Loud sounds of banging and fabric being ripped echoed through the cottage. She was very glad that she wasn't inside. All the windows were open, and now and then a small plume of dust would stream out and catch the sun in a gross rainbow effect that had Sarah wincing.

She'd clean the house meticulously that evening. And the next morning. And every day until she no longer found dust on everything. Which would probably be for the next couple of months.

She reminded herself that it would all be worth it in the end. Being on Celfare meant getting the data from Billy for a game-changing project that would literally change the world for the better if her calculations were correct. And if that meant living through a massive renovation project, so be it.

Her phone chimed with the familiar ringtone that she had assigned to only one person. She snatched up the device, sucked in a calming breath, and answered.

"Hi, Mum!"

"Hello, I'm having to call you earlier than planned because I have a very important meeting later this evening."

Angela Campbell only ever had very important meetings. She was never otherwise engaged or double-booked. And Sarah's weekly phone calls were always the first thing to be discarded when something else came up.

"That's okay," Sarah said automatically. "How are you?"

"Exhausted," Angela replied. "Honestly, you'd think trying to get ministers to listen to reason would be easy when it came pre-packaged with votes, jobs in their constituency, and the promise of making the world a better place for their children. But it seems not."

"Sounds tricky." Sarah lowered her laptop lid. She knew her mum was about to embark on a long speech about her latest foolproof method to save the environment, and therefore the world, if only people would listen to her.

Angela was the kind of person who was either adored or avoided. There was little space in between. The militant environmentalists that Angela had met and aligned herself with some years ago worshipped her as a goddess. They told her what she wanted to hear and hung on her every word. They'd taken someone with an already inflated ego and created a narcissist.

Sarah loved her mum but wasn't blind to her faults.

Angela launched into an explanation of her latest scheme to disrupt networks. She'd recently become fascinated with the idea of being a disruptor of things. It was no longer enough to lobby companies or governments. Creating mayhem was the loudspeaker she used these days. Sarah didn't agree with the methods, but her opinions didn't register on her mother's radar.

Sarah closed her eyes, leaned back in her chair, and put her feet on the table. If she was going to listen to her mother, then she'd be comfortable doing so.

"What's all that noise?" Angela suddenly asked.

"Oh. We're, um, having some work done to the cottage."

"Be careful with tradespeople, dear," Angela said in a lecturing tone. "Get at least three references, and don't pay them for materials in advance."

Sarah rolled her eyes. The chance of getting references from a tradesperson was very unlikely, and she'd never be stupid enough to pay for materials in advance.

"Natalie's doing it herself." The lie slipped off Sarah's tongue easily. It always did when it came to her mother. It had started when she was younger and got fed up with her mother's lectures. Angela had a habit of naturally assuming that Sarah was an idiot. Sarah had developed the habit of lying to her mother at any opportunity to protect her own sanity.

"Oh, is she handy?" Angela asked. "That's an excellent trait in a person. I always wished that you'd be a little more handy with things, but you never knew which end of a hammer was which."

Sarah bit the inside of her cheek. She wanted to point out that maybe things would have been different if she'd been taught something as a child. But she knew that route was pointless. Every route was pointless. Eventually, it all came back to the same thing: Sarah being a disappointment in one way or another.

Pippa poked her head out of the kitchen door. When she saw Sarah was on the phone, she looked apologetic and gestured that she'd go back inside again. Sarah held up her hand to request that she wait.

"Sorry, Mum, I have to go. Natalie needs my help. Can we catch up later?"

Pippa raised an eyebrow at apparently being called Natalie but said nothing and waited patiently in the doorway.

"Of course, dear. It will have to be after my round table at the weekend. I'll drop you a message with my schedule. Anyway, must dash."

Angela hung up the call before Sarah had time to say goodbye. She lowered her feet from the table and placed the phone down with a thump.

"Natalie?" Pippa asked with a confused expression.

"My perfect, fake girlfriend," Sarah confessed.

Pippa blinked. "Oh, you're…"

"Gay. Yeah."

Pippa's brow remained furrowed. "A fake girlfriend?"

Sarah stood up and tidied her paperwork. Anything to avoid Pippa's gaze as she told the sad story of her love life.

"My mum is a bit judgemental. She thinks I'm going to be alone forever. Her words, not mine. I created a girlfriend, so she wouldn't worry about me." She sighed. "And to shut her up, if I'm honest."

"And that's Natalie?" Pippa clarified.

"Yeah. Natalie's great. She's handy, which I'm apparently not. She's kind, funny, and has her life together." Sarah leaned her hands on the table, lowered her head, and closed her eyes in defeat. "Sounds stupid, I know."

"Not stupid, no. I'll admit that I'm not sure why you're lying to your mother about such an important part of your life, but it's not my place to say."

Sarah itched to explain. But explaining her mother was an impossible task. You had to experience Angela Campbell to understand her, and no one had the experience that Sarah did.

Sarah looked up. "Anyway, did you need me for something?"

Pippa nodded. "I need to turn the water off to remove some carpet that has been nailed into a pipe."

"Nailed into a pipe?" Sarah repeated, sure she'd not heard correctly.

"Accidentally, but yes. Whoever was having fun nailing the carpet down rather than using gripper rod nicked a water pipe. It's okay as long as the nail is there, but when I remove it, it's going to be a problem."

Sarah felt her heart beat a little faster at the idea of nails in water pipes. Surely that meant water leaking, and potential flooding. But Pippa looked calm, almost amused by the discovery.

"Can it be fixed?" Sarah asked.

"Oh, absolutely. I have some copper pipe in the van. I'll just turn the water off, drain the system, and replace that piece of pipe. As long as you're okay for the water to be off for an hour or two?"

Sarah smiled. "Just like that."

"It's easy when you know how," Pippa said.

Sarah didn't know how. Didn't have a clue. She felt useless, a remnant of having recently spoken to her mother. Even during their good conversations, Sarah often felt worthless in the shadow of her mother. Angela didn't value Sarah's education or her work. Quite the opposite. Sarah had squandered her chances, according to Angela. She'd taken the wrong educational path and ended up working for the devil. The only right direction would have been to follow her mother and become another one of her fanatics.

"Are you okay?"

Pippa's voice broke through Sarah's spiral of doubts and self-chastisement.

Sarah shook the thoughts away and nodded. "Sorry. Um, yes, yes, turn the water off. No problem."

Pippa's eyes bored into Sarah for a long few seconds before she nodded and returned to the house. Sarah let out a sigh. She needed to not let her mother get under her skin. However, that was easier said than done.

She checked her watch. It was time to get some more data

from the shed. She picked up her notepad and pen and peeked into the cottage to see Pippa heading up the stairs. It was the perfect opportunity to disappear for a few moments, and the chance to push thoughts of her mother out of her head was a welcome one.

Until her next phone call.

CHAPTER EIGHT

Pippa opened the window and looked at the hinge. It had come loose from the runner and would be an easy fix.

"It was fine, and then it wasn't," Rowena Findlay explained for the sixth time since Pippa had arrived less than five minutes ago.

Pippa opened the window wide and guided the hinge back. She closed the window and listened out for the sound of the mechanism popping back into place. When she heard the satisfying sound, she opened the window again.

"Just a problem with the hinge. I'll tighten it up so it doesn't slip again."

"Thank you, Pippa. I was worried the window might have fallen. It just slipped and then it was hanging and I didn't know what to do."

"That's what I'm here for."

Rowena had called at nine o'clock that evening and sounded panicked. Apparently, she was closing her window to prepare for bed when something had happened and she couldn't close it. The elderly woman sounded rattled, and Pippa had reassured her that she'd be there within a few minutes. Mr. Findlay had died some years before, and Rowena had been living alone in her bungalow in the middle of town ever since.

Pippa visited the bungalow at least once a month to fix something or help with a new purchase. The last time she'd been called out was to install a new curtain rail.

"I'll make you a cup of tea," Rowena said. "Sorry for calling you out so late."

She was out of the dining room and in the kitchen before Pippa could say anything. She suspected that the cup of tea was as much for Rowena to have some company as it was a thank you for Pippa's service.

She crouched down to her toolbox and ran her finger along the row of neat screwdrivers. Finding the perfect size, she pulled it out of the line-up and tightened the screws on the hinge. While the kettle boiled, she did the same for the other hinge and the window in the living room just in case.

Ten minutes later she was sitting in the wingback armchair she still considered Mr. Findlay's with a mug of tea and a slice of Dundee cake on the side table beside her. For someone who had been going to bed, Rowena seemed remarkably prepared with tea and cake.

If she didn't know Rowena was incapable of such things, she'd assume the hinge had been tampered with as an excuse to get Pippa to come over.

"So, you're spending a lot of time at Hillcrest Cottage, I hear?" Rowena asked.

"I am. There's a lot of renovation work needed."

"Been there every day for the last two weeks, I hear," Rowena continued.

"Yes. As I say, a lot of work needing to be done."

"I hear that there's a pretty young one living there," Rowena said.

"Sarah." Pippa picked up the small plate and fork and cut off a piece of cake.

"Little rainbow flag on her car." Rowena sipped from her teacup and looked at Pippa over the rim.

"I hadn't noticed." Pippa ate a piece of cake. She'd noticed. And she'd also had confirmation of Sarah's sexuality from the woman herself. She wasn't surprised that others seemed intrigued by Sarah's presence on Celfare. She was new and young and kept to herself. All of which meant that the local gossips were desperate to know more about her. The small detail of the rainbow flag on Sarah's car had no doubt set tongues wagging at a rate that could have started fires.

"I don't believe you," Rowena said.

"Did you break that hinge?" Pippa asked.

She was confident that Rowena wouldn't know how, but the set-up seemed just a little too perfect.

"Of course not. My window broke. I called you. I'd planned to ask you to come and cut back the apple tree, and I was going to talk to you then, but this seemed like as good a time as any."

Pippa rarely regretted her decision to move to Celfare. The only issue was that people like Rowena had known her since she was a child and sometimes struggled to treat her like the adult she was.

When she'd first met Rowena, she'd thought her an old woman. Now, some forty years later, she realised with horror that Rowena had been younger than Pippa was now.

"She seems very nice," Rowena added.

"She is very nice," Pippa said. "But I'm just helping her with renovations. There's nothing more to it."

"You don't want to be alone forever," Rowena said. "I miss my David every single day, but if I was younger, then I wouldn't waste my life. He wouldn't want me to."

Pippa ate a slightly bigger piece of cake, hoping to finish and wash it down with a cup of tea in short order so she could leave without being rude. She didn't want to argue with Rowena, and she certainly didn't want to explain her singledom to anyone. To do so would inadvertently suggest that Pippa's grief was somehow more pronounced than anyone else's, and that wasn't something she wanted to say to an elderly widow.

"It just seems that the Lord has provided you with an opportunity to have someone in your life again."

Pippa ate another piece of cake. She was halfway through. When she'd got home that evening she'd never expected to later be eating her way through a Dundee cake towards freedom.

"I don't think the Lord has anything to do with it," Pippa said in between bites of cake.

Rowena wasn't ordinarily the religious sort, only when it served a purpose for her. She never attended church, nor was she one for prayer. But if something happened that she thought was fortuitous, it was often down to God. Pippa had long ago given up on any lingering faith she might have once had. Loss of a loved one had a tendency to throw people either into or out of religion, as she'd discovered when she'd first joined a bereavement group back in Bournemouth. The group had done little but squabble about whether or not there was a divine plan that the departed were supposedly part of. She'd attended two meetings before deciding there was little solace to be found in them.

"I appreciate your worry," Pippa said. "But I'm fine, really."

Rowena regarded her for a moment. Her gaze fell to the nearly finished cake. Pippa could sense the cogs in her mind were turning, but she feared they were turning in entirely the wrong direction.

"Oh!" Rowena said. A smile started to appear on her face. "You're both taking it slow. I understand. You don't want all the local gossips to be pressuring you. That's understandable. I'll keep your secret, of course."

Pippa opened her mouth to issue a denial but knew it was too late. Rowena had misread her discomfort and assumed she was already in a relationship with Sarah. It was a much better story to tell Louise, Marie, and the other members of the unofficial Celfare gossip committee.

Any denial Pippa issued would only reinforce Rowena's notion, but she knew she still had to try.

"There's nothing between us. I'm just helping her with renovations." Pippa polished off the last piece of cake and picked up the mug of tea. She was a few swallows from being able to escape, but it seemed useless now that Rowena had spent the time constructing her own fantasy.

"I see." Rowena tapped her nose with her finger. "Nothing between you."

Pippa rolled her eyes. The lack of anything happening on Celfare was a blessing and a curse. They didn't have all the drama of a big city, but it did mean that sometimes a little idle gossip needed to be created by some to relieve the boredom.

"I better get going." She drank half a cup of tea in one go and carried the cup and the empty plate into the kitchen. "Thank you for the tea and cake."

Rowena joined her in the kitchen, opening her handbag in search of her purse.

"We'll settle up when I see you next week," Pippa said. She wanted to leave before Rowena's imagination conjured anything else up. They shared a quick goodbye, and moments later Pippa was outside and in her van.

"Well, that could have gone better," she mumbled to herself.

It had been years, and she was still not quite used to her life being so interesting to others. At first there had been a lot of chatter about why she had come to Celfare and when she might leave again. As the months drifted by, people became used to the idea of her staying. After half a decade had passed, they'd finally stopped ruminating on her personal life.

She knew that it came from a place of love. They wanted her to be happy. But Pippa was a private person, especially when it came to the topic of her widowhood.

Rowena didn't mean any harm, but Pippa still felt irritated by how the evening had turned out. Instead of heading home, she drove to a nearby beach where she could watch the sun set and be guaranteed some peace and quiet.

❖

Sarah sat on the flat-topped rock and watched the tide coming in. Celfare had its issues, but the incredible beaches were something she'd miss when she returned to London. The warm day had turned into a perfect night with just a hint of a breeze. She'd taken to walking along the beach of an evening, partly for exercise but mainly for fresh air. Hillcrest Cottage was full of dust every evening with the work Pippa was doing.

The beach was usually quiet. Now and then she encountered a dog walker who greeted her, but usually she had the beach to herself. Sometimes she walked by the water, and sometimes she sat on one of the many rocks and thought about her day. Once she sat in the abandoned wooden fishing boat just because she could.

"Hello again."

Sarah turned to see Pippa walking across the beach towards her makeshift seat.

"Hey. Did you miss me already?" Sarah asked.

Pippa chuckled. Sarah enjoyed the rich, throaty sound.

"It's only been six hours," Pippa said after a glance at her watch.

"Wow, you could have lied, you know."

"I missed you terribly." Pippa grinned. "But I'll leave you to it—I just wanted to say hello. Have a nice evening."

Pippa turned, and Sarah instantly missed her company. Before she had a chance to think about what she was doing she called out, "Hot chocolate?"

Pippa paused and looked over her shoulder. "Sorry?"

Sarah held up a Thermos flask. "Would you like some hot chocolate?"

Sarah watched indecision skitter across Pippa's face. She was about to retract her offer and allow Pippa to have a private walk along the beach when Pippa approached the rock and took a seat next to Sarah.

"I've never said no to hot chocolate of an evening," Pippa confessed.

"I knew you were smart." Sarah poured the drink into one of the two cups that came with her Thermos, suddenly happy that she had spent the extra pound on the fancier flask.

They sat in silence for a few moments, each cradling their drink and looking out to sea.

Sarah eventually broke the silence. "Do you walk along the beach often?"

"Rarely," Pippa confessed. "I used to come here all the time, but I stopped, and now I hardly ever make the effort. When I'm here, I wonder why not. You?"

"I'm here every evening. It's still new to me. And my house is full of dust in the air."

Pippa chuckled. "I did warn you."

"You did. I'm not complaining—I know it needs to be done. But I've developed a cough that would make a Victorian miner proud."

Pippa turned to face her, distress clear in her expression.

"It's not that bad," Sarah said. "I keep the windows open and spend time outside while it all settles. The vacuum cleaner will never be the same, though."

"Make sure you keep those windows open," Pippa instructed.

Sarah nodded and smiled to herself. Some might think of it as lecturing, but Sarah could see it was watchfulness. Pippa cared. And Sarah liked that.

"So, what brings you out here?" Sarah asked.

"Fresh air and distraction."

"Distraction from what, if I may ask?"

Pippa took a sip of hot chocolate. "I was ambushed by one of my regular clients. She called me at nine o'clock about a broken window hinge. Then she used the opportunity to quiz me about things. Tea and cake were all prepared."

"Did she break the hinge on purpose?" Sarah asked.

Pippa laughed. "I wondered that, too. I doubt it. I think she has the mild malevolence needed to do it, but none of the knowledge."

Sarah took a sip of her drink, and they eased back into a comfortable silence. Pippa had been working at the cottage for two weeks, and they were both finding their feet in their relationship. But a question niggled at Sarah's mind.

In the end, she decided to just ask. Pippa could always say if she didn't want to reply. It wasn't as if she was some wilting violet.

"What did she quiz you about?"

Pippa stared out to the sea, and Sarah could feel the internal war happening within her. She sat quietly and allowed Pippa the time and space to decide if she wanted to share whatever it was that had caused her to decide on an evening walk to clear her mind.

"My grandfather lived on this island his entire life," Pippa said. "I visited him all the time when I was a child. Summer holidays, Christmas and New Year, even some half-terms if I begged my parents enough. When I was older and went to university, I spent a lot of spare time here. All of that was many, many years ago. But a lot of the people who knew me then still see me as a child, or at the very least a naive young woman."

Sarah couldn't imagine anyone thinking of Pippa Kent as naive. To Sarah she was confident and completely in control at all times.

"I came to live here permanently six years ago," Pippa continued, "a little while after my wife died."

The words hit Sarah hard. She struggled to fully process them. "I'm so sorry for your loss." The words were automatic. She knew they meant little, but she had nothing else at her disposal.

"Thank you." Pippa continued to look out towards the waves. Sarah wondered if that was to keep her emotions in check. "I made a choice to come here because I wanted to be alone. I wanted to forget my old life with Kim. But there are people on Celfare who think they know what's best for me, or think they understand what I've been through and what I should do with my life."

"People love giving advice," Sarah said.

"They do. But after six years I had really hoped that they'd stop and they'd leave me to it." Pippa sipped her drink. She looked at Sarah with a small smile. "I should really know better. I'm sorry for bringing this to you."

"It's fine. We're friends, right?"

Pippa chuckled. "Well, rumour around here has it that we're more than friends."

Sarah blinked. "Where did they get that from?" Her heart raced. Panic set in as she feared her secret crush was visible for all to see.

"I'm in and out of your house all the time," Pippa said.

"You're doing work for me," Sarah spluttered.

She felt caught red-handed for reasons she couldn't fathom. She'd deliberately pushed aside all thoughts of Pippa being anything more than a contractor helping her to renovate Hillcrest Cottage. But somehow the locals were inside her head and knew exactly what she'd been initially thinking.

"Well, you and I know that. But this community gets quite bored sometimes. They saw a rainbow flag on your car and put two and two together," Pippa explained.

"And got sixteen," Sarah said. "I'm sorry if that's put you in an awkward situation."

"It's fine."

Sarah didn't know if that was confirmation that she'd been placed in an awkward situation or not. She supposed Pippa had meant it to be ambiguous. She couldn't help but feel bad that her presence had somehow caused some drama for Pippa.

As she processed what Pippa had told her, she couldn't help but ask herself if Pippa had been single for six years. It sounded like it. She wanted to know more, but it wasn't her place to ask. While she did consider them friends, she didn't know if Pippa felt that way. She presumed not. Sarah was probably nothing more than another client to her.

"What should we do?" Sarah asked.

"About?"

"The rumours."

"Oh." Pippa smiled and shook her head. "Nothing. If you deny it, they'll claim that we protest too much. Best to just ignore it. A more interesting piece of gossip, true or otherwise, will come along soon enough."

Sarah knew that was the best way to deal with rumours but also felt offended that she was the topic of conversation amongst people she didn't even know. Especially considering they had unwittingly unearthed a desire that Sarah had initially struggled to keep under control.

"Good thinking."

Pippa finished up her hot chocolate and handed the empty cup back to Sarah. "Thank you for the drink—it's nearly as good as my mother used to make."

"Nearly?" Sarah asked, grinning at Pippa's perma-honesty.

Pippa shrugged and smiled back. "She was an exceptionally good hot chocolate maker. Keep practicing." She winked and stood up. "I better go and have that walk, or it will be dark."

"Enjoy. See you in the morning."

"See you then."

Pippa walked away, and Sarah watched her go, safe in the knowledge that Pippa couldn't see her staring. While Sarah had done what she could to put her attraction to Pippa to one side due to the small matter of the secret underwater data centre just out to sea and the fact that Pippa seemed wholly uninterested in her. That didn't mean she didn't enjoy looking now and then.

Sarah sighed and turned away. She looked out at the water and reminded herself of her schedule for the following day. She had back-to-back meetings with her team in London, and Pippa was planning to finish installing the upstairs electrical sockets. For the first time since she'd moved into Hillcrest Cottage, she'd have all new cabling and outlets. In other words, she wouldn't need to wince and hold her breath every time she plugged in an expensive device.

The cottage no longer felt like an axe swaying above her head. She no longer jumped at every creak and thud. Slowly it was starting to feel like home, and she knew she had Pippa to thank for that.

Chapter Nine

Pippa lifted the floorboard and looked into the floor space with a torch. As she'd suspected, there were more redundant cables that needed to be removed now that she had replaced most of the wiring. Hillcrest Cottage was a prime example of a property that had undergone decades of patch repairs by people who didn't properly clean up after themselves.

New pipes ran beside old pipes when the old ones should have been removed. Floorboards were hammered down with multiple nails and had become splintered to the point where the nails no longer gripped the joists. While the renovation project was a big one, it was the little things that bothered Pippa, the things that were just poor workmanship.

She'd been working in Hillcrest Cottage for four weeks now. All of the electrics had been replaced. Bill McFarlane was coming the following day to install a new gas boiler to the new pipework which Pippa had installed. The old carpets were up, and the floorboards were being repaired or replaced. She'd fixed the draughty windows and found the source of the noisy joist in the loft space. The upstairs shower room had been completely replaced upon discovering the leaky pipes in the wall, which had caused a lot of hidden damage. Her job list was going down quickly, and her client was looking more comfortable and happier each day.

Every morning Sarah greeted her with a mug of coffee and a warm smile before heading off to work. The week before, Sarah had painted one of the spare bedrooms, and it had been turned into her home office.

Pippa still didn't know precisely what Sarah did. She spent a lot of time on the phone, and while Pippa wasn't eavesdropping, she did catch the odd discussion while she worked and found that she only understood around half of the words that Sarah used. *Server loads, paths, uptime,* and *CFD* were terms bandied around frequently.

Whatever it was that Sarah did, she appeared to be very good at it. Phone calls came in thick and fast, and Pippa often heard Sarah calmly talking to people and issuing instructions.

Sarah often walked around with an earpiece in while on a call, and when she did, Pippa couldn't help but glance up from her work and watch. Sarah was clearly very passionate about her job, and that vibrancy lit up whatever room she was in. It had been a long time since Pippa had last shared a space with someone so animated. She thought she preferred her own quiet life, but as the days and weeks ticked by, she realised that Sarah's enthusiasm made her smile.

Sarah was often smiling, and Pippa found herself doing the same in her company. Being around Sarah reminded her that a smile didn't need to be reserved for a happy event or a greeting—it could just come naturally and even be a default setting.

Pippa had found herself looking in the bathroom mirror one morning and wondering why her face naturally fell into a slight scowl. Had it always been that way? Had it happened six years ago and never recovered?

She tried to push the thought away, but it lingered in her mind. Every day she went to Hillcrest Cottage, and every day she came home satisfied that she'd ticked off a few more jobs and got Sarah a little closer to living in a home she liked rather than feared. She wasn't sure when making Sarah happy had become such an important thing to her.

It was natural after spending so many weeks together that they had formed a friendship of sorts. They spoke of the renovations but also about Celfare and the interesting people who lived there. Sarah joked about the lack of a good restaurant on the island, and

Pippa playfully pointed out the fresh produce and the recently deep-cleaned oven.

The days were filled with more smiles and laughter than Pippa had been used to, something she was reluctantly enjoying. Reluctant only because she knew it couldn't last.

She heard Sarah rushing down the stairs. Sarah was always rushing about. She seemed full of energy and was always flitting around the house and even the garden. At the last moment, Pippa realised that the floorboards in the hallway were up and Sarah had likely not seen them.

Panic washed over her, and images of Sarah plunging her foot through the gap in the floorboards and becoming injured flashed through her mind. Pippa dropped her tools and jumped to her feet. There was no time to issue a verbal warning, Sarah was moving at such a speed that she'd never be able to hear and react in time.

Sarah reached the last step and turned to enter the hall. Her foot disappeared into the hole at the same moment that Pippa wrapped an arm around her and lifted her away from the broken boards and to solid ground.

Sarah gasped. Pippa was glad as it covered the whimper that escaped her lips as Sarah's hands wrapped around her shoulders to steady herself. Sarah's body was pressed against Pippa's as she looked down at the lifted boards.

"Oh," Sarah said. "Thank you for the save."

"Sorry, I should have let you know. I usually put up a safety line."

"No harm done." Sarah's hands softly squeezed Pippa's shoulders, and she took a step back.

Pippa quickly let go. She couldn't believe that she had forgotten to tell Sarah about the danger or put up her ever-present safety line. Sarah had lightly mocked her for the safety precautions she took. A piece of electrical tape to mark an exposed wire, safety tape to prevent entrance to a room, signage depicting all kinds of dangers. Sarah had called Pippa a one-woman health and safety department. And she was right—for a handyperson service she probably had gone overboard with the amount of time she spent on safety equipment. But somehow, she had forgotten to stand up her safety line when there was a real danger lurking at the bottom of the stairs, out of sight.

"Good thing you have quick reflexes. I'll be more careful on the way up." Sarah smiled and hopped over the remaining hole and made her way into the kitchen.

Pippa stood still and took a few breaths to try to return her heart rate to normal. It hadn't been the fear of Sarah injuring herself that had caused the spike, though that had been the worry initially. It was the feel of Sarah's body against hers, and Pippa's own unexpected reaction to it.

Sarah's shampoo was still noticeable in the air. Pippa realised that her hand was shaking lightly. Swallowing, she headed out of the front door to the privacy of her van. She stood by the open back doors and stared at the equipment inside without really seeing any of it.

It would have been so easy to hold Sarah closer, to have whispered in her ear, to have kissed her.

"Stop it," she murmured under her breath.

She leaned her head against the door. She wasn't oblivious to Sarah's attractiveness. She'd noticed it on day one, and she continued to notice it every time they met. It wasn't something that she'd wanted to notice. In fact, it was something that she wished would go away. Not Sarah, just the feelings that Sarah stirred within her.

Pippa had decided a long time ago that love wasn't for her. She'd experienced love in all its glory once before. Nothing else would come close, and if it did, it might break her. Love was a dangerous thing, once lost. Pippa had been burned once, and she didn't want to feel that way ever again.

She was happy in her own company away from the potential dangers of love, no matter how tempting the object of her interest. She sucked in a deep breath to calm herself and push aside any residual feelings that didn't belong before heading back into the house.

CHAPTER TEN

Sarah looked at the newspaper and sighed. Her mother had written an opinion piece in a national broadsheet, and Sarah wasn't entirely sure that she wanted to read it. When they'd last spoken, her mother had been a little quieter than Sarah was accustomed to, which generally meant trouble.

Now Sarah understood the short call. Angela had written an essay about how big technology companies were killing the planet and needed to be taxed off the face of the earth as punishment.

It was a commonly held view, and even Sarah agreed that the CEO of Swype, Tom Morgan, and his contemporaries deserved enormous tax bills to go with their enormous wealth. Tom apparently did give away most of his money to various charities, but it was never enough for some. While newspapers shared his eye-watering net worth, that didn't equate to actual money in the bank. But facts never sold newspapers.

She felt eyes upon her and looked up to see Pippa standing in the doorway.

"Sorry to interrupt," Pippa apologised, walking into the room. "I wanted to know if you'd ordered those new door handles or if you wanted me to get Matt to pick them up from the mainland tomorrow."

"I tried to order them," Sarah said. "But when I put in my delivery postcode the website just laughed at me and wished me luck. Could you ask Matt to get them?"

Pippa chuckled. "Sure. Do you think you'll ever learn that you can't get things delivered here? You know this is an island, right?"

Mischief swirled in her eyes, and Sarah grinned back.

"I will continue to try," she said. "If I keep trying, someone might see that there's demand. And where there's demand, there's supply. Or at least an enterprising person who is willing to try. I won't be happy until I see an entire army of delivery drones sweeping over the beach like a swarm of bees."

Pippa laughed. "I think I know a few dozen people on the island who might have something to say about that."

"Probably," Sarah agreed. She turned the paper around and held it up for Pippa to see. "My mother."

Pippa took the paper and looked at the picture. "I see the family resemblance. Professor Angela Campbell? I feel like I've heard that name."

"You might have heard her ranting with Project Earth."

"Project Earth?" Pippa frowned for a moment. "Oh, those people who storm motorways to protest people using cars?"

"That's them. They believe in disrupting people from sleep-walking into the destruction of our planet." Sarah repeated the phrase that fell out of her mother's mouth nearly every conversation they had.

Pippa glanced up from the article. "She's not particularly complimentary about your boss."

"No. I spend about a quarter of my time at work apologising for things she's said. Or things she's encouraged Project Earth followers to do. Like the time when they picketed a delivery centre because they'd calculated—incorrectly, I might add—the carbon footprint of the site. Employees couldn't get into the building, so they couldn't work and didn't get paid. I agree with some of the things they are campaigning for, but some of the methods cause more harm than good."

Sarah's phone rang the familiar tone she had assigned to the woman in question.

"Speak of the devil," Sarah said. She picked up the phone. "Hi, Mum."

"Sarah, I meant to tell you I'm in the papers today, but I completely forgot. Just a few words, you know what it's like."

It was a three-page spread, definitely not a few words and definitely not something she'd forgotten about. This was typical of her mother, doing whatever she pleased without giving Sarah any warning and then requesting forgiveness later. In her own way, that was. She'd never admit to doing anything wrong or potentially making things awkward at work for Sarah.

"I did see your picture, but I haven't read it yet," Sarah said.

"I wouldn't," Pippa mumbled under her breath as she continued to read.

Sarah bit back a smile.

"Well, it obviously won't be to your taste, dear," Angela continued. "But Martin and Alejandro at PE really thought we needed to make a fresh effort to wake up the masses."

Martin and Alejandro spent all their time pandering to her mother and had done for the last twenty-five years. They'd been so excited to have a qualified scientist willing to use her voice to further their cause that they had happily given her anything she wanted. The two men had swept in and taken Sarah's mother away from her when she was in school. Sarah could barely remember a time when the men weren't mentioned on a daily basis as if they were gods of some kind.

"I was looking in my diary to schedule a speaking engagement and two things jumped out at me," Angela continued as if she hadn't recently dropped a journalistic bomb on Sarah's career.

"Yes?" Sarah asked, hoping to end the call soon so she could read the article and then call into work and apologise yet again for her mother's loud protesting.

"You've been up on Celfare for nearly eight weeks."

"That's right, almost two months."

"Which means you've been living with Natalie for eight weeks, and she's not thoroughly sick of you yet." Angela laughed heartily at her joke. "Who would have thought that was possible?"

It was simple teasing, but it hit Sarah hard. She felt a few tears track down her cheek and quickly wiped them away. Pippa frowned. Sarah waved away her concern.

"And if she's so hearty, then I have to meet her," Angela continued.

Sarah sipped some water to disguise the fact that her mother's casual words had caused such offence. She would never understand why Sarah would become upset with something she meant as a joke. However, Sarah knew that underneath the veil of the joke was the reality that her mother didn't understand how anyone would choose to stay with Sarah for long.

Sarah recalled when she was just nineteen and still dating men that her mother had practically forced her to go on a date with a creepy man that Sarah had met online. He'd turned up on her doorstep unannounced in a way he thought was romantic and Sarah thought was downright creepy, not to mention manipulative.

Angela had taken her to one side and instructed her to accept his flowers and go out with him. When Sarah had said she wouldn't, her mother had pointed out that there was no queue of people lining up at the door. She'd suggested that Sarah should go to dinner with him simply because he'd driven a long way.

Fifteen years had passed, and still Sarah could remember the words her mother had said and the suggestion that she needed to take whatever she was offered. Even if it was a potential stalker who had used his hacking skills to find her home.

"We'll try to get to London in a couple of months," Sarah said. She took another sip of water and clutched the glass to her forehead, hoping to relieve some of the headache that was forming below the skin. "We'll look at our schedules and see if you can squeeze us in for a lunch or something."

"That brings me to the second thing I noticed upon perusing my diary," Angela said, a note of smugness to her tone. "I'm free next Thursday. And I've decided that I'm coming to see you! I'm looking forward to trying out that spare bedroom you spoke about last week. Won't that be lovely, dear?"

The glass slipped from Sarah's fingers and thudded on the

wooden floorboard. Water splashed up her leg, but she barely noticed.

"H-here?" Sarah asked.

"Yes. Next Thursday. It's a devil to get to, but I made all the arrangements. I'm very much looking forward to seeing your new home. And meeting Natalie, of course."

"No!" Sarah stood up and nearly fell over. "No, um, Thursday's not good for us. We're...there's a thing—"

"Well, I'm sure you can cancel whatever this thing is in order to introduce your girlfriend to your mother. It's all booked now, Sarah. Please, don't be awkward and throw my whole schedule out. It will just be a few days. Don't you want to see your mother?"

"Of course I want to see you, it's just—"

"Dear, my taxi is here. I have to go. Don't worry yourself. I'm sure I'll adore Natalie. I'll call you tomorrow."

The line went dead. Sarah dropped into her chair and blinked a few times.

"No, no, no," Sarah mumbled. Her breath caught in her chest. Cold raced through her veins like icy tentacles.

"Sarah?" Pippa's voice was distant. Panic was rising within her and all she could hear was a strange ringing in her ears. "Sarah? What is it?"

It was only the sound of Pippa's worry that pulled Sarah back from the abyss of dread. Her eyes started to focus again. Pippa was crouching beside her, a hand on her shoulder and concern-laden eyes boring into her.

"Sarah?" Pippa's voice almost trembled with alarm.

"She's coming here," Sarah whispered.

"Your mother?" Pippa asked. Her voice was soft and calming, and Sarah clung to it like a lifeline, ignoring the sound of alarm bells in her ears.

"Yes."

"That's good, isn't it? It will be nice to see her?"

"No. It will be awful," Sarah confessed. "She's...difficult. She hates me. And she wants to meet Natalie."

Understanding flickered in Pippa's eyes. "Ah. That will be tricky. Can you tell her that you broke up?"

The dam finally broke, and Sarah couldn't control the tears. Everything had been going so well, and now it was about to crumble around her. Without a reason to stay on Celfare, Angela would encourage Sarah to come home. When Sarah didn't, Angela would become suspicious. Not to mention that Angela would assume that Sarah was to blame for Natalie leaving her, and that would have to be what happened because why would Sarah break up with Natalie after saying how wonderful she was?

As if her mother needed any more ammunition for destroying Sarah's confidence. Any other mother would take their child's side, but *her* mother would immediately ask what Sarah had done wrong. She'd done it before when Sarah had suffered a break-up.

There was no way out. When her mother decided to do something, she followed through. Her mother was on her way, and Sarah's self-esteem and job would soon be in ruins.

❖

Pippa didn't know what to say. Sarah seemed to be utterly shell-shocked by the idea of her mother coming to visit. Pippa didn't know anyone who disliked their mother so much they emotionally shut down at the very thought of it. She knew she should just leave Sarah to it, but she couldn't stand to see her in such distress.

"Sarah?" she repeated.

Sarah just continued to stare into nothing with wild eyes.

They'd spoken a little about Professor Campbell before, and Pippa had gotten the impression that the relationship was very broken. Sarah appeared to lie readily to her mother, something that Pippa couldn't understand. She'd had the best relationship with her parents and had been devastated when they passed away. She knew not everyone was as lucky as her, but she couldn't imagine ever shaking with fear at the prospect of a visit.

"Sarah, please, speak to me. Is it really that bad?"

Sarah laughed. It was a bitter sound that caused Pippa's stomach to churn.

"It's that bad. My mum…she…" Sarah drifted off and then laughed again. "She will love this. It feeds into her picture of me. Useless. Unlovable."

"I'm sure your mother doesn't think that you're unlovable," Pippa said.

Sarah wiped at her tears and chuckled to herself. "She does. She's said as much. I once told her that my girlfriend had left me for someone else. I must have lost my mind to think that I'd get any emotional support from her."

"What did she say?"

"She said she was sorry but not all that surprised," Sarah said. "She told me I needed to try to be less unlovable if I wanted to keep someone around."

Pippa's mouth fell open. She couldn't imagine anyone saying that, never mind a mother to her daughter.

"One of a hundred examples," Sarah said. "As far as my mother is concerned, I'm wasting my life and my potential. She wanted me to settle for an ex who cheated on me three times, because at least she kept coming back."

Pippa swallowed. She didn't know what to say to that. Sarah's mother was clearly a piece of work. Not that it was her place to say such a thing.

"And now she's coming here. She's going to have a field day when I tell her Natalie's gone. And she's staying here. Morning, noon, and night. Opportunities to tell me how much of a disappointment I am. And it won't just be about work this time—no, she'll have her second favourite topic of how I can't manage to hold on to a relationship."

Pippa couldn't understand how Sarah was struggling to remain in a relationship. Or how someone had cheated on her three times. Pippa had only been in her orbit for eight weeks and grew to like her more and more each day. The initial attraction still lingered in the background, but these days it was Sarah's outlook on life, dry sense of humour, and intellect that kept Pippa wondering how Sarah could possibly be single.

"Can you put her off from visiting?" Pippa asked.

Sarah shook her head. "No, once she's decided to do something, then she's doing it. And she's been curious about Natalie. Damn, I shouldn't have spoken about her so much."

Pippa wanted to agree but knew now wasn't the time.

"Maybe if you were honest? Told her that you were upset because of what she has said about your previous relationships?"

Sarah shivered. "No. That will make things worse. She doesn't understand how her words hit. She's clueless. I've tried to ask her to be kinder, but she just thinks that she's being honest. She values honesty. More than people's feelings."

"Can you pretend you're sick?" Pippa started to scrape the barrel. Anything to fix the predicament that Sarah had gotten herself into.

Sarah shook her head. "It wouldn't stop her from coming. I'm…just going to have to face the music. It's not like I'm going to find a girlfriend in the next few days, and definitely not one who would be willing to lie to my mother like this."

"No, I don't imagine that you will." Pippa picked up the dropped glass and put it on the table, impressed that it didn't break.

"Is there an actor for hire on Celfare?" Sarah asked, sounding only half joking. "Or an escort service?"

"Yes, now you mention it, there is a lesbian escort service," Pippa said.

"There is?" Sarah's eyes widened.

"Of course there isn't."

Sarah sagged back into her chair.

"Besides," Pippa added, "what are the odds that you'd find anyone to exactly match your description of, what was her name, Natalie?"

"I never described her," Sarah said.

Pippa sat on the edge of the desk. "Why not?"

"Because I hardly get to speak about anything when I'm talking to my mum. She's always preoccupied with her work, and I'm only allotted a few minutes here and there. She never asked any details about Natalie, and I never had a chance to offer them. All she knows is that Natalie lives here, and I came here to live with her."

It hurt to see Sarah so broken. Pippa struggled to reconcile her own relationship with her parents and what Sarah seemed to have with her mother. She wondered if Sarah had anyone that she could rely on in place of her mother. Presumably not if she was also single. It made no sense that Angela thought Sarah unlovable, even less that she'd actually say such a thing. Pippa recalled the newspaper article she had skimmed—the tone had been harsh and patronising. Maybe it wasn't preposterous to think that such a person would say such things to her daughter. The thought hurt. Sarah deserved better—she deserved kindness and respect. But instead she was reduced to tears by harsh words that seemed to echo back for years.

"I wish I could help." Pippa stood. "And I'll be here while she is, so at least you'll have a friendly face."

"You might want to hold off on coming while she's here," Sarah said. "It won't be pleasant."

"I don't mind." Pippa shrugged. "I've dealt with far worse, I'm certain. Anyway, I'll go and call Matt about those door handles."

She was halfway down the stairs when she heard Sarah call her name. She paused and turned to see Sarah hurrying down the hallway with an expression she couldn't read. She wrung her hands and bit her lip.

"Yes?" Pippa asked. Something was off but she couldn't quite decipher what it was yet.

Sarah stood at the top of the stairs and looked down at Pippa pleadingly. "Perhaps…you?"

"Perhaps I…?" Pippa asked, still not catching on to what Sarah could possibly be asking.

"Could be…Natalie?"

Pippa couldn't help but laugh.

"It's not funny," Sarah said. "Please?"

Pippa shook her head and continued walking down the stairs. "I know you're desperate but even you must see the humour in that?"

Sarah followed her downstairs. "Not at all. You're the only

person on the island who knows me. You spend most of your time here anyway. You're a lesbian. You're my ty—You're a perfect candidate. The locals think we're together anyway—you said so yourself. Please, I really need your help."

Pippa paused in the doorway to the kitchen, her back to Sarah. It was a terrible idea. Probably the worst she'd heard in a long time. It could only end in disaster.

She slowly turned around. She contemplated the request from several angles, but every single one came back to the same conclusion.

"I would consider it if I believed we could pull it off," Pippa said. "But it's madness. It's something from a bad movie."

Sarah shook her head. Pippa could see wild desperation in her eyes. "It's not. Think about it—she'll only be here a few days. We get on well, you kinda know me, and I kinda know you. How hard can it really be? It's not like it's an immigration interview—it's just my mum."

Pippa chuckled. "Just your mum? You've changed your tune from less than ten minutes ago."

"Please, Pippa. Really, I need your help with this. If my mum gets here and there's no girlfriend, then she'll never let me live it down. My life will be a nightmare because it will be mentioned all the time. She'll tell all her friends. I can't stand the idea of it. I don't mind being alone. Really, I don't. I don't mind not finding someone to love. But having my mum think I'm never going to find anyone because I'm"—she waved her hand over her body—"me? I can't take it. Not when there's a way to stop it. Just a few days. A little pretending. She'll never know. She'll spend most of the time talking about herself, anyway."

Pippa felt cold and her chest constricted. She hated that Sarah seemed to have such a poor excuse for a mother. Hated more that Sarah was reduced to begging her to go through with a plan that surely could never work. Most of all, Pippa hated that she actually couldn't help even if she wanted to. She wasn't about to lie to Sarah's mother and pretend to be someone else. She had no acting ability, and that was the absolute least of her concerns.

She let out a sigh. Sarah looked absolutely broken. She wished she had an answer, one that didn't involve her pretending to be Natalie.

"I wouldn't even know where to begin," Pippa admitted.

Sarah's eyes widened with hope. Pippa quickly shook her head to dampen any expectations Sarah might have.

"And I don't think it's a good idea. But I'm sure we can come up with something between us," Pippa conceded. "Why don't you come over tonight for dinner? A few hours to digest this news, and I'm sure we'll find a solution. And I'm actually rather a good cook."

A ghost of a smile skittered across Sarah's face but was lost in the shadow of depression as quickly as it arrived. Pippa felt heavy guilt at not being able to come to her rescue. It wasn't a feeling she enjoyed. Fixing things, finding solutions, calculating ways forward, they were the things that Pippa enjoyed most. Not being able to immediately say that she could fix things caused a lump in her throat.

"Thank you," Sarah said, her voice practically a whisper. "I'd like that."

Distress was written all over her face, and Pippa struggled to look at her. It hurt to see Sarah upset and know there was little she could do to help.

"We'll come up with something," she said, reassuring Sarah.

Pippa needed space and time, but she was sure that she'd be able to find a solution. Maybe even one that Sarah liked. Right now she needed to escape Hillcrest Cottage because the need to pull Sarah into a comforting hug, tell her that it would all be okay, and promise to do whatever it took was far too great. Her saviour complex was out of control, and knowing that Sarah needed her was more than she could stand.

"I need to go and get these door handles ordered." Pippa grabbed at an excuse to leave. "I'll see you tonight?"

"You don't have to," Sarah said, her voice still small.

"I want to. We're friends, right?"

When Sarah had said the words to her just the other week, Pippa hadn't been entirely sure what they were. She'd never made friends easily. Kim had always been the one to meet new people, and Pippa simply tagged along. But Sarah had called them friends, and Pippa certainly liked Sarah's company.

Sarah smiled, and Pippa felt a little weight lift from her shoulders.

"We are," Sarah agreed.

"Good." Pippa returned the smile. "See you tonight."

"I'll be there." Sarah tucked a lock of hair behind her ear. She was starting to look calmer and more like herself. The redness in her face was fading to pink, and the tears had dried even if her eyes remained watery.

Pippa felt a swell of pride and relief followed by some fear. She didn't have a plan, and she had precious little time to come up with one. She'd already worked out that the most likely way forward was for Sarah to tell her mother that Natalie was no longer around. But it wouldn't solve any of the problems and, if Sarah was right, would create more fodder for her mother.

All Pippa could do now was to offer moral support and stand by her side like a real friend would. It didn't feel like enough, but it was the best that she could do.

CHAPTER ELEVEN

Sarah parked outside Pippa's house. She'd never seen the house before, hadn't even known where Pippa lived until she asked for directions. The brick cottage was picturesque with the original wooden front door and small windows. Outside a garden was in full bloom with rose bushes and lavender. Love and attention were clearly lavished on the home, and Sarah couldn't help but wonder if her own would ever look the same.

She picked up the wine bottle from the passenger seat and got out of the car. A woman she didn't recognise passed her and didn't even attempt to hide her curiosity as she looked from Sarah to the wine to Pippa's home.

Sarah smothered a smile. The local gossips would have something to talk about now. She wondered how the innocent gesture of two friends sharing a meal would be twisted and how quickly it would happen. Precious little happened on Celfare, so she wasn't entirely surprised that rumours had started to swirl. Rumours that would be cemented if Pippa went ahead with Sarah's ridiculous scheme to attempt to fool her mother.

It was just ten minutes after Pippa had left when Sarah realised that she'd asked far too much of her new friend. The silence of Hillcrest Cottage had been suffocating and quickly focused her nervous energy on the fact that she had gone too far.

Her mother was no one's issue but Sarah's. It was wrong to ask Pippa to lie to protect her own sanity. Even if she dearly wanted to.

She'd created the lie, and now she was going to have to deal with the consequences and apologise to Pippa for even suggesting her ludicrous plan.

She entered the country cottage style garden and knocked on the door. Her mouth felt dry. She'd rehearsed what she wanted to say to Pippa multiple times on the way over, but now that she was here, she found the embarrassment of what she had asked creeping up to record heights. The door opened. Sarah held her breath and willed the nausea to pass quickly.

"Come in." Pippa smiled warmly and stood to one side.

Sarah entered the hallway and looked around at the immaculate decor with interest. She'd always known that Pippa had an eye for design, but the attention to detail was incredible.

"You have a beautiful home," Sarah said. She handed over the bottle of wine.

"Thank you. And thank you for the wine." Pippa gestured towards the kitchen with the bottle. "Come through, I'll pour you a glass."

The kitchen was warm and welcoming with patio doors that led out into the back garden. It was small, as to be expected in a cottage of that age, but clever design had made good use of the space. A large table by the open back doors was the centrepiece and looked to have been created out of one large piece of wood. Sarah wondered if Pippa had made it herself.

Pippa gestured for Sarah to take a seat at the table while she opened the wine.

"I wanted to apologise," Sarah said.

"What for?" Pippa dug around a cutlery drawer and retrieved a corkscrew.

"For asking you to pretend to be Natalie. It was wrong—I shouldn't have put you in that awkward position. I was in shock, I guess. I'll face the music with my mother. I've done it before, and I'll do it again. I'm just sorry if I made things weird by asking that of you."

Pippa opened the wine bottle with a pop. "Not weird at all. Maybe a little unexpected. But I'm glad you've seen reason. I really don't think we'd be able to pull it off. And maybe a clean sheet is just what you and your mother need to fix this rift between you. Maybe some honesty will clear the air."

Sarah started to chuckle at the notion that there was anything at all that could clear the air between herself and her mother. Before long, the chuckle turned into outright laughter. It was sweet that Pippa seemed to think there was any way to redeem the mother-daughter relationship, which had long ago deteriorated beyond any repair.

Pippa poured two glasses of wine and smiled at Sarah's laughter. "Is that really so funny?"

"You don't know my mother," Sarah said.

"That's true. Although, after reading that article this afternoon and her name ringing a bell with me, I'm sorry to say I googled her."

Pippa placed a glass of wine in front of Sarah.

"Thank you," Sarah said. "What did your search uncover?"

Pippa was uncharacteristically quiet for a woman usually so happy to speak her mind. A frown appeared on her forehead as she seemed to struggle to verbalise what she wanted to say. In an apparent bid for more time, she returned to the oven and checked the contents. The smell of salmon wafted through the room, and Sarah felt her stomach grumble with excitement.

Her nerves had left in a few short minutes in Pippa's company, and Sarah marvelled at how easy it was for her to relax and feel at home around someone she hardly knew.

"Obviously I don't know her as well as you," Pippa finally said.

"Very diplomatic." Sarah sipped some wine and waited for Pippa to expand on her thoughts. She wondered what Pippa had uncovered in her Google searches. Probably her mother's speaking engagements, maybe some of the protests she'd been a part of. No doubt she'd seen the famous interview she gave where she turned up covered in the blood of Mother Earth, a PR stunt that had gone viral and achieved exactly what Project Earth had desired.

Angela Campbell loved the limelight and being worshipped by Project Earth. Every outlandish statement she made and every crazy PR trick she pulled achieved both news coverage and more adoration heaped onto her by the people who had placed her on a pedestal.

Sarah knew her mother wholeheartedly believed that she was doing the right thing and fighting to save the planet. But she also knew that there was a healthy dose of people-pleasing and a need for more attention attached to her actions.

"She seems a little difficult," Pippa confessed.

"Understatement, but I'll allow it." Sarah chuckled again.

"I hate how much upset she caused you," Pippa said. "And I'd dearly like to help if I can. But I don't think my pretending to be Natalie would fool her. She's your mother—she'd see through it in an instant."

Sarah smiled tightly. It was impossible to explain to someone who had been blessed with a more conventional relationship with their mother that she and her mother shared DNA and a surname but little else.

It hadn't escaped her notice that they were different to other mothers and daughters. She'd spent much of her childhood wondering if it was her fault that they didn't have a close bond and do the things society had taught her they should do. It had taken years and a stack of psychology books to finally acknowledge that she wasn't to blame for her mother's emotional distance.

Her mother had had little interest in Sarah as a child and even less as an adult. Sarah felt shame to admit it to herself and had never gone as far as to say it to someone else. To do so would feel somehow scandalous. She carried guilt that she was to blame for the relationship breakdown, even though she knew in her heart that it had started before she could possibly shoulder any blame for such a thing.

Pippa naturally thought that her mother would see through any lie Sarah told, as so many other people would assume, simply because she was her mother. And mothers did that kind of thing. Mothers were supposed to have a sixth sense.

Like so many others, Pippa obviously assumed all mothers loved their children without hinderance or question. It was impossible for those people to grasp the possibility that Sarah's mother didn't know Sarah at all.

"What will you tell her?" Pippa asked.

Sarah took another sip of wine. "I…I'm going to tell her that Natalie broke up with me. I think that's slightly less humiliating than saying Natalie never existed."

Pippa's expression was neutral, yet Sarah could feel the disappointment.

"My life would be a living hell if she knew Natalie—"

Pippa raised her hand to cut off Sarah's explanation. "It's entirely your choice. You don't need to justify it to me. It's between the two of you. I could see that your mother is a…formidable woman. I'd like to help if I can. Maybe my presence would soften her a little? Surely she can't be so bad around company."

Sarah wanted to laugh again but managed to hold back. Not a lot stopped her mother from expressing an opinion. The presence of another person certainly wouldn't. But Sarah appreciated the offer and would happily snatch it up for her own sake.

"I think she'll be about the same as she always is," she admitted. "But I won't lie—I'd appreciate the company."

"I could come with you to the ferry," Pippa offered. "Then you could tell her about Natalie straight away. I can be your friend offering you support following your breakup. That seems reasonable and might stop her from saying anything too terrible."

Sarah didn't want to break Pippa's optimism. Or sound defeatist. She knew her mum would happily say whatever she wanted, whether Pippa was there or not.

"Maybe we could even stop for afternoon tea at Maisey's," Pippa suggested. "I could ask your mother some questions, and that would keep her attention diverted for a while."

Sarah stood up and walked over to Pippa with her arms outstretched. Pippa hesitated for only a split second before pulling Sarah into a hug.

"Thank you," Sarah said. "Really. I can't tell you how much I appreciate this."

Pippa held her in a loose embrace. "It's not entirely selfless. I do love the afternoon teas at Maisey's."

Sarah laughed and let go. She took a small step back and looked Pippa straight in the eye. "Seriously, though. Thank you."

Pippa smiled shyly and averted her gaze. "You're welcome." She took in a deep breath and looked up. "Maybe we should eat outside. The weather is nice, and we rarely get the opportunity to do so on Celfare. What do you think?"

"Sounds great."

Pippa explained what to move where, and Sarah set about moving cutlery and placemats to the patio table outside while Pippa watched over the meal.

The garden was surrounded by a high brick wall covered in climbing plants, which was probably built the same time as the cottage. It felt secluded and comfortable, miles away from any problems anyone might have. Sarah thought if she had such a garden that she'd spend all her time in it.

In fact, if her mother was even half as terrible as she suspected, she might well pitch a tent in Pippa's garden to escape her.

It was sweet that Pippa thought that the acerbic Angela Campbell could be somehow distracted enough to forget that Sarah had yet another broken relationship in her wake. It would take more than that to sway her mother off course. If there was criticism to be given, an *I told you* to be dealt, then an afternoon tea wouldn't stop the freight-train-style delivery her mother used to deliver such thoughts.

Her mother would be extremely disappointed with Sarah's inability to remain in a relationship, and she wouldn't be afraid to say so. Pippa's support was welcome, but Sarah knew that it wouldn't soften her mother's reaction. She felt a little guilty at possibly misleading Pippa but knew that any words would be directed squarely at her. All Pippa risked was having to watch Sarah squirm while her mother handed out her judgements.

❖

Dinner had been eaten, the dishwasher rumbled quietly in the background, and Pippa was enjoying an evening of company in a way that she couldn't recall having done for years. After they'd eaten dinner, the wind had started to blow a little harder. It would have been easy to go indoors, but Pippa hadn't wanted to spoil the mood. She'd popped inside and brought out two blankets, and they'd agreed to wrap up against the chill and carry on talking.

She'd expected the meal to be a little awkward after telling Sarah that, despite her best efforts, she couldn't come up with a plan, aside from somehow putting Angela Campbell off the idea of coming to visit, which was apparently unlikely.

Thankfully, Sarah had calmed down considerably since she'd last seen her and was now even apologising for initially asking Pippa to be Natalie. Since then they'd eased into casual conversation, and Pippa couldn't believe the difference between the intelligent, compassionate, and funny woman who sat in front of her and her mother.

Pippa had vaguely recognised the name Professor Angela Campbell the moment Sarah handed her the newspaper article. It hadn't been until she'd gotten home and consulted the internet that she was fully reminded of who the woman was. The term *eco warrior* sprang to mind, but more than that, Professor Campbell was a snob who appeared to love the sound of her own voice. She was a woman who used her intellect and educational standing to further her own goal, which Pippa determined to be her own fame.

When Pippa had found a playlist of YouTube videos, she'd noted the professor had a lopsided smirk, which grew when a crowd applauded her words or when she was introduced to a stage to speak. There was something about the expression that put Pippa on edge.

She'd never been one for putting people on pedestals. Everyone had flaws, some more than others. Pippa had always thought that fans could only lead to a swollen ego. It certainly appeared to have done so in the case of Sarah's mother.

Seeing the reality of Angela Campbell had made Pippa's mind up. Leaving Sarah to the mercy of the woman who frequently shared questionable so-called facts with impressionable young audiences wasn't going to happen on Pippa's watch. Even if it meant an uncomfortable few days spending more social time with Sarah than she would have usually.

The more Sarah spoke about Angela, the more toxic Pippa realised the woman was. It was clear that Sarah was not exaggerating and seemingly held no malice towards her mother. If anything, Sarah seemed to have resigned herself to the odd relationship they had forged.

Pippa still didn't understand why Sarah had taken to lying. She understood that Angela was a tricky person to deal with but didn't see how potentially giving her more ammunition could possibly help. But then, Pippa had always been honest. Sometimes to a fault.

"What will you say happened between you and Natalie?" Pippa asked.

Sarah shrugged. "She probably won't ask. I'll just say that we've split."

"Surely she'll want more details than that?"

Sarah chuckled. "I keep telling you—I'm not her favourite subject. She didn't ask how we met, doesn't know anything about Natalie. She never asked. And I never offered."

Pippa shook her head in despair. "I just don't understand that."

Sarah peeked a hand through a gap in the blanket she was wrapped up in and picked up her wine glass. "You'll understand when you meet her. I love her, but she's the most selfish person you're ever likely to meet."

Pippa worried her lip. Something had been on her mind for the last few hours, and she just wasn't sure she knew how to approach it. It wasn't important, just curiosity that she couldn't satisfy.

"What?" Sarah asked, already seemingly attuned to her.

Pippa smiled. "It's silly, don't worry."

"Go on," Sarah encouraged.

She felt odd asking but knew that if she didn't, she'd wonder about it, and she hated a mystery. "It's just, I find it strange that you asked me. I mean, I know you were desperate, but would your mum really believe that you were with someone like me? Someone as old as me?"

Sarah leaned her head back against the high-backed patio chair and looked at Pippa with a smile. "You're the perfect age."

She rolled her eyes at the line. "You don't even know how old I am," Pippa said.

"Forty...one?" Sarah guessed.

Pippa stuck a finger in the air.

"Forty-two?"

Pippa prodded the air a little.

"Forty-three?"

"In the interest of saving time, before we both turn into pumpkins at the stroke of midnight, I'm forty-eight. Wouldn't your mother be a little concerned by a...How old are you?"

"Thirty-four."

"By a fourteen-year age gap?"

Sarah simply laughed. "No. It wouldn't be the first time. I like an older woman."

Pippa couldn't help but look away as her heart fluttered at that tantalising piece of information. Not that she understood why someone as young and full of energy as Sarah would be interested in someone older.

She decided that it was best not to ask, just in case they walked into even more uncomfortable territory. She needed to steer the conversation back to safety.

"You seem to be settling into island life well. Aside from missing the convenience of next day delivery."

"Sometimes I'll accept *any* day delivery," Sarah joked. "Honestly, how do you get used to it?"

"It does take a while," Pippa admitted. "You have to just let go of your past life and accept that this is how things are now. You need to lean in to it."

Sarah leaned in a little closer. "I know, but sometimes"—she lowered her voice and whispered sensually—"don't you just wish you could...order something and it would arrive the next morning?"

Pippa laughed. "I used to. But not these days."

Sarah chuckled and leaned back in her chair. A serious expression crossed her face this time. "You said you moved here after your wife died."

"I did."

"Why?" Sarah asked. Her tone was soft and unpressured. Pippa didn't believe Sarah was unaware of the weight of the question and appreciated the light tone that gave Pippa a way out if she didn't want to answer.

She didn't usually talk about her decision but suspected that her most fragile truth would be safe with Sarah.

Pippa considered what to say. She'd never explained what had happened and how she had felt at the time. Not to anyone else and not even to herself. Never having verbalised the events of the time meant that she was now having to think about things that she had attempted to bury long ago. It didn't feel as uncomfortable as she thought it might. Probably because it was Sarah asking.

"We lived in Bournemouth," Pippa began. "We met there. I was working as an architect, and she was the project manager at the school where we were bidding to build a new wing."

Pippa remembered the very first time she had laid eyes on Kim. It was a meeting with at least twenty people crammed into a conference room, but she had only had eyes for Kim. For the first time in her life she had stumbled over words and found herself completely consumed by this beautiful, enigmatic woman who sat before her.

"She was incredible," Pippa said. "The first time I saw her, I knew she was something special. I knew I'd never met anyone like her before. But I also knew nothing about her, whether she was straight, or even married with kids. Nothing. But I was completely infatuated. I'd never felt like that before."

"I can't imagine you infatuated," Sarah said. Her words were soft and kind, and a touch of a smile graced her features.

"I didn't think I was capable of it," Pippa agreed. "She asked me out. Which was good because I was such an emotional mess that I don't know if I ever would have managed it."

"Can't imagine you being an emotional mess, either," Sarah added.

Pippa laughed. "No, I suppose not. I was young and very different to who I am now. Definitely tainted by what happened."

A rush of cold consumed her at the memories. She shivered and pulled the blanket tighter around her. She tried to mask her discomfort by shifting a little in her seat.

"She died. And up until that moment I think I'd always thought that younger people died of road accidents, or illness that had been around awhile and slowly withered them. I logically knew that people died of accidents around the house, but I honestly never expected it."

She sighed and looked up to the sky. The memories were always with her, but now they felt more pronounced, despite the gaps in her recollection that lingered. She would always remember the kind words of the paramedic who sat with her, but his face remained a mystery. She had no idea if he was young or old, Black or white. His calm voice soothed her when she woke from nightmares, but beyond that he was a ghost.

"A loose wire was all it took," Pippa continued. "She likely never knew what happened. A split second and she was gone. By the time I got home, she'd been gone awhile. For some reason, I acted as if she could be saved. As if it wasn't absolutely obvious that she was dead. I don't think I could accept it. I called for an ambulance, performed CPR until they arrived. Even though I realised that it was far too late."

Sarah wordlessly stood up and moved her chair closer to Pippa's. She sat back down again, this time right beside her in a silent offering of comfort.

"I'd never thought about love before in much detail," Pippa said. "I loved Kim with all my heart and never considered what that meant. When she died, I understood what people meant when they say they lose a piece of themselves when someone passes. We had fourteen years of absolute bliss, and then I had to pay the price."

"Pay the price?" Sarah asked.

"Not everyone is lucky enough to have what I had," Pippa

said. "Some people settle for someone—some never find someone to be with. I found my perfect person. Everything was so easy, we just fit together, and life was wonderful. But I later realised that my life was so absolutely wonderful because I'd allowed myself to fall completely in love, to give a piece of myself to someone else. And that meant that when she left me, I didn't feel whole anymore. It's a price you have to pay for such love, I think."

Sarah remained quiet, and Pippa couldn't read her expression.

"I don't want to hurt like that again," Pippa confessed. "I moved away from our old life because everything reminded me of her. My memories were changing from seeing her laughing over a glass of wine at a friend's birthday party to…that day. I didn't want that. I didn't want to replace those memories. I wanted to keep things the way they were. And I wanted to be alone."

"So you came here to Celfare."

"Yes. It seemed suitably remote."

"It's certainly that," Sarah agreed. "I'm sorry that you lost the love of your life."

"Thank you. I'm glad for the time together that we had."

Sarah picked up her wine glass and held it aloft. "To Kim."

Pippa smiled and raised her own glass. "To Kim."

They tapped their glasses together and took a sip. Pippa looked up at the sky and wondered what Kim would say about her decision to move away. She'd probably accuse her of hiding. And she'd be right. But that wasn't going to change Pippa's mind.

Very few people had the capacity to understand what she had been through. She'd never really understood the meaning of the word *heartbreak* until she had gone through it herself. There were times when she thought the pain would kill her. It was a price to be paid in exchange for wedded bliss. A price she didn't want to pay again. Now she kept herself and her heart locked away.

CHAPTER TWELVE

Sarah looked at her reflection in the bathroom mirror and sighed. She looked drawn and exhausted. And her mother would no doubt comment on it.

She'd spent the last few days preparing for her mother's sudden visit. It meant hurrying up with some of the decorating, making up a guest bedroom, and building flat-pack wardrobes, chests of drawers, and bedside tables. The flurry of activity to get the house ready for her mother was tiring, and she knew it probably wouldn't be good enough either.

"It will be fine," Sarah told her reflection. "It's just a few days."

She'd contemplated telling her mother that Natalie had left her before she arrived but had not felt brave enough to do so. She'd tried to convince herself that it would be better face to face. That hopefully the shock would slow her mum's commentary down. Or perhaps, just perhaps, she'd think better of it and say nothing at all.

Sarah smiled bitterly. She knew that was incredibly unlikely.

It wasn't that her mother was ever going out of her way to be cruel. She was just painfully honest. Very painfully sometimes.

Sarah wished, not for the first time, that she had called the whole thing off. A bout of norovirus would have kept her mother away. But she knew in her heart that it would only delay the inevitable.

It was too late to waver now. Her mother was on her way, and everything was in motion. The ferry was halfway into its journey, and nothing but poor weather would turn it back now. Sarah hadn't been able to sleep and had taken a stroll along the beach that morning and was taken by how calm the water had been. It made sense that on a day where she'd half-heartedly wished for storms, the sea had been the calmest she had ever seen it.

With one final glance at her reflection, and an acknowledgement that there was little to be done about her appearance, she turned off the bathroom light and strolled through the cottage.

Everything to do with Sarah's work was currently under lock and key in a box beneath her bed. It might have been overkill, but she couldn't risk her mother finding out about a data centre sunk off the coast. Her mother wouldn't be reasoned with. She'd claim it was killing the ocean, and therefore the planet, and would probably end up on the nine o'clock news shouting about it to the world.

The very thought caused Sarah's stomach to lurch.

She'd worked hard on this project, and the idea of Billy being destroyed, by her own mother no less, was more than she could take. She didn't know what she'd do if the project was taken away from her. It wasn't just a job—it was a campaign to make the world better. Data centres were a necessary evil in the world, but they didn't have to be that way. She believed they could be sustainable and not damage the environment one bit.

She chuckled to herself. Maybe the apple hadn't fallen that far from the tree after all.

The cottage was as good as it was going to get. Sarah knew that negative comments would be made, but there was little she could do now. Even if she'd made it perfect, her mother would find something to point out.

She headed out to the garden shed for one last check on Billy before she'd be relying on remote telemetry while her mother was in the house. She'd have to go out to the shed now and then to get some of the data, but she'd need to limit her visits, or her mother would surely notice her new and unexpected fascination with the bottom of the garden.

As always, she looked around before entering the shed. There was no one around for miles, but she still checked just in case the postman or a hiker happened to be nearby.

It was still strange to be so far away from people. She was

used to constantly hearing the noise of other people, from traffic to neighbouring doors closing in her apartment building. Now she was truly alone and in the middle of nowhere. More surprisingly, it wasn't as bad as she thought it would be. In fact, she was starting to appreciate the quiet, which was punctuated only by the sounds of nature.

Inside the shed, she closed and locked the door. Server lights blinked rhythmically to show the transfer of data, and a quiet hum of the machines felt almost soothing despite her frayed nerves.

She walked along the row of equipment, reassuring herself that it would be okay for the short period of time she was gone. These days she visited the shed five to six times a day to check Billy's vital statistics. Pippa thought she was extremely keen on short power walks around the garden.

Sarah felt bad for lying to Pippa but knew that the secrecy of the project was absolutely essential. Loose lips sank ships. Or in this case, loose lips could unsink an experimental data centre, cost Swype millions of pounds, put back an important project at least half a decade, and almost certainly leave her unemployed.

She placed her hand atop the satellite router. "I'll be back soon. Be good while I'm gone."

She silently hoped there would be no emergency signal sent that would require her to run out to the shed and switch any stacks or move the data load. Of course, she'd do it if she had to. But it would be nice if her plan would just run smoothly without any unexpected bumps instead.

Something that she had little hope would happen.

❖

"Take a breath," Pippa instructed.

Sarah hadn't realised that she'd been holding her breath the whole while as she watched the ferry slowly manoeuvre into the dock. She felt sick with nerves. It was happening—her mother was about to arrive. The two of them sharing the same space had rarely been a good idea. From when Sarah had been a teenager to the present day, it had always been a struggle for them to be in each other's company. Sarah wished that wasn't the case but had enough evidence to know it was the truth.

"Sarah." Pippa tapped her arm.

She sucked in a deep breath and pushed herself up from the metal railing. Holding her breath when stressed was something that she did without knowing.

True to her word, Pippa had met her by the dock with the intention of trying to be a human shield to protect Sarah from the Arctic judgement that was about to arrive.

Nervousness had completely washed over Sarah. Spending time with her mother was one thing, but preparing to tell the lie about breaking up with the perfect, though entirely fictional, Natalie just made things worse. And then there was the biggest secret of all just lurking in the sea. The fear that her mother might find out about Billy was enough to cause Sarah's hands to shake.

"It will be fine," Pippa said.

Sarah wanted to say that it wouldn't be fine, but she felt as if she'd already been negative enough. She'd spent the last couple of days telling Pippa that nothing was good enough for her mother and attempting to warn her of all the terrible things that might fall out of Angela Campbell's mouth during her visit. Pippa hadn't argued, but there had been a tinge of disbelief in her gaze.

Sarah suspected that Pippa thought she was overreacting. Sarah didn't need to defend herself. Her mother was coming, and with that would be all the proof she needed. Pippa seemed to think that a mother's love was unconditional and that Sarah was simply misreading her mum's attitude. But Pippa would find the truth out soon enough.

The ferry slowly moved forward into position. Ropes were thrown over to the dockside staff, and the engine made stuttering noises as the ship moved back and forth to come to a safe stop. The gangway-bridge was lowered, and pedestrians started to walk off the ship.

Sarah spotted her mother quickly. She looked tired and angry, probably not impressed with the amount of time it took to dock.

"Here we go," she muttered under her breath. She walked towards the arriving passengers and waved to attract attention. "Hi, Mum!"

Her mother spotted her and walked over, eyes already rolling. "You'd think they'd never done that before." Her mother gestured to the ship behind her. "Back and forward, back and forward. Do they have any idea how much fuel they burn while they dither? It's not like it's difficult, surely."

She parked her wheeled suitcase and lifted her chin to examine Sarah head to foot. "You look unwell. Are you ill? Please don't be sick—I have a series of important meetings after this."

"I'm just tired." Sarah tried to brush away the lacklustre greeting. She felt Pippa's presence just over her shoulder and waited a moment for her mother to stop complaining for long enough so that she could introduce her.

"You don't know tired until you've been through what I've been through," her mother continued. "I had an awful time in that terrible guest house last night. Would you believe that they didn't have any vegan options for breakfast? I had to cobble something together."

Sarah could well believe that a small guest house in the middle of nowhere wouldn't have a vegan breakfast option on hand. Her mother often didn't advise locations of her dietary requirements simply so she could complain bitterly when they didn't stock what she wanted.

"It's disgusting." Her mother sniffed. "They expect me to eat meat, I suppose? When did you last get your hair cut, dear?"

"Last week."

"I suppose it's hard to find a good hairdresser on an island."

Sarah bit the inside of her cheek. She'd been expecting her mother to be on form, and she wasn't going to be disappointed.

"I suppose it's too much to hope that you've found a new career since we last spoke?"

It was a question her mother asked frequently. It was often phrased as a joke, but Sarah knew that it was heartfelt. It would make her mother's day if Sarah left Swype.

"No, sorry. I'm still a Swype employee and proud," Sarah said.

"Pity. But if you want to waste your education, then I suppose you can't be stopped. Even if it does mean I have a lot of explaining to do to my colleagues and fans."

Sarah sucked in a quick breath, forced out a smile, and turned to Pippa. "Mum, this is—"

Pippa stepped forward and put her hand out. "Hello, Professor Campbell, I'm Natalie."

Thankfully, her mother was too distracted by Pippa's greeting to notice Sarah's mouth falling open. *What is she doing? This isn't part of the plan. How are we going to pull this off?*

"Oh, I didn't see you there," her mum said. A fake smile was plastered onto her face, and confusion was clear. "You're not quite what I expected."

Sarah winced at her mother's sharp words. She wanted to pull Pippa to one side and tell her that she didn't need to do this, to ask what she was thinking, and to apologise for everything that was about to come.

"You're not exactly what I expected either, isn't that funny?" Pippa said. She turned to Sarah. "I need to get back to work, but why don't you two go and have afternoon tea at Maisey's? It would be nice for you both to catch up. They do a very good vegan cream tea."

"Oh, do they?" her mother asked, suddenly intrigued. "Well, I am a little hungry."

"That's settled then," Pippa said. "I'll meet you both at home later. Would you like me to drop your case off at home?"

Pippa already had her hand on the handle of the suitcase.

Sarah's mother hesitated a moment, swept up in the sudden change of plans. "Um, yes, I suppose that would be a good idea."

"Sarah, do you have the car keys?" Pippa asked, sweeping the bag up and walking over to Sarah's car.

Sarah told her mother that she'd be right back and rushed after Pippa.

They opened the boot of the car and Pippa slid the case into place.

"I'm sorry, I shouldn't have said that, but I couldn't stand the way she was talking to you," Pippa said. She was still smiling as they were only a few metres away from the subject of their discussion.

"It's okay, I know the urge to shut her up," Sarah said. "What do we do now?"

"We tell her I lied, or…we run with it, and I try to be Natalie." Pippa put her hand on Sarah's elbow. "I'm so sorry. I don't know why I did that. I just…I couldn't help myself. The way she spoke to you, I just…Is this normal?"

"This is fairly mild," Sarah said. "I tried to warn you."

"I'll admit that I thought you were being a little dramatic."

"Well, surprise! This is my mum. What do we do?" Sarah could tell that her mother was becoming curious about their ongoing discussion.

"Go and have afternoon tea with her. I'll swing by my place to pick up some things and will drop them at yours. I practically live at yours anyway, what will be the difference?" Pippa said.

"We'll be sharing a bed, for one," Sarah pointed out.

A blush touched Pippa's cheeks. "Yes, well, we can be adults about it. Not in that sense, I mean. We can keep our hands to ourselves."

"Are you sure that you're okay to do this?" Sarah asked. "The time to back out is right now."

"I know." Pippa closed the boot of the car. "I did it, and I'm happy to go through with this. Just…call me Natalie." Pippa leaned in and grazed her lips on Sarah's cheek. "Give me at least an hour to make it look like I live at yours," she whispered in Sarah's ear. She stood back and waved. "Lovely to meet you, Professor Campbell. See you this evening."

Sarah watched the car drive away. She still felt the residual warmth on her cheek and knew without a doubt that she was blushing. Pippa's kiss had been the lightest, most innocent of touches, but it had completely shaken her.

She turned and looked at her mother. The dreaded visit was about to have another layer of complexity added to it. On the bright side, she now had someone to shoulder the weight with.

❖

Pippa exited Sarah's car and rushed into her house. She still didn't know what had possessed her to suddenly change her mind and take on the persona of Natalie. Angela had been so much more than she'd expected. Her words were sharp and exact, cutting away at Sarah's happiness and confidence with precision. From her position just behind Sarah, she had watched as Sarah had become smaller. Her shoulders tightened while her body slumped. She looked depressed and dejected, and Pippa couldn't stand the thought of it.

At the back of her mind was the knowledge that soon Sarah would provide the biggest piece of ammunition to her mother in the form of her break-up with the wonderful Natalie. In that second, Pippa could see the future.

If Angela revelled in telling Sarah that her newly cut hair was inadequate, then she would have struck the virtual lottery to know that her daughter had been dumped.

Pippa had acted with only a moment's thought. A deep-seated desire to protect Sarah was all it took. That, and the knowledge that she could pretend to be someone else for a couple of days.

She'd gripped Angela's hand a little harder than she ordinarily would have. She'd stared a little deeper into her eyes. She wanted to convey that she wouldn't accept Angela's attitude towards Sarah any longer. She hoped that she'd conveyed *I'm here, and I'm watching you.*

It had all been instinctual, and now she'd thrown them both into something they hadn't had time to plan for.

"So thoughtless," she mumbled to herself.

She climbed the stairs two at a time to pack up some belongings. She had an hour to make it look like she lived at Sarah's. That definitely meant clothes and toiletries, but she couldn't think what else. It would be impossible to move everything she owned.

"Books," she decided aloud. She pulled a suitcase down from the top of the wardrobe and threw a handful of books from the shelf in her bedroom into the case. Clothes were next, just enough for a few days. She could replenish easily enough.

Her mind was a blank. She simply couldn't focus on what she needed to do. All she could think of was how she was going to convince Angela that she was Natalie. And how she was going to survive pretending to be Sarah's loving, perfect girlfriend.

She wondered if she even remembered how to be with someone. What was clear was that she'd thrown Sarah into a lie she wasn't prepared for, and it was up to Pippa to make sure that it worked.

Chapter Thirteen

Pippa held the book tightly and waited. Her heart was beating so loudly that she was sure others would be able to hear it. Thankfully, she was alone. For now.

She'd raced around Hillcrest Cottage and placed a few personal items here and there to make it look like she lived there and had done for some time. Her clothes she left in the suitcase, placed atop Sarah's wardrobe. It felt too personal to be placing her clothes next to Sarah's.

After that she texted Sarah to ask if they would like to be picked up from town. Sarah had quickly replied to say that her mother wanted to walk and that they were on their way back. Pippa had read the text several times, searching for any clues. She didn't know if Sarah was angry at her for her sudden decision to change all their plans. She wouldn't find out until they managed to get some time alone, and she had no idea when that might be.

There was nothing she could do except be the best Natalie that she could be, something she had no idea how to do and hadn't prepared in the slightest for.

In an attempt to distract herself, and to look as if she belonged in the house, she'd decided to sit in the living room with a book. The book was open, and she was looking at the page, but not a single word was being processed by her brain.

Every second felt like an hour as she waited to see if she'd be found out. Pippa wasn't used to lying. It just wasn't in her nature.

Now she had to be good at it if she wanted to protect Sarah. There was no way to back out now.

The door opened, and Pippa's heart started to beat even faster. She could hear the irritated tone of Angela Campbell's voice, and a wave of sorrow for Sarah swept over her. The last hour and twenty minutes had been stressful, but she imagined that it was nothing compared to sitting and sharing afternoon tea with the pompous and opinionated woman.

"So this is it," Sarah said. "Home sweet home."

Pippa put the book to one side and stood. She entered the hallway and watched Angela looking around with a critical eye. Pippa met Sarah's gaze and was relieved to see a tight smile offered in her direction. Sarah looked exhausted—emotionally drained, Pippa imagined.

"Did you have a nice tea?" Pippa asked.

Angela ignored her. Instead of replying, or even looking at Pippa, she continued her inspection by walking into the kitchen.

Sarah turned to Pippa. "Mum had a chat with the owner to find out about the source ingredients for the vegan tea." Her tone was light and neutral, but her expression said it all. She'd been mortified.

"You've not finished decorating the kitchen, have you?" Angela asked.

Sarah looked ready to pop. Pippa placed a hand on her shoulder.

"Let me," she whispered. She entered the kitchen. "Not quite. There's more plasterboard work to be done, so we can continue the painting. We've only replaced half the doors."

"Looks odd." Angela placed her handbag on the dining table. "But I suppose you girls know what you're doing."

"We do." Pippa gestured to the kettle. "Can I get you a drink?"

"Just water." Angela sat down and continued to look around the room as if she was attempting to locate the source of an unpleasant smell.

Pippa got her a glass of water and placed it and a coaster in front of her.

"Sarah tells me that you're doing the renovations yourself."

"Yes." Pippa decided to keep her replies short. There was less chance she'd misstep if she did.

"That's very impressive," Angela said. "It's not an easy task, I'm sure."

"It takes a bit of knowledge and experience," Pippa agreed, thankful that Angela finally seemed to be shifting towards a positive tone.

"Which I can see you have," Angela said in an obvious dig at Pippa's age.

Pippa bit her tongue to stop from saying what she wanted to. She didn't want to stoop to Angela's level. Or let her know that her words had hit their target.

Angela stood. "I think I'll have that nap that you suggested before we eat dinner, Sarah. This headache is persistent."

"Okay, Mum. I'll show you upstairs."

"I'll find it," Angela said.

"Okay, it's the second on the left," Sarah said. "I hope you manage to get some sleep."

"Doubtful." Angela kissed the tips of two of her fingers and pressed the fingers to Sarah's forehead. She turned to leave the room, pausing in the doorway to say, "Nice to meet you, Natalie." She gave Pippa a once over with her eyes that suggested it hadn't been very nice at all.

Pippa and Sarah stood in silence and waited for Angela's footsteps up the stairs to fade away and the click of the guest bedroom door to close. Sarah sagged in relief.

"Oh. My. God," she whispered. "I forgot how much drama she is in person. Or she's gotten worse."

"She has a headache?" Pippa asked.

"Supposedly. She said it was because breakfast was stressful. She stayed in some tiny little guest house and didn't tell them that she has special dietary requirements. She ate breakfast, but she says it wasn't enough, and not starting the day right has given her a headache. If she does have a headache, it's probably more because she got herself into a snit with the owner of the guest house."

Frustration flowed off Sarah in waves. Pippa gently took hold of her upper arms.

"Breathe," she instructed.

Sarah sucked in a short breath and then started talking again. "You know, I warned her that the cottage was still a work in progress. She's going to complain about everything. If she'd seen it at the start, she would have had a heart attack."

"A deep breath," Pippa instructed.

Sarah sucked in a deeper breath. "And she told me I look ill. Like, the first thing she said to me."

"Well, you don't look ill," Pippa said. She wanted to tell Sarah that she looked as beautiful as always but held back. "You're allowing her to get under your skin. I know it's hard, but you need to try to rise above it."

Sarah's eyes finally met hers. "You're right. I do this to myself."

"No. She plays a role, you just let her get to you," Pippa said.

Sarah nodded quickly. "I do. I just don't know how to stop."

"Let's prepare dinner," Pippa suggested. "If she does have a headache, then food will help."

"Yes. Good idea." Sarah stepped away and picked up a folder from a shelf. "I downloaded a load of recipes of things she can eat. Mum's vegan, but she's also very particular about where the food has come from. No flying in a tomato from Spain, it has to be grown locally."

Pippa could believe that. It also now made sense why Sarah was driving around every farm shop on Celfare buying produce for the last couple of days. She watched Sarah inspecting each recipe to find the perfect one for that evening. Her nose ruffled, and deep frown lines appeared between her eyes. Stress was radiating from her.

Pippa wished that she could take it away but knew that little would dent the strong desire to receive some maternal support and affirmation that Sarah clearly wished for. Sadly, Pippa suspected that it didn't matter how hard Sarah tried as Angela seemed like the sort of woman who would find fault no matter what.

It was clear that Sarah knew that on some level but had yet to fully accept it. Sarah still bent over backward for Angela's acceptance and the possibility of a crumb of a compliment. Pippa didn't know if she should focus her attention on getting Sarah to stop trying or Angela to soften.

She found herself staring at a beautiful woman tying herself in knots to please the clearly unpleasant. She wanted to hold her and tell her that Angela's opinion meant precious little. Pippa felt her eyes widen in surprise at the unexpected longing.

"Greek-inspired cauliflower stew," Sarah said.

"Sounds delicious. I'm sure she'll love it," Pippa replied.

Sarah threw her head back and laughed. "I'm sure she'll have something to say. We live in hope that she might eat it." She picked up a knife from the knife block. "How are you with chopping?"

Pippa took the knife. "I'm an expert."

"Of course you are." Sarah placed a chopping board on the worktop. "Show me your skills."

❖

Dinner was painfully awkward. Angela had appeared ten minutes before it was ready and cross-examined Sarah on the meal and all its components. Even when Sarah assured her that everything was locally sourced, Angela seemed displeased.

Pippa had to bite her tongue when Angela completely cleared her plate and then had the audacity to declare that she hadn't been much of a fan of the dish. Sarah had looked broken as she cleared the plates away.

Now Pippa sat at the dining table with a woman she had only known for a short period of time and was already certain she disliked more than anyone she had ever met before. She reminded herself that this was Sarah's mother, and no matter how mean she appeared, she was important to Sarah. There was also the possibility, however slim, that she had simply met Angela on a bad day. Pippa herself had been a beast to deal with for several weeks after Kim had died. That terrible time had given her insight into not judging others too harshly or quickly without knowing all the details. Even if that was hard in the case of her current company.

"So," Angela said.

It was a word and a tone that rarely led anywhere positive, and Pippa braced herself for whatever question was about to come her way.

"You and Sarah met online?" Angela asked.

"That's right." Pippa had already decided to be as vague as possible. There was no need to decorate a lie with unnecessary details. Sarah had given her a quick, whispered rundown of what she thought Pippa might need to know while they had prepared dinner. It was precious little, and Pippa was again surprised that Angela seemed to care so little about the details of her daughter's life.

"Do you often date people from the internet?" Angela continued.

Pippa sipped her wine and then replied, "No, never."

"What was it about Sarah that made you change the habit of a lifetime?"

Pippa did her best to maintain a neutral expression despite the very sharp questions being dispatched in her direction. With Sarah in the kitchen doing the washing up with the radio on, Angela was taking her opportunity to quiz the stranger she shared a dining table with. Pippa wondered if she might do the same if she ever had children. She assumed, and hoped, that she'd do so with considerably more tact.

"We spoke a lot and found we had a lot in common," Pippa said.

Angela raised an eyebrow. "Really? You seem quite different."

Pippa knew that she couldn't deny the obvious. The gap in years between them was the most visible sign of their differences, but even beyond that it was clear that there were many. Even so, Pippa still felt closer to Sarah than she did to most people.

"I suppose we just work well together because we have the right differences and the right similarities," Pippa replied.

Angela's expression stated clearly that she didn't believe a word. "You are different from what I expected."

"Older?" Pippa asked.

"Yes. And I don't see this magnetic connection that Sarah spoke of. I was expecting you to still be in the honeymoon phase from the way she spoke on the phone."

Pippa tried to hold back her frustration at Angela's blatant rudeness. "Well, we do have a guest to think of."

"Oh, don't mind me." Angela smirked and sipped her wine. "Just pretend I'm not here."

Forgetting about Angela's presence wasn't on the cards. The woman was like a shadow that lingered, even when she wasn't in the room.

Pippa picked up the empty wine bottle. "I'll just get a fresh bottle—I'll be back in a moment."

"Oh, I'm not drinking any more this evening," Angela said.

"I am," Pippa replied.

She entered the kitchen and went straight over to Sarah. "She's questioning our relationship," she whispered in Sarah's ear.

Sarah's eyebrows rose. "Why?"

"We don't appear to be in our honeymoon phase. Or have a magnetic connection. And I'm old." Pippa huffed. She knew she was older than Sarah, that much was obvious for anyone to see. But she didn't need it to be pointed out by Sarah's mother. "How old is she, anyway?"

"I'm not answering that," Sarah said.

Pippa sighed. It meant there was precious little difference in their ages. Not surprising but equally not a fact that cheered her up at all.

"We'll have to ramp things up," Sarah said.

"Ramp things up?" Pippa wasn't entirely sure how she felt about that. She was already struggling to appear unaffected when Sarah casually touched her. Ramping anything up might be a struggle.

"Yes, you know, seem more loving. It's easy." Sarah finished the washing up and wiped her hands dry on a cloth. Before Pippa had a chance to say anything, Sarah walked back into the dining room.

"Shall we go for a walk along the beach?" Sarah suggested loudly.

CHAPTER FOURTEEN

Sarah sucked in a deep breath of fresh sea air and enjoyed the few moments where her mother wasn't complaining about something. As irritating as her mum could be, she found peace in nature and became a completely different person when surrounded by natural beauty.

It was hard not to get lost in the beauty of Celfare's coastline, from sandy beaches, to pebbles, to cliffs. It had it all. Sarah knew she'd miss it when she got back to London.

After a few minutes of walking, Pippa had fallen behind and was taking some photographs on her phone. Sarah suspected that she simply wanted a break and was using that as an excuse as she presumably already had a million photos of the beach.

"She's not at all what I expected," her mother said.

"What did you expect?" Sarah asked.

Her mother shrugged and looked out at the water. "Not her."

"Because she's older?" Sarah fished.

"Maybe."

"I've dated older women before."

"I know." Her mother plastered a smile on her face. "Maybe it's not her age. I'm not sure. As I say, I didn't expect her. I'm sure I'll get to know her better soon, and it will all fall into place. You seem happy."

"I am." She wasn't, but she could pretend. Pretending was an instinctual reflex when it came to conversations with her mother.

Sarah had pretty much given up on the idea of finding someone to slot neatly into her life. It had become easier to just be alone.

A phone started to ring. Her mother looked at her expectantly.

"Not me," Sarah said.

Her mum patted her pocket. "Oh, I forgot I'd even brought it with me." She looked at the screen. "Oh, it's Martin."

Sarah resisted the urge to roll her eyes. Of course it was Martin. He couldn't leave her mother alone for more than a few hours. It seemed his calls increased in frequency when he knew Sarah was around. Probably worried that Sarah would somehow break through his hypnotic hold over her mother. Sadly, Sarah knew she had no such power.

Her mother answered the call and sped up a little along the beach. Sarah stood still and watched her mother walking away. The sound of her laughter swept along the beach. Sarah tried not to be hurt by how her mother's mood had instantly lightened when one of her Project Earth fanatics called.

"Who's she talking to?" Pippa asked, catching up to where Sarah stood.

"Martin. He's one of the leaders at Project Earth."

"Well, he knows how to make your mum laugh," Pippa said.

"Probably fluffing up her ego." Sarah took Pippa's arm and started walking again.

Pippa pocketed her phone and placed a warm hand on Sarah's where it clutched at her bicep. "She's not looking at us."

"She will," Sarah said.

She'd seen the way her mother looked at them. Doubt was written all over her face. Sarah didn't think that she suspected their relationship was a ruse, just that they were mismatched. The assumption angered Sarah all the more. Pippa was a catch, and Sarah would be lucky to have her. Unless her mother suspected that Sarah was just wrong for Pippa, which was just as likely, considering who they were talking about.

"Far be it from me to say anything negative about the woman who gave you life—"

"Please do," Sarah encouraged. "I've spent years on and off wondering if it's just me. It would be nice to have some confirmation."

"She's quite…difficult."

Sarah chuckled. She clutched Pippa's arm a little tighter. "She is."

"I had hoped to be a kind of buffer, but I think I'm making things worse. She doesn't like me," Pippa added.

"You're not making things worse—she'd be far worse if you weren't here," Sarah said, reassuring her. "And she doesn't like most people, so you're in great company."

Sarah kept a steely eye on her mother and noticed that she was about to turn around. Sarah stopped walking and used her grip on Pippa's arm to pivot her. She moved in close and placed her lips on Pippa's.

Pippa stiffened. They'd talked about the need for an occasional peck on the cheek but never in any detail. This was categorically not a peck. This was a kiss. One which Sarah was very much in charge of as Pippa had yet to respond.

Sarah let go of Pippa's arm and slid both her hands up and over Pippa's shoulders and interlaced them behind her neck. She leaned in closer, pressing her body against Pippa. Something woke Pippa up, and she felt arms snaking around her back and holding her close. A moan escaped Sarah's lips.

Pippa pulled away. Her eyes were wide, and her cheeks were flushed.

"I think she got an eyeful of that," Sarah said, sneaking a look at her mother over Pippa's shoulder. Anything to ignore how attractively ruffled Pippa looked.

"Good," Pippa murmured. She stepped back. "I think I'm going to head back. I have a couple of phone calls to make, probably best that your mother doesn't overhear them."

"Hiring a hitman?" Sarah winked.

"Not yet. Give me a few more days." Pippa glanced in her mother's direction and then looked away again. "I'll see you at the house."

She was gone before Sarah had a chance to say goodbye. She bit her lip and watched the retreating the figure. Had Pippa been uncomfortable with the kiss? The opportunity for her mother to see them was just too good to pass up. During their quick discussion about how to handle things as they prepared dinner, Pippa had seemed happy with the idea of kissing and whatever else they needed to do to be convincing. Or at least had little to say against it.

Sarah frowned. Now that she thought about it, Pippa had nodded and agreed to whatever she had suggested. She wondered if that was Pippa being comfortable with the idea or just going with the flow. It was too late to find out now.

"Sarah?" her mother called.

She sucked in a breath and turned to catch up to her.

"Martin says hello."

"Cool." Sarah shoved her hands into her pockets and walked alongside her. "Everything okay?"

She didn't really care, but her mother was positively beaming as she always did when she came off an ego-expanding phone call from one of the men who knew exactly how to get what they wanted from her.

"Martin wants me to tour the universities again," her mother explained. "He's started arranging a schedule. It will be arduous, of course, but so worthwhile."

"Didn't that not go so well last time?"

Sarah recalled her mother's fury when some of the talks were picketed by students who felt that Project Earth's methods went too far. Apparently, it was perfectly okay for her to tell people to stand up for their beliefs, as long as they didn't believe something that countered what she was trying to tell them. Students weren't as impressionable as Project Earth had hoped.

"There are always those who need convincing," her mother said.

"I don't think they needed convincing, Mum. They agree with what you are saying, just not necessarily the methods you suggest. Not everyone agrees with disruption politics."

"They'll have to eventually. It's the only way to get things done."

Sarah ground her teeth. She didn't believe that at all and knew her mother would fight the point with her dying breath. They'd never see things the same way when it came to that topic.

"Where did Natalie go?"

"She's headed back to do some work," Sarah said.

"What does she do?" her mother asked for the first time.

"She runs a handyperson service."

"Here?"

"On Celfare, yes."

"Is there much call for that?"

"Yeah. She's pretty busy."

The huge project of renovating the cottage had taken up a lot of Pippa's time, but occasionally she disappeared to help others. Sarah had felt guilty for monopolising the best handyperson on the island. Pippa had reassured her that she'd be able to manage her schedule.

Her mother's eyebrows were still raised in displeasure.

"She's a qualified structural engineer," Sarah added.

Pippa hadn't spoken much about herself, but she had mentioned that the handyperson service was only part of her income and that the bulk of it came from consulting for her old firm. Sarah hoped that the whiff of qualifications and a career her mother could respect would soothe the worry lines on her face.

"Then why is she here?" Angela asked. "Don't tell me she's retired."

Angela said the word as if it was a curse. The idea of retiring appalled her. If one no longer needed to work, then it was time to volunteer for the greater good. Leisure time was simply selfish in her view.

"No, she still works in structural engineering now and then."

Sarah certainly couldn't tell her mother about Pippa's ex-wife. In fact, Sarah knew it was best to say as little about Pippa as possible. Every lie came with its own potential new trip hazards, especially now that Pippa wasn't there to hear what had been said.

"How many universities will be included on this tour?" Sarah asked, knowing her mother would love the opportunity to go back to talking about her own career.

❖

Pippa opened the news application on her phone for the fifth time just in case there was anything new to read. She'd been hiding in the downstairs shower room for half an hour, checking her email, looking at the news, checking what was happening on Facebook, and organising her photos. Anything to delay the inevitable.

Sarah had scoffed at the idea of Pippa sleeping in a sleeping bag on the floor. Apparently, they were both adults and sharing a bed would be the obvious choice. They weren't on a reality television show or characters in a romantic comedy, Sarah had added—they were real people, and real people could share a space without there being any awkwardness.

Pippa hadn't wanted to give Sarah the impression that she was uncomfortable with the idea, even though she did have some reservations about sharing a bed.

Especially after the kiss on the beach.

Having Sarah pressed up against her had been a surprise. Pippa had spent a few seconds surprised that she barely remembered what a kiss felt like. And then a few more seconds reminding herself what to do when engaged in one. When Sarah had moaned, Pippa had stepped away because it was that or slip her tongue into Sarah's open mouth. The instinct had shocked her to the core. She'd not felt that way since Kim. No one had ever come close to making her feel that way. She'd made sure of it.

She'd known from the start that pretending to be in a relationship would be tricky, but it appeared that she'd seriously underestimated by how much.

After they had all returned from the walk on the beach, Angela had stated that she was ready for an early night. Sarah had quickly agreed that she was also tired. Pippa suspected that Sarah was happy to simply have the first day of the torturous visit finally over.

While mother and daughter had gone upstairs to use the main bathroom to get ready, Pippa had hidden in the downstairs shower room. She knew that time was running out and that Sarah would be sending a search party if she didn't head upstairs soon.

Turning off her phone and looking at her reflection one last time, she took a deep breath and unlocked the door. She'd spent hours in the cottage recently but still found it a little disorientating to be locking up and turning the lights off downstairs before heading up to bed.

She paused in front of the closed door to the main bedroom. It didn't feel right to charge in without knocking. But if she knocked, then there was a chance Angela would hear. In the end she decided to open the door slowly and walk in with her eyes closed. She felt foolish but knew she'd feel far worse if she accidentally walked in on Sarah in a state of undress.

She heard a snort of a laugh from Sarah. "You can open your eyes."

Eyes open, she saw Sarah sitting up in bed with a book in her hands. Her face was clean of make-up, and her hair hung loosely around her shoulders. Pippa closed the bedroom door.

"I didn't know if..."

"I get changed in the bathroom. You can come in and out of here without worrying about that," Sarah explained. She peeled back a corner of the duvet and winked. "Come to bed, honey."

Pippa swallowed at the joke. She deliberately kept her face hidden in the dim light as she plugged in her phone to be charged overnight. She got into bed, lay on her back, and stared straight up.

A few weeks before, when she was filling in cracks and painting the ceiling, she'd never expected to be in bed looking up at it.

She risked a look to her side. Sarah was wearing a tank top and seemed engrossed in her book. True to her word, she was casually not concerned about sharing a bed. Pippa wished she could bottle some of that confidence. Sarah was a mystery. In some ways she was uncertain and timid, but in other ways she seemed to be comfortable in her own skin and oozed assuredness.

"What are you reading?" Pippa asked.

"Just something for work." She closed the book and showed Pippa the cover.

"Digital transformation, web application social engineering," Pippa said. "I have no idea what any of that means."

"You're not missing much. I wouldn't call it a page-turner." Sarah opened the book again and continued reading. "If you want to pretend that you're working late tomorrow and can't join us for dinner, feel free. I know this can't be much fun for you."

"Oh, do you want me to stay away?" Pippa had done her best but was aware that Angela was a tough person to fool.

Sarah closed her book again and looked down at Pippa. "No, not at all. I'm giving you an out. I'm so grateful that you're here. But I feel bad asking you to stay when she's in this much of a bad mood."

"Am I the one causing that bad mood?" Pippa asked.

"No. I think she's had some bad feedback about her article. This happens all the time. She writes something to split the room and feels great about how she's going to disrupt things. Then the wrong thing gets disrupted, or she gets some negative commentary, and she gets angry because things didn't go her way." Sarah went back to her book. "This happens a lot."

Pippa looked up at Sarah and noticed that her eyes shone in the light from the bedside lamp. She'd either been crying recently or was trying to hold back tears. Pippa had no idea which, but the thought of it made her even more determined to stay close. If she could deflect any of Angela's animosity, then she would.

Watching YouTube videos of Angela Campbell had only marginally prepared her for meeting the woman in person. Pippa had thought that she might be tricky but had discovered that she was downright rude, probably even cruel at times. She wouldn't leave Sarah to deal with that alone.

"I have some work to do early in the morning, but I'll be back to help prepare dinner," Pippa said.

Sarah smiled. "Thank you. I really appreciate that."

"Try to get some sleep. You'll feel better," Pippa said.

"One more chapter." Sarah picked up a bookmark with a small

reading light attached to it and switched off the bedside lamp. "Night, Pippa."

"Goodnight." Pippa turned to her side, away from Sarah, and closed her eyes.

She didn't know when sleep would come but assumed it would take a while. Her heart was in turmoil in a way she hadn't experienced for a long time. The more she tried to push aside her feelings, the stronger they seemed to grow.

Giving in to them wasn't possible. She was helping a friend, nothing more. They might be sharing a home, even a bed, but it didn't mean anything, and she had to make sure it stayed that way. She had to keep her emotions in check. If she didn't, then she would be taking advantage of Sarah's trust in the worst possible way.

Most of all, she didn't want to get into a relationship. The potential for heartbreak was too high. The last one nearly killed her, and she swore to never put herself into that position again.

She sighed as quietly as she could, scrunched her eyes up, and tried to push all such thoughts out of her head. The sound of pages being softly turned soothed her to sleep.

CHAPTER FIFTEEN

Sarah woke up and instantly felt a wave of panic rush over her. Pippa was gone. She snatched up her phone and looked at the clock and realised that she had to hurry. She jumped out of bed and rushed across the room to slightly open the door.

Downstairs, she heard conversation. Her heart thudded. She raced down the stairs. Her mother was often up early in the morning, and the moment that Sarah realised she was alone in bed, she knew Pippa and her mother were downstairs together. Alone.

She'd entered the kitchen before she realised that she was wearing nothing more than a pair of very short shorts and a tank top. Sleeping beside Pippa in the skimpy nightwear hadn't felt problematic due to being tucked up in bedding. Walking into the kitchen was a little different. Of course, her mum had seen it all before, but it was patently obvious that Pippa hadn't as her eyebrow rose and she quickly got up from the dining table and went to the sink.

Sarah hoped that her mother hadn't noticed Pippa's strange reaction. Despite her panic over what the two had been talking about, she felt a bubble of pleasure that she'd caused such an obvious reaction in Pippa.

"Morning," Sarah said. She pulled a mug out of the cupboard and started to make herself a large cup of very strong coffee. She knew she'd need it. "Sleep well, Mum?"

"Quite well."

It was a glowing review and meant she'd slept like a log and was feeling well-rested. That was a bonus that Sarah hadn't expected.

"I have to get going." Pippa approached. Her gaze was firmly on the floor to avoid looking at Sarah.

"Okay, sweetie, have a good day." Sarah leaned in and gave Pippa a kiss on the cheek.

"You, too." Pippa smiled tightly and then quickly left, saying a brief farewell to her mother before the front door clicked closed. Sarah hoped she'd be back, that her mother hadn't scared her off permanently.

She returned to making her coffee. "What would you like to do today?"

"Oh, I don't want to be a bother," her mother replied.

"You're not," Sarah said. "I'm looking forward to having the day off and spending some time together."

It was a blatant lie, and she was fairly sure her mother knew it. It was a kind lie, she reminded herself. The truth was that her mother had probably only visited out of curiosity and a misplaced sense of duty. She'd rather be at home. Sarah would rather be at work. Neither of them enjoyed each other's company, but they pretended for the other's sake. It was a strange dance that they'd performed for years, each very aware of the other's real thoughts but conforming to some kind of societal requisite.

"What would you like to do?" her mother neatly batted back.

"We could have lunch at a cafe in town." Sarah looked over her shoulder and saw that her mother's teacup was still full. "Do you want some more tea? Something to eat?"

"No, thank you. Natalie was very attentive."

"She's good at looking after people," Sarah agreed.

The silence from the dining table was deafening. Sarah finished making her drink and took a seat. She was desperate to know what the two had spoken about but wanted to appear casual about it.

"What time did you get up?" She wasn't too proud to fish for information.

"Oh, you know me, up with the sun. I performed some yoga in my room and came downstairs around six thirty. Natalie was already here—she said she had an early start. You look tired still. Are you getting enough sleep?"

Sarah sipped her coffee. No, she wasn't. The last few days she had been stressed about her mother's arrival and working hard to get the house in good order for her. Last night she had read the most boring book she had in order to calm her racing heart at sharing a bed with Pippa. She'd read for over an hour and a half with her tiny reading light until she thought she heard Pippa's breathing become deep and rhythmic.

Even then, sleep hadn't come easily. Worry that her mother didn't quite believe their ruse and that she was asking too much of Pippa had kept her tossing and turning through the early hours.

"I'm fine," she replied. "What would you like to do this morning? There's the beach, or we could go to the other side of the island where it's rockier if you fancy hiking. There are a few shops in town but nothing much."

"Actually…" Angela looked down at her teacup. "I was thinking of having a walk on my own, if that's not too rude? I'd like to ramble a bit. It's rare that I'm in a place like this, and I want to take advantage of it. Especially before it gets too hot. Maybe we could meet up for lunch. Did you say there was a cafe you recommend?"

"Yep. Annie's, it's pretty good. Nice menu and plenty we can both eat." She got up and put a slice of bread into the toaster. "And of course, it's fine if you want to have a walk on your own. It's your holiday."

Relief at not having to entertain her mother for a few hours collided with the fact that her mother would be wandering Celfare alone and could bump into any number of locals who could blow her deception sky high. But it wasn't like she could keep her mother a prisoner. If she wanted to go and walk in the countryside, then Sarah could do little about it, except perhaps warn Pippa that her mother was on the loose and could turn up anywhere.

"Wonderful. I think I'll get ready and will head out soon. Do you have a Thermos I could borrow?"

"I do." Sarah opened a cupboard and placed the flask on the dining table.

"Thank you, darling." Angela kissed the tips of her fingers and pressed them to Sarah's forehead before heading back upstairs to get ready.

She let out a sigh and leaned on the countertop. Her mother hadn't said how long she'd be staying yet. She'd mentioned that she had an open ticket and the world was her oyster, speaking engagements aside, of course. Sarah hadn't pressed her on the matter, claiming that she was just happy to see her. But the truth was that not having a definitive end to the visit was draining. It could be an extra day—it could be several.

She imagined it wouldn't be that long as her mother no doubt had more interesting things to be doing. Experience told her that it would last until they had a massive argument or until her mother felt her maternal duties had been completed.

There was little Sarah could do but wait and see which one would come first.

❖

Pippa's phone softly rumbled on the desk. She looked at the text from Sarah. *Target is on the loose. Stay safe out there!*

Pippa laughed. She hit the call button and held the phone to her ear, already forgetting about the calculations she had promised Lawrence.

"Morning," Sarah said.

"Good morning again," Pippa replied. She leaned back in her office chair, a grin on her face. "So, she's on the loose?"

"Yep."

"Do you know where?"

"No, she wanted to go for a walk on her own," Sarah said.

"Well, you couldn't pass up an offer like that."

"Exactly. I wanted to warn you in case you came across her today."

"Thank you, I appreciate the warning." Pippa sat forward and accessed her email. "Actually, I need to talk to you about the kitchen renovation. The doors that we thought would match have a twenty-six week wait."

Sarah's laugh caused Pippa's smile to grow wider.

"Sounds like we need new doors," Sarah said. "I'm not waiting twenty-six weeks for some cupboard doors."

"I thought you'd say that. And I'd like to point out that this is a manufacturer delay and nothing to do with the fact you live on Celfare."

Sarah chuckled some more. "I don't believe you. I suspect the manufacturer took one look at where they'd have to ship the doors and pretended it would be a twenty-six-week delay. I'm sure if I still lived in London, I'd have them tomorrow."

Pippa felt a lump in her throat form at the thought of Sarah moving back to London. She didn't know what Sarah's long-term plans were—she'd deliberately not asked. To ask would be to admit that she didn't want Sarah to leave.

"Oh, absolutely, delivered by someone on a moped being paid one pound fifty." Pippa played along. "Do you remember your second choice for the doors?"

"No, they were named after a city," Sarah said.

"They're all named after cities." Pippa picked up the brochure and leafed through the pages. They'd chosen Oxford as a first choice and Winchester as a second. She'd known Sarah would forget.

"Oh. Which ones had the cornery thing?" Sarah sounded distracted, and Pippa could picture her squinting up at the ceiling, deep in thought.

"You decided you didn't want that," Pippa reminded her.

"Did I?"

"You did. Do you want me to come over with the brochure as your mother isn't there?"

It wasn't necessary. Pippa knew what Sarah had chosen. She was using Sarah's forgetfulness as an excuse to see her, although she masked it to herself by pretending that she was actually double-checking that Sarah was happy with the choice before she placed the order.

"Would you mind?" Sarah asked. "I'm sorry. I'm no good with names."

"It's not a problem at all. We never made a decision on taps anyway. I haven't seen one that has a rubber glove tied to it, so you might need to rethink your aesthetic."

Sarah burst out laughing, and Pippa smiled happily at hearing the lyrical sound. "Look, it seemed logical at the time." Sarah defended herself for the tenth time. "When do you want to come over?"

"Now? Who knows when your mother might return from terrorising the innocent citizens of Celfare."

"Sounds great. I'll put the kettle on!"

Pippa said goodbye and hung up the call. She felt a little bad for her deceit, but it quickly passed at the warm feeling of knowing she'd see Sarah again soon. It had only been an hour, but she already keenly missed being at Hillcrest Cottage. She reasoned that it was natural after spending so much time there recently. She was a creature of habit, and it took a while for her to acclimatise to a change. The truth, of course, lurked at the back of her mind— it wasn't anything to do with a change in schedule. It was Sarah. Funny, casually beautiful, occasionally unpredictable Sarah.

"Stop it," she told herself.

Thinking that way wasn't helpful. She needed to stop and focus on the tasks at hand—helping Sarah with the final renovations of Hillcrest Cottage and somehow pretending to be the impossibly perfect Natalie. She was quite sure she'd failed at that second one, at least in Angela's eyes. But she'd carry on and do her best to help Sarah out of the sticky situation that she'd made.

She snatched up the brochure and car keys. The figures for Lawrence could wait.

❖

Pippa approached the front door to Hillcrest Cottage and paused for a moment. She'd been about to knock when she recalled that she had a key and was probably expected to use it. She opened the door and called out, "Hello!"

"In the kitchen," Sarah replied.

Pippa closed the front door and silently hoped that Angela wouldn't be back too soon. Partly for Sarah's sake but also for her own.

She entered the kitchen and stopped dead for a moment. Sarah had her back to Pippa while she prepared two drinks. She wore a towelling robe, and her hair was damp. Sarah was more covered up than she had been that morning when she came downstairs in a tank top and some extremely short shorts, but that didn't matter. Pippa's heart raced. It was the second time that Sarah's appearance had caused a physical reaction in her, and she knew she needed to get a grip.

"Hey, thanks for coming over," Sarah said. She turned around and handed over a cup of tea to Pippa.

Pippa took the cup. "No problem. How are you doing?"

Black smudges of exhaustion lingered under Sarah's eyes. Her demeanour was slumped and saddened. Angela had taken her toll quickly.

"I'm okay. Just…waiting for it to be over. I had a long shower to try to get some of the muscle knots out, but no luck. Muscle knots after less than a day!"

"I'll be out of your hair shortly," Pippa promised.

"Oh, not you." Sarah placed her fingers on Pippa's arm. "You're the only thing keeping me sane at the moment. I just would like to know when she's thinking of leaving."

"Can't you ask?"

Sarah laughed. "The guilt trip that would lead to isn't worth having the answer."

Pippa could easily imagine that Angela would happily use the innocent question as an excuse to make Sarah feel bad. "I could ask—she hates me already."

Sarah walked into the living room and gestured for Pippa to follow. She sat on the sofa and rubbed tiredly at her eyes.

"I appreciate the offer, but I think it would have the same result. Sorry I'm a mess today."

Pippa sat next to her, placing the mug of tea and the brochure on the coffee table in front of them. "You're not a mess."

"I have mirrors these days. I know what I look like." Sarah tucked a loose lock of damp hair behind her head. "Anyway. Taps?"

"Have you tried talking to her?" Pippa asked.

"We talk, just not about anything important."

"Exactly. Have you tried telling her how you feel? Explaining how she makes you feel?"

Sarah sighed softly and leaned back into the sofa. She looked small and thoroughly beaten up. Pippa wanted to fix it, wanted to ask Angela what the hell she thought she was doing. Wanted to take Sarah in her arms and tell her that it would all be okay.

"Mum…" Sarah stopped and scrunched up her face. She looked thoughtfully at the ceiling. "Mum isn't like a lot of people you know. She just doesn't work in the way you expect people to work. You can't reason with her. I don't want to say she isn't normal, because what is normal? It's just that she doesn't follow the rules you expect. She doesn't care about niceties. She's ruled by her ethics, and they may not be the same ethics that you or I share."

"But surely if she knew she was hurting you by the way she acts and the things she says?" Pippa reasoned.

"She's not going to change the things she says. She'd tell me I need to toughen up. Or that I was picking on her. She doesn't see anything wrong with what she says."

Pippa shook her head. "I just can't see how she is oblivious to the fact that she's clearly upsetting you. Maybe if I—"

"No. Absolutely not. Trust me, Pippa. I've been here a hundred times. Over the years, I've said things and other people have said things, and it just makes matters worse. There's nothing to be done. Sometimes relationships are broken beyond repair, and that's where we are. I don't like it, but I've come to accept it." Sarah sat up. "Please, promise me you won't try to fix this."

Pippa reluctantly nodded. She still felt that an honest conversation with Angela was the right thing to do, but she recognised it wasn't her place. She also knew that she was causing Sarah additional stress, which was the absolute last thing that she wanted to do.

"Understood." She picked up the brochure. "Can I interest you in some kitchen renovation therapy?"

Sarah smiled and edged forward a little. "Yes, please. It's a shame we can't get those new cupboard doors, but I was thinking about changing one of the cupboards, so this might have been fate."

"You think a manufacturing delay is fate?" Pippa grinned.

"Fortuitous, then." Sarah took the brochure from Pippa and quickly flipped through the book. She got to the end and then started her way back to the front again. "Why can I never find anything in these books?"

Pippa took the brochure from her and calmly found the right pages. "Because you flip through at one hundred miles an hour."

Sarah took the book back. "How my mum thinks that we don't sound like we've been living together for weeks, I don't know. We sound like an old married couple."

Pippa chuckled. "We do, don't we?"

Sarah looked at the book carefully, appearing to read the descriptions of the various products. "Thank you, by the way."

"For?"

"For doing this. Being Natalie."

"I'm sorry I threw you into it without warning." Pippa apologised yet again.

"It's okay. I'm glad to have you here. It's nice to have someone agree that she's hard work. I'm just sorry that I'm taking you away from your work. And your house."

"You don't need to be sorry, I offered. And I'm sure your mother will be bored of us soon." Pippa hoped that would be the case, anyway.

It wasn't simply being out of her own home that was making the visit exhausting. It was watching Sarah go from being carefree and relaxed to tense and on the verge of tears. Pippa's hero complex was forefront in her mind. She'd spent a lot of time thinking of ways to solve the issue of the broken mother-daughter relationship and was no closer to finding a solution. Worse than that, she knew Sarah didn't want her to try to help.

"Why did we say no to Ipswich?" Sarah asked.

"You said it was too shiny," Pippa reminded her.

"Did I?" Sarah lifted the brochure and peered at the image.

They fell into a comfortable pattern as they had done so many times before while researching building materials, paint swatches, and designs. Sarah would pick out options, Pippa would explain how practical they were, and together they'd cost up each option. In between they'd joke about outlandish designs they saw. It had become a fun pastime for Pippa. Something that she would often leave to her clients, she was now fully engaged with.

She'd picked the door handles, vetoed a particularly ugly banister rail, and scribbled a few designs for the garden. Sarah appreciated her feedback, and Pippa was happy to give it, even when she wasn't charging for her time.

It was ludicrous that Angela didn't see them as a couple, because Pippa hadn't been this close to someone for years, a fact that caused a knot to form in her stomach.

Somehow ninety minutes passed. Sarah seemed brighter and more like her usual self. Pippa couldn't help but make comments to get Sarah to laugh, or even to playfully poke her in the ribs to soften the effect when her jokes were a little sharp.

The back door opened, and Pippa felt her heart sink at the realisation that Angela was back. She started to turn towards Sarah to share a last private moment before Angela started to complain about something.

Sarah was already moving. But not to get up as Pippa had expected. Instead, she straddled Pippa's lap, wrapped her arms around her neck, and started to kiss her.

Pippa's brain knew that it was all an act, but it had forgotten to tell her heart, which was now slamming against her ribcage with equal parts excitement and panic. Sarah's soft lips were on hers, her hands clamped to her face. There was no question that Sarah wanted her mother to discover them in a passionate act. Which meant that Pippa had to react, or the entire effect would be blown.

Ignoring the desire to run her hands up Sarah's bare thighs, which straddled her own, she instead wrapped her arms around Sarah's back and pulled her closer. She tried to listen for any further sounds that Angela might make, but it was useless as Sarah's panting breath and moans filled the space.

Pippa felt her head spin. She wanted to enjoy the kiss but knew that would be wrong. Sarah was playing a game and expected Pippa to be doing the same. Pippa couldn't take advantage of her new friend in that way. But how could she possibly respond to the kiss and not feel the effects of it? She wasn't made of stone.

Thankfully, Angela must have entered the room because Sarah very suddenly broke the kiss. She rested her hands on Pippa's shoulders and looked over her head.

"Oh, I'm sorry, Mum. Didn't hear you come in," Sarah said.

"It's the middle of the day, dear."

Pippa struggled to look away from Sarah's partially covered heaving chest that was right in front of her face. She needed to get out of there. Needed to save her blushes and calm her soaring blood pressure.

"We've done worse in the middle of the day, haven't we?" Sarah asked. She leaned back a little and looked down at Pippa.

Pippa looked up at her and found her breath taken away. Wide eyes, swollen lips, red cheeks. She didn't know what to say. Couldn't have spoken even if she did.

"I'm going to use the bathroom, and when I come back, I hope you'll be decent," Angela said.

Sarah chuckled softly. "I think that convinced her."

Pippa attempted to look behind her.

"She's gone," Sarah confirmed.

"I…have to go." Pippa made a move to stand up. Sarah got off her and stood up, too.

"I'm sorry, I saw the opportunity and thoug—"

"It's not that," Pippa lied. "It was a good idea. It will definitely help to convince her. I've just lost track of time. I have a client."

"Oh, do you have time to stay for lunch?"

Pippa wanted to stay, wanted to be the human shield she was

supposed to be to protect Sarah from her mother's harsh words. But she couldn't. Her emotions were so unsettled that she wondered if she'd be able to form a sentence when Angela returned.

"I'm sorry, I'm already running late." Lying to Sarah felt terrible, but Pippa had to get out of there.

"Are you sure that you're okay?" Sarah asked. Tiny frown lines marred her forehead.

"I'm fine," Pippa lied again. "Just feeling guilty about leaving you alone."

"I'll be okay," Sarah said.

"I'll be back as soon as I can." Pippa grabbed her keys and her jacket and fled.

CHAPTER SIXTEEN

I'm feeling so much better," Sarah's mother proclaimed for the fifth time since she had returned from her walk. "Fresh air! It's so important. It's easy to forget."

Sarah nodded her agreement.

Her mum had clearly decided to ignore the whole walking-in-on-her-daughter-and-partner business and had immediately suggested lunch in town. Apparently, she'd worked up an appetite during her walk and was also keen to treat Sarah, as an apology for her moody behaviour the previous day.

Sarah wasn't about to turn down a free lunch, nor an apology. It was rare that her mother ever apologised for anything. Sarah would have rather driven into town but knew that her mother preferred to walk—better for the environment and better for her health. And so they were walking along deserted country lanes with her mother telling her about everything she'd seen during her walk. Every animal, every flower, every cute cottage, and every glimpse of the deep blue sea that surrounded Celfare.

She'd lightened up considerably and Sarah couldn't help but feel a weight lift from her shoulders. Most times they were together, it ended in an argument.

"What kind of food does this cafe serve?"

"A bit of everything. Sandwiches, quiches, some hot food," Sarah said. "I've only been there once."

"I would have thought that you and Natalie would have been out for more meals. It seems you haven't been anywhere."

"We haven't really," Sarah admitted. "We're kind of home-bodies."

"She's not cheap, is she?" Her mother ruffled her nose in dis-taste.

"No, she's not cheap."

"Has she bought you any gifts? Jewellery?"

"Mum!"

"What? I want to make sure that she's treating you well."

"Treating me well doesn't mean buying trinkets, Mum." Sarah sighed. "We're not in an old-fashioned heteronormative relationship. She's not the man. I don't want her to buy me jewels. Well, I wouldn't mind if she did, but I'm not expecting anything. And it's not a barometer of our relationship."

Her mother made a confused face but said nothing more. Her mother rarely dated. When she did, she expected the man in question to shower her with gifts, open every door, always drive, and generally treat her like a queen. Many a potential partner had been cut loose because he didn't follow the rules. For someone so forward-thinking in some ways, she was stuck in the past in others.

They walked in silence the rest of the way and soon arrived at the cafe. They were seated at a window, which overlooked the marina. Fishing boats bobbed on the calm water, having long since returned from their early morning journeys. Sarah thought they looked picturesque but was quietly waiting for her mother to complain about the damage the fishing industry did to marine wildlife.

Miraculously, nothing was said. Her mother even thanked the waitress for handing her the menu. Sarah let out a relieved sigh. It looked like lunch would not be as stressful as the previous day. Maybe fresh air had been the elixir she'd needed all along.

"Oh, what a marvellous selection," her mother exclaimed upon opening the menu. "It is rare to see so many vegetarian dishes in a place so…bijou."

"Yes, and a lot of it is locally sourced," Sarah added.

"So I see." Her mother appreciatively examined the menu.

Sarah looked out of the window. She'd already decided on a

toasted panini, and she didn't need to look at the menu. Although food was the last thing on her mind. She wished Pippa was with them if only so she could apologise for her poorly thought through plan of kissing her senseless on the sofa.

She'd given the idea all of one second of thought before planting herself on Pippa's lap. Worries that her mother was on to them had lingered in her mind, and suddenly the perfect way to convince her that they were an item was presented right in front of her. The only problem was that she had no time to warn or even ask for permission. And then she'd started to get lost in the kiss. Pippa's arms around her, the feel of her body pressed up against hers, the sound of her own moaning in her ears. It had been a lot. Sarah had wished that her mother would simply walk in for a fresh bottle of water and then leave them to it without ever breaking the moment.

But afterwards Sarah had realised that she'd put Pippa in an impossible situation. No wonder she'd all but run away and had yet to reply to Sarah's text message. She hoped that she'd be able to spend some time alone with Pippa later so she could apologise.

"Did you read my article?" her mother asked.

"I did," Sarah confirmed. She didn't want to talk about the article—it was a sure-fire way for the good mood between them to evaporate.

The waitress returned and they placed their orders. They sat in silence for a few minutes until their drinks were served. Sarah knew she should open a conversation, but she had no idea what to say. She didn't want to ruin the mood. Things were going well. She wanted to enjoy it for as long as possible.

"I received some negativity about it," her mother continued.

Sarah sipped her juice. "I'm not surprised."

"Some nobody on social media brought up that my daughter works for Swype."

"Well, that's never been a secret," Sarah replied.

In fact, her mother had often told people about her daughter working for the devil if only to garner some sympathy from her sycophants.

"It undermines my work, Sarah."

"Your work is yours and mine is mine," Sarah said. "We're mother and daughter, but we're different people. If people can't understand that the—"

"Of course they don't understand that. If I can't convince my only daughter to stop killing the planet, then how am I going to convince businesses and governments? It was amusing for a while, but enough is enough, Sarah."

Sarah sat back in shock at the unexpected outburst. "What are you saying?"

"I'm saying that you have to leave Swype. You can get another job, darling. But this world is the only one we have. There's no second planet for us to move to when we destroy this one. How can I possibly do what I need to do if people think I can't even convince you to do the right thing?"

"Now hold on—"

"Sarah, do you know how much CO_2 Swype pumped into the atmosphere last year?"

"I'm not having this discussion again." Sarah shook her head. Her body tensed. This was not the calm lunch she had expected. In fact, it was looking like an ambush.

"Sarah, please. Martin says that my influence is waning because more and more people are realising that my own daughter is the enemy."

"*Martin* says?" Sarah shook her head. "Wow. Martin really thinks your followers will stop following you because I'm working for Swype? And you're actually…What? Asking me to leave my job? Because of him?"

"Don't call them followers. It's not a cult."

"It is to some. You know that. Answer the question—you want me to leave my job because of something Martin has told you?"

"I want you to do it because it's the right thing to do," her mother asserted.

"For you!"

"You can get another job—you're bright and talented. Put those talents to good use for a change."

"I am!" Sarah clamped her mouth shut before something about her current project slipped out. "I can't believe you. You came here solely to get me to leave Swype, didn't you?"

Her mother's expression said it all. It was nothing to do with seeing her, or meeting Natalie. It was a plan to get Sarah to change her job from the very start. The sudden change of attitude had nothing to do with fresh air—it was simply a ruse to attempt to leverage her and get her own way.

Sarah could see it now. Her mother had embarked on the whole trip with the mindset of getting Sarah to leave Swype. She had been thrown by the long journey and the fact that Natalie wasn't who she had expected. A call from Martin the previous evening and a walk that morning and reinvigorated her and focused her on her mission.

Suddenly she was smiles and compliments. And Sarah had fallen for it. Because she was so desperate to believe that her mother could be a nice person, could be a nice person to *her*.

"You're unbelievable." Sarah shook her head. She looked out of the window and willed the tears that threatened to fall to stay where they were. She didn't want to add to her humiliation by crying.

"Do you even read any of those articles I send you?"

"The biased articles written by fanatics with an agenda? No, I don't. Do you ever read the articles I send you, explaining what Swype is doing to improve its environmental credentials? The articles about awards we have won for doing just that?"

"Trinkets given by charities who want money, you mean," her mother retorted. "You're gullible, Sarah. Always have been."

"I was gullible to think that you came here because you actually cared about me."

"Of course I care about you." Her mother rolled her eyes.

Sarah swallowed. The words should have carried care and authenticity, but instead they were flippant. Lip service and nothing more. Her mother was shaking her head in the same way that she had done when Sarah was a child seeking comfort.

In an instant she flashed back to a time when she'd fallen off her bike and had run to her mother, who had refused to cuddle her.

Instead she told her that it was a life lesson. She'd told Sarah to be more careful and that someone wouldn't always be there to soothe wounds.

She doesn't care about you, Sarah told herself. *When will you actually learn that and stop expecting her to be something she isn't?*

Sarah stood. She grabbed her coat from the back of her chair.

"Where are you going?" her mother asked.

"I don't know." Sarah tossed the house keys on the table. "Let yourself in when you get back."

"Sarah!" her mother called after her as she ran from the cafe.

She wasn't sure why she jogged through the town. It wasn't as if her mother cared enough to come after her. But she jogged nonetheless. She didn't know how much time had passed when she started to feel drops of rain hitting her face and mingling with her tears.

She looked up at the dark sky and rolled her eyes.

"Just perfect," she muttered.

❖

Pippa pulled out of the local school where she had spent far too long fixing a faulty plug socket. Her mind had been elsewhere, and she'd only just managed to follow along with the conversation she'd been having with Andrew Hayes. She was throwing herself into work again, that much was clear.

She hadn't looked at her phone. She knew she'd have a text message or a voicemail from Sarah after she ran out on her earlier. As much as she might wish that she could be subtle, it absolutely wasn't one of her strengths. Sarah would have easily realised something was wrong, and Pippa wasn't sure how to handle the situation.

Rain started to fall on the windscreen in large splats. It had been getting darker over the last few minutes, and it appeared that they were about to have a heavy summer storm. She put the windscreen wipers on full and slowed down the car. The rain was coming down so heavily that it wouldn't be long before the narrow lane started to fill with water.

Her emotions were as turbulent as the weather. Thoughts of Sarah collided with memories of her grief after Kim's passing. Living on Celfare was supposed to allow her to carry on with her life without fear of becoming entangled with someone again.

And then Sarah arrived.

They had come together gradually until they were suddenly thrown together. Pippa knew that she could have pushed her feelings aside if things had stayed as they were. The renovations would have ended, and the distance would have given Pippa the chance to step back and take stock of what was happening. Instead, they were thrown together with little time for Pippa to breathe, never mind understand what her confused heart was going to feel next.

She noticed a figure walking along the side of the road. The camber of the tarmac meant they were walking in several inches of water and the tented coat over their head was probably doing precious little to keep them dry.

Pippa slowed down as she approached. The figure turned around, and Pippa gasped at the sight of Sarah. She was completely soaked through, and the light make-up she wore streaked her face. She looked like she had been walking for a while, and there was a dull lifelessness in her eyes that sent a chill through Pippa.

She leaned over and opened the passenger door.

"Get in," she called when Sarah didn't even move.

The instruction seemed to shake Sarah out of whatever daze she was in, and she got into the car.

"I'm going to get the seat wet," Sarah said.

"I don't care. Are you okay? Why are you out here? Where's your mother?" Pippa looked up the road to see if she could see anyone else out in the storm.

"Having lunch, I imagine."

Pippa had no idea what had happened, but as much as she wanted answers, she could see that Sarah was in no state to give them. She simply shivered and stared blankly ahead.

Pippa turned the heat up to full and continued driving.

"I don't want to go home," Sarah said after a few moments.

"I'm taking you to mine," Pippa said.

Sarah fell back into silence. Pippa gripped the wheel and reminded herself to stay calm. Soon enough she'd be at home, and she could care for Sarah and get her into a place where she could explain everything. But for now, Sarah needed calm and security, and that was something Pippa was happy to provide.

❖

The rain had stopped by the time they arrived at Pippa's home. Sarah stood in the hallway, still dripping wet and shivering with cold. Pippa didn't have any change of clothes for Sarah, so a shower would probably leave them in more of a pickle than they were currently in.

She picked up several large bath towels from the linen cupboard and handed two of them to Sarah. The others she put into the tumble dryer to warm them up. When she returned to the hall, Sarah was holding the towels but still looked like she was miles away.

"Sarah?" She picked up one of the towels and wrapped it around Sarah's shoulders. "Talk to me. Please. You're worrying me."

Recognition flickered in Sarah's eyes. Whatever trance she'd been in seemed to slowly float away. She pulled the towel closer around her shoulders.

"I'm sorry."

"Don't be. What happened?"

Pippa guided her into the living room. She took the other towel from Sarah's hands and placed it on the sofa to soak up some of the water when she sat down.

"Mum happened," Sarah said. She looked at the sofa. "I don't want to ruin your furniture."

"I don't care about the furniture." Pippa gestured for Sarah to sit down. "What happened?"

Sarah sat down on the towel. She shivered a little and wrapped the other towel tighter around her.

"She was being so lovely. All this talk about the fresh air making her feel better. She was going to buy me lunch as an apology for being a complete cow yesterday. Then she starts telling me that working for Swype is undermining her."

Pippa sat next to her. "What did she mean by that?"

"Oh, we've been here a hundred times. Swype is the big bad monster. My mum is trying to tell people to save the planet. But, allegedly, when people find out that I work for Swype, they don't believe a word my mum says. After all, if she can't convince her own daughter to do the right thing…"

"That's nonsense."

A sob burst from Sarah. "Right? I mean, we go through this all the time, and she makes me feel like I'm losing my mind."

"You're not losing your mind."

"She came here because she wanted to try to get me to leave my job," Sarah said. "She didn't come here to see me. To meet you. Because she cares about me. None of that. She came here because she wants me to leave my job so I stop being an embarrassment for her."

"She cares about you," Pippa said.

"She doesn't!" Sarah snapped. "She doesn't. And I need to get that into my head. Because every time I think she does, she goes ahead and proves to me that she doesn't. Like, I'm incapable of realising that my mother never wanted to have children. Never had the gene that other mums have. Her career is all she has, and that trumps me every time. The sooner I understand that, the sooner I can stop giving her the power to hurt me."

Pippa swallowed. She didn't want to agree with Sarah, desperately didn't want to paint the relationship as broken beyond repair. But she had to wonder if maybe it was. If Angela really had come all this way simply to try to convince Sarah to leave her career, then Pippa could understand Sarah's broken heart.

If it was true, then it was deeply manipulative. Sadly, Pippa thought it was also entirely possible, having now met Angela.

The tumble dryer beeped to indicate it had finished its short cycle. Pippa jumped up and went to get the towels. When she returned, she took the wet towel from around Sarah's shoulders and replaced it with two heavy, warm towels.

"Thank you," Sarah murmured.

Pippa sat next to her and put a hand on her back. "I wish there was more I could do."

"There isn't," Sarah said.

Pippa hesitated a moment before asking, "Do you think maybe you *could* leave your job? Is it worth all this grief?"

Sarah chuckled. "It's a slippery slope. What next? Move house? Cycle to work? Eat certain food? Donate half my salary to Project Earth? I've been here before."

"When?"

"When I was a teenager. And for a brief period in my twenties when she got her claws into me again." Sarah pulled one of the towels off her shoulders and dried her face. "There was a time where I desperately wanted my mum to notice me. I did everything I thought she'd want me to do. Became a vegan, worked for a charity, went to watch her speeches. I marched in protests and even helped with some of the disruption. I lay down in front of an oil tanker once."

Pippa blinked. "Sounds dangerous."

"It was. The idea was that we'd all come running out of the woods and throw ourselves to the ground in front of the tanker. I think some people wanted to be injured, even die. Then the story would be bigger. The message was always that the story is king. If you got injured or killed, then you died getting your message out there. And I was totally on board with that for a while."

Pippa felt a shiver of fear chase up her spine at the thought of Sarah being so reckless with her life. "What changed?"

Sarah folded the towel into a ball and hugged it to her chest. She turned to Pippa. "I realised that she didn't care. I'd done what she wanted me to do, and that meant I was a completed project. A tick in the box. She moved on to the next person she wanted to convince. I'm aware that I sound like a needy child, but I suppose I was. I wanted her to be proud of me."

"It sounds like you wanted your mother to acknowledge you—that's perfectly normal," Pippa said.

Sarah shrugged. "I started to pull away from her. I guess I was feeding off the negative attention at that point. I was completely alone. I didn't have any friends—they were all too scared of my mum. No family to speak of. Just the two of us. I was starved for attention, and at first I thought doing what she wanted me to do would get her to see me. Then I realised that doing the opposite was the answer."

Pippa couldn't think of an easy solution to the bruised relationship. It seemed as if they had both been through so much, and their different personalities and goals were at odds every step of the way. Still, she wished Sarah could experience a parental relationship like the one Pippa had enjoyed growing up and into adulthood. It grieved her to think that wasn't possible.

"I think I just need to accept that she doesn't love me in the way I'd like her to," Sarah said softly. "I'm not enough for her."

Pippa placed her fingers under Sarah's chin and forced her to meet her eyes.

"You're enough. Don't ever think that you're not. Your mother is a tricky woman—that much is very obvious. But don't think it's your fault. If she can't see how incredible you are, then that's her fault, not yours." Pippa sighed. "I'm sorry that she came all this way to attempt to manipulate you. You don't deserve that."

Unshed tears shimmered in Sarah's eyes. The air between them was charged. Pippa knew she should lower her hand to break the connection between them, but she couldn't. Sarah started to drift forward, and Pippa realised she was about to be kissed. She prepared herself to enjoy and return the kiss that was incoming, despite a small part of her screaming to not become emotionally invested. The voice had become smaller and smaller over the weeks with Sarah, diminishing to not much more than a whisper of late.

Sarah jolted back. Her eyes widened as if she had suddenly woken up from a daze. The almost-kiss hung in the air between them. Pippa had no idea what to say or do. Her heart was overwhelmed with emotions, some new and some that she had been pushing down for years.

Sarah stood up. "I should get back home. Thank you. For the ride. And the towels."

"I'll drive you." Pippa stood as well.

"It's fine, I can walk." Sarah picked up the towels and folded them neatly.

"But the rain." Pippa turned to the window and was almost disappointed to see shafts of sunlight hitting the puddles in the garden.

"It's fine, really." Sarah handed the towels to Pippa. "It will be good to walk and clear my head before I see her again."

Pippa stood uselessly with an armful of towels and no idea what to do or say next.

Sarah quickly pressed a kiss to her cheek. "Thank you again. I'm sorry about all of this, I really am."

Before Pippa had a chance to respond, Sarah had left, and the front door was clicking closed behind her. She stood aimlessly still for several moments. Her brain and her heart were at war.

It was becoming painfully clear to her now that she'd fallen in love with Sarah. She wasn't sure when it had happened, but there was no more hiding it. Seeing Sarah in distress tore at her soul. Wanting Sarah to be happy had become her number-one priority. Feeling Sarah's lips on hers sparked a desire like no other.

"Damn, damn, damn," she muttered under her breath.

She'd promised herself that she would never feel like this again. Some might call it irrational, some might call her a coward. Pippa knew she was being practical. A part of her died the day Kim had passed. And that part of her had never returned. If she was to protect herself, then she had to make sure that could never happen again.

She'd loved and paid the price. She couldn't love again.

CHAPTER SEVENTEEN

Sarah lifted the doormat and picked up the spare key. She let herself into the house and called out for her mother a couple of times. Relief washed over her when she was greeted by silence. Somehow she'd made it home first, despite her long walk in the rain and spending time with Pippa.

She quickly pushed aside thoughts of Pippa. She'd nearly kissed her, and that wasn't okay. Pippa was simply being kind and had helped her so much, but that didn't mean anything more than friendship. Pippa had been clear about that, and Sarah needed to respect the boundaries. Even if boundaries were very confusing at the moment, not least because of the way Pippa sometimes looked at her. Sarah was sure something was there, but then why did Pippa push her away? It didn't matter. Now wasn't the time to explore anything of that nature. She had to focus on the problems immediately on hand and not create new ones.

Realising she had a few precious moments alone, she headed to the kitchen and out the back door. She looked around to check that she wasn't being watched and entered the shed at the bottom of the garden.

"Hey, Billy," she said to the random blinking lights of servers and monitors. "How are you doing?"

She opened the laptop lid and looked over some of the data. A smile curled at her lip at the confirmation that her project was not only working but positively thriving. Years of research had gone into the work, but there was nothing like building and testing the real thing. Many previous tests had sent Sarah and her team straight back to the drawing board, but Billy was working well so far. There was a way to go, but Sarah couldn't help but feel positive.

"I wish I could explain you to her," Sarah said.

She turned around and looked at the lights which blinked rhythmically, indicating uploading and downloading data being sent through millions of processes to ultimately reach a small island off the Scottish coast.

Her mother would never understand what an achievement Billy was. All she would see was a metal tube being dropped into the ocean and the damage that might cause. The fact that tens of thousands of data centres currently on land could soon follow Billy on a deep dive adventure and substantially reduce the amount of pollution heating up the planet wouldn't register on mother's radar at all.

Her mother dealt in absolutes. You were either helping to save the planet, or you were aiding in its destruction. Making something better than it was wasn't a solution. Making data centres less damaging to the environment would mean little. It was simply taking something bad and making it slightly less bad.

Nothing Sarah could do would make her mother proud of her. It was a simple fact that she was struggling to cope with.

She spent half an hour burying herself in work, enjoying the quiet peace that the shed afforded her. No one knew she was in there, and she was able to relax for the first time in a couple of days. As much as she relished every moment, she knew it couldn't last. Eventually she would have to come out and face the music.

After taking a few deep breaths, she discreetly left the shed and walked around the garden to approach the cottage from the front. A few more deep breaths and she opened the front door. This time she didn't need to call out to see if she was alone. Her mother sat in the living room with a book in hand and making no move at all to acknowledge Sarah's arrival.

"Hi, Mum," Sarah said.

"Mmm."

It wasn't a greeting, but it wasn't complete silence, and so Sarah would take it. She went into the kitchen and put the kettle on.

"Tea?" she asked.

"Please, dear."

It was painfully polite and stilted, but they'd danced this dance a thousand times before. It was either cold silence or frosty civility. Thankfully they had both chosen the latter on this day.

Sarah made two cups of tea and delivered one to her mother, who barely registered her.

"I'm going to go up to the office and get some work done," Sarah said. "Call me if you need me."

Her mother hummed her understanding but didn't look up.

Sarah rolled her eyes. Maybe they hadn't quite reached civility yet.

She took her cup of tea and went upstairs. She closed her office door and put some headphones on, taking herself back to her teenage years. It would be impossible to count how many times Sarah had sat in her room with music blaring through headphones in an attempt to ignore her mother and whatever argument they'd recently had.

So far the visit had been painfully familiar. Nerves had jangled beforehand, anger had spiked during her mother's pointed criticism, and now they were no longer talking. It was a pattern that Sarah should have predicted, but even so, it put her on the back foot. It was because she always hoped for the best, and deep down she hoped her mother would miraculously become the mother that Sarah secretly wished she would be.

It never happened. Of course it wouldn't. Sarah ended up devastated by her mother's harsh words and critical examination of the failures of her life. And time and time again, she never learned her lesson. So the next time the same thing happened, she was not only upset at her mother but angry with herself.

"Stop it," she murmured under her breath.

She knew from bitter experience that if she didn't get herself together soon, then she'd start crying. Thankfully, her email inbox was full to bursting, and there was plenty to occupy her. Burying herself in work had become a lifesaver and probably accounted for her dismal social life. But at least she was happy and proud of the work she did.

She didn't know how much time had passed when she heard the sound of distant conversation in the quiet gap between two songs. She paused the music and looked at the clock. She was surprised that nearly two hours had gone by.

She removed the headphones and cocked her head to the side to decide if she'd actually heard something or if it was simply the television, a phone call, or her mind playing tricks on her.

She heard voices and closed her eyes to focus. They was coming from outside, so she walked over to the window and looked down to see Pippa and her mother having a conversation in the garden. They were sitting at the patio table, each with a cup of tea in her hands. Panic surged through Sarah. The window was open slightly, so she stood as close as she could while ensuring that she couldn't be seen.

"I just suggested that she might like to think of other career opportunities," her mother said.

"Sarah loves her job," Pippa replied. "She's very passionate about it. Surely, you want to see her happy?"

"Of course I do!"

"Well, this makes her happy," Pippa said calmly. "She's good at what she does. Most of it goes over my head, but I know she's well-respected. She receives so many calls a day where she has to guide people through things."

Sarah smiled to herself. She didn't know that Pippa was that aware of her work. She felt pride that Pippa thought she was good at her job.

"That may be—"

"I would have thought you'd be proud of her," Pippa said.

"Well, of course I am. Very proud. She has an excellent mind and a good work ethic."

Sarah felt her lip wobble with emotion. She would have given anything for her mother to say that without prompting and to her face. But she'd accept it this way.

"You should tell her," Pippa said. "You're both remarkable women, but you have very different passions. You're different people. I know you argued today, and I'd hate for your visit to end on a sour note. I'm not suggesting you apologise—I'm just suggesting that you let Sarah know that you're proud of her. Because she doesn't know."

"That's ridiculous. She knows."

"She doesn't know," Pippa repeated.

"I think I know my daughter better than you."

Sarah bit her lip in frustration.

"I don't believe you do," Pippa said. "And I only say that because I'm trying to fix that."

Sarah heard the scraping of a chair. She risked a quick glance and noticed that Pippa had left the table. She hurried back to her office chair as she heard someone entering the house and climbing the stairs. She quickly put her headphones back on and waited, her heart pounding.

A few moments later there was a quiet knock on the door.

"Come in," Sarah called, hoping she sounded calm.

The door opened, and Pippa stepped in.

Sarah took her headphones off. "Hi."

"Hi. How are you doing?" Pippa entered the room and closed the door behind her.

Sarah shrugged. "I'm okay. Giving her some space."

"I talked to her."

Sarah's first thought was to act as if she didn't know that. But enough lies had been told. She had no reason to mislead Pippa. In fact, she wanted Pippa to know that she appreciated her efforts. Hiding in her room listening to music had sent her back to her teenage self and she didn't like it.

"I heard," Sarah confessed. "Thank you for trying."

Pippa smiled softly. "I don't know what good it will do. She's a hard woman to influence."

"She is. It made me feel better, though, so thank you."

"You know what else would make you feel better?"

Sarah had a couple of thoughts but pushed them aside and shook her head.

"Getting out of those clothes that you took an unplanned

shower in, having a real shower or a relaxing bath, and then eating a delicious home-cooked meal."

Sarah felt her cheeks heat up. She'd been meaning to get changed out of these clothes. She'd dried out quickly enough from the walk home in the sun. Not that that was much of an excuse. She'd been so frustrated by her mother's snotty behaviour that she hadn't wanted to leave her room. The apple hadn't fallen far from the tree in that regard.

"Sorry, I lost track of time."

"No need to apologise," Pippa said. She folded her arms and looked at Sarah.

It took her a few minutes to realise that Pippa was waiting.

"Oh, I…um, I was going to…" She gestured to her laptop.

"Hide in here for as long as possible, I know." Pippa walked over to the desk. She placed her fingers on the lid of the laptop. "Everything saved?"

Sarah nodded, and Pippa closed the laptop.

"Would you like me to run you a bath?" Pippa offered.

Sarah wished she would stop being so kind, so perfect. It was making it all the harder to remember the distance she needed to keep. This was surely more than being a friend? This was drifting into something else. Maybe Sarah's instincts were right, and Pippa was feeling the same way she did. But Sarah didn't know for sure, and that conversation wouldn't be an easy one.

"No, I'll jump in the shower," Sarah said. "Sorry for being gross."

Pippa chuckled. "Not gross at all." She sniffed the air playfully. "Maybe a little ripe."

Sarah rolled her eyes and refused to rise to the bait.

"Dinner in one hour," Pippa said, turning to leave the room. "I'm going to have every item approved by you-know-who before it goes into the oven."

"Sneaky, I like it. And thank you for making dinner, I really appreciate it. What would I do without you?"

"Commit a murder?" Pippa deadpanned. "Oh, and we agreed on a movie night."

"Oh, that…sounds quite nice, actually." Sarah had been mentally preparing herself for more silent treatment. At least now a movie would smother the tense environment.

"It will be," Pippa promised. "We agreed on a movie, a comedy. It will be a nice and relaxing evening."

Sarah swallowed down her emotions. Pippa was going out of her way to make things better, and Sarah didn't know what she'd done to deserve such kindness. Before she had the chance to formulate an anywhere near appropriate thank you, Pippa left the room.

❖

Pippa sighed contentedly. The atmosphere wasn't friendly, but the coolness between Sarah and her mother had warmed considerably. Angela was curled up in the armchair with a blanket around her, occasionally sniggering at the movie. Pippa had suggested that she pick something to watch, and that had definitely been the right choice.

Sarah sat next to Pippa, a blanket over her lap with a bag of popcorn atop it. Now and then, Sarah would lean into Pippa, and Pippa would put her arm over her shoulder, and they would sit like that for a while until Sarah shifted again.

It was all an act, Pippa had to remind herself.

Angela was able to see them clearly, and Sarah was simply keeping up appearances. The fact that Pippa enjoyed the warmth of her company was completely irrelevant. She needed to talk to Sarah that evening. Needed to explain why nothing could happen, even if it was clear to everyone that she had feelings for Sarah. Feelings that she was working hard to bury.

It wouldn't be easy, especially when the movie ended and they had to share a bed once again. Pippa felt exhausted. She hoped she wouldn't accidentally move closer to Sarah in the night. That was one of the things that had kept her awake the night before. Now she was far more tired, emotionally and physically.

Angela was a hard women to like. Not that Pippa was trying that hard. But out of respect for Sarah, she had been as polite as she could muster. Pippa watched Angela as she watched the movie. She couldn't fathom how someone could be so ignorant of their own flesh and blood. Sarah seemed to think that Angela just wasn't built to have children, and Pippa was slowly beginning to think that might be true.

Pippa had made the decision to try to push Angela along to get her to see how her behaviour was affecting Sarah. She didn't know how successful she had been, but the smile Sarah had rewarded her with for even trying made her feel as if she had won a prize.

When the movie ended, Pippa offered to clean up. Sarah and Angela went upstairs to get ready for bed as they had done the night before. Rather than use the dishwasher for the second time that evening, Pippa washed the few dishes and cups by hand.

As she washed up, she looked out of the kitchen window into the darkness. It felt so familiar and domestic. She'd cooked a family meal in the kitchen just hours before. Conversation had been stilted and the atmosphere chilly, but it had reminded Pippa of what family could be. She'd been alone for a very long time, deliberately so. Being thrown into a family dinner had been a lot easier than she'd expected.

It reminded her of Kim for so many reasons. That first day when their eyes had met and Pippa had fallen immediately for her was etched in her memory, which was now stronger than ever. She hadn't realised then that it was love, but it had become clear in the following days and weeks. She'd never thought it possible that she could just fall in love at first sight. Anyone who had ever told her such a thing could happen had been treated to a low chuckle and a shake of her head. Until it had happened to her.

It had never happened since, and Pippa was resolved that it could never happen. Her guard was up. She'd never experience love at first sight again because she was wary of love and constantly making sure that it wasn't lurking around any corner.

It hadn't been love at first sight with Sarah, but that was because Pippa was working as hard as she could not to form attachments. But that didn't mean that Sarah hadn't managed to unwittingly work her way around those high walls, and now she resided in a special place in Pippa's heart.

Something that caused Pippa palpitations for multiple reasons.

She heard a sound behind her and turned to see Angela. She had a thick coat on and wore hiking boots and a woolly hat.

"Heading out?" Pippa asked.

"Yes. It's a clear night," Angela explained. "The light pollution in England is terrible, and it's a rare treat to be able to see the stars. I thought I'd go out and enjoy them while I have the opportunity."

Pippa looked through the window and up at the bright stars. She'd not given them much thought since moving to Celfare, but she had to agree that they were impressive.

"Wrap up warm," Pippa advised.

"I will," Angela said. "Goodnight."

Pippa finished the washing up, and a few minutes later she heard Angela quietly leaving through the front door. She finished clearing up and turned off some of the lights, leaving the hallway light on for Angela when she returned before heading upstairs to bed.

CHAPTER EIGHTEEN

Sarah paced the bedroom. The evening had gone better than she'd expected, but she was still very aware of her mother's eagle eye on them. Pippa might have thought they were doing a great job of fooling her, but Sarah knew better.

Angela Campbell was a scientist. She watched, she waited, and then she declared her findings. Her mother's subtle watching of them meant she suspected something was up and was busy gathering evidence.

If she wants evidence, I'll give her evidence, Sarah thought.

The door opened, and Pippa entered the bedroom. Sarah immediately held up her hand to silence Pippa. Pippa raised her eyebrow but smiled indulgently. Sarah gestured for Pippa to sit on the chair in front of the dressing table and again indicated for her to remain quiet.

Pippa did as she was asked and sat down. She wore the same pyjamas she had the previous evening, baggy cotton trousers and a long-sleeved top. Sarah had opted for something similar, following Pippa's reaction to her usual sleep shorts.

They sat in comfortable silence for a while, even if Pippa did look bemused at being ordered to silently sit at the dressing table. Sarah looked at her watch and decided enough time had passed. She approached the bed and gently swayed it so that the headboard tapped the wall. She counted a few seconds and then did it again.

Pippa let out a splutter of laughter upon understanding what she was doing.

"Shh!" Sarah threw over her shoulder before shoving the bed into the wall again.

"I'd never damage the paintwork like that," Pippa whispered.

Sarah turned and glared at her. Pippa simply laughed as quietly as she could manage. Sarah returned her focus to the bed and this time slammed it into the wall a little harder. Every few seconds she shoved the bed into the wall and tried to ignore the sound of stifled laughter from behind her.

"That's a very heteronormative rhythm you have going there," Pippa whispered.

"Shh!"

"Sarah—"

"Shh!"

"Fine," Pippa whispered. She picked up a book from the dressing table and started to read.

Sarah returned to hitting the bed against the wall. She knew it looked ridiculous, but surely her mother would think they were having sex, and that would go a long way to convincing her that their relationship was real.

The thought that her mother could discover their lie was nearly as soul destroying as the actual truth that Sarah couldn't hold on to a relationship. If this silly little act could prevent that embarrassing situation, then she'd gladly do whatever she had to do.

In between the thrusts of the bed, she let out a little moan. She turned to look at Pippa.

Pippa looked at her over the top of her book.

"You do it," Sarah whispered.

"Absolutely not," Pippa said.

Sarah moaned at the wall and then turned back to Pippa and gestured for her to follow suit.

"Did I mention your mother has gone for an evening stroll to admire the stars?" Pippa said at normal volume.

Sarah stopped dead. "You mean she's not here?"

Pippa lowered the book and shook her head. "Nope. Went out around ten minutes ago."

"And you let me?"

"Yes. You shushed me."

Sarah narrowed her eyes. "Well, you still could have told me."

Pippa grinned. "I suppose I could have."

"That's mean." Sarah put her hands on her hips.

Pippa nodded. "It was, but you did shush me, so I feel like we're even."

Sarah wanted to argue but knew that Pippa was right. The idea was ridiculous, and she *had* told Pippa to be quiet.

"Can we talk?" Pippa asked.

The mood turned serious. Sarah sat on the bed and pulled her legs up to sit cross-legged. She nodded for Pippa to continue.

"It can't have escaped your notice that this…ruse is developing into something more," Pippa said. "I'm not the best person you could have chosen for this acting role, we all know that. I'm not able to casually kiss you without looking affected. I can't pretend I'm not surprised to see you in shorts. I'm not immune to you, Sarah. I know we're starting to drift together, and I know that some of that is my fault. I don't want to give you mixed messages, but it's important that you know that…there can't be anything between us."

Sarah tried not to look crestfallen. Pippa was trying to be kind by not allowing her to think there was something there when there wasn't. But it was still a shock to suddenly be hearing it so clearly.

"Is this because I nearly ki—"

"No." Pippa shook her head. "Not that in isolation. It's because of…everything. We're in an awkward situation. And I want to continue helping you with this act, and I will—I just want to make sure that things are clear between us. I don't want any hurt feelings. Any more than there needs to be."

"I understand." Sarah swallowed. It all felt so deeply uncomfortable. She wasn't used to having such open discussions about matters of the heart. Maybe it was a generational thing, but she was used to tiptoeing around the subject of feelings, not tackling them head-on in such a direct, uncomfortable way. Maybe it was a Pippa thing.

"I'm sorry if I hurt you," Pippa said, picking up on Sarah's obvious discomfort.

"It's okay. You have a right to your feelings. I'm glad you've been upfront with me. It saves any confusion." Sarah stood up and went to her bedside drawer under the guise of getting bed socks that she didn't particularly need. "I'm sorry if I made it difficult for you."

"You didn't," Pippa said.

"I did," Sarah insisted. "You're just…You're kinda my type. But I get that I'm not yours, and that's fine. I get it. No harm done."

She triumphantly pulled out a pair of bed socks and hoped that would be the end of the conversation. Putting your heart out there was difficult at the best of times, but now it felt completely destroying. All she wanted to do was turn the lights off and be left to stew in her own embarrassment.

"That's not it at all."

Pippa's voice was so soft that Sarah wondered if she'd heard correctly. She turned to look at her and just waited for Pippa to say more. With a sigh, Pippa stood up and wrapped her arms around her middle. She walked over to the window and looked like she was trying to find words.

"In another time…" Pippa trailed off.

Sarah worried her lip between her teeth. She didn't know what to say or do. The emotional turmoil was coming from Pippa in waves. She longed to comfort her but knew she had to keep her distance. And she really didn't want to do anything to distract Pippa from whatever she was about to say.

"Losing Kim…" Pippa paused again.

Sarah wondered if Pippa could hear her heart slamming in her chest. She started to feel light-headed at the tense atmosphere.

"I loved," Pippa said. "I loved fully. I didn't even consider there was another option. And when I lost Kim, I broke apart. I'm not trying to undermine the grief that anyone else has ever felt, but for me it was the most painful thing I have ever endured. There were times when I thought I could die of a broken heart. I promised myself to never allow myself to feel that way again. Maybe there is something broken in the way I love. Like an alcoholic who can't enjoy a single drink without it turning into a problem. I fear that I can't love without being destroyed if that love was to ever end." She turned to face Sarah. "Does that make any sense?"

"Sort of," Sarah said. She didn't agree with Pippa, but she could understand how someone might feel that way.

"I'm not blind to your beauty or how well we fit together. And most importantly how this might have been different in other circumstances. But I can't, Sarah. And I know I must be confusing you because of the mixed signals I'm giving you. But I wanted to be clear. I value your friendship."

"So you're going to be alone...forever?" Sarah asked. "That's your plan?"

Sarah had intended to say nothing further to save her own embarrassment. The sooner the conversation was over, the better. But she couldn't believe that such a sensible and intelligent woman had decided to never be with anyone ever again. She didn't doubt that Pippa's loss was painful, but to swear off love ever again was surely taking protecting your heart too far.

Pippa's expression hardened. "Yes."

"Okay." Sarah shrugged.

"No, don't brush it off like that. What were you going to say?" Pippa stepped forward.

"No. You know what you want to do. It's up to you. I appreciate the honesty, really. I'm glad we know where we stand. And I value your friendship, too. Even if you did let me simulate a sexual encounter when there's no one to hear it." Sarah sat on the edge of the bed and put on her bed socks. She climbed into bed and looked at Pippa. "I'm tired—can we talk about this in the morning? If there's anything more to talk about?"

Pippa looked like she wanted to say more, but thankfully she shook her head. Sarah burrowed into the duvet, turned to her side, and closed her eyes. The sooner the day ended, the better as far as she was concerned. A few seconds later she felt Pippa climb into bed. After a few moments of adjusting the duvet, the light went out.

Sarah tried to push all the thoughts and feelings out of her head, but her mind raced. Thoughts of Pippa and Kim deliriously happy and in love clashed with the thought of Pippa being broken in two by her loss. Sarah couldn't begin to imagine what either felt like. She felt young and inexperienced in a way she had never done before.

What she mainly felt was heartbroken. Pippa was ending things before they started for her own benefit with no understanding that Sarah couldn't just switch off her feelings like that. With no acknowledgement that Sarah might have any feelings at all.

Pippa wanted to protect herself from a broken heart, but all she had managed to do was break Sarah's instead.

CHAPTER NINETEEN

Pippa woke up to an empty bed. She rubbed tiredly at her face and sighed. She realised that she'd inadvertently hurt Sarah the previous evening but knew that she'd had to say the things she'd said. She stretched and got out of bed, hardly eager to start the day, but she couldn't lounge in bed forever.

As she walked past the window, she saw the subject of her thoughts walking down the garden path. Pippa frowned. There was something suspicious about Sarah's manner. From the hurried steps to the looking over her shoulder, she clearly didn't want to be seen. She disappeared around the corner to where Pippa knew the garden shed stood.

She'd never been in the garden shed. Or anywhere near it. Sarah had been keen to point out that it was empty and she wanted to keep it that way. Pippa had thought it a little odd at the time but hadn't thought on it since. Now her curiosity was piqued.

She got dressed and used the bathroom before heading downstairs to greet Angela, whom she had heard moving about in the kitchen. She wondered how much longer Angela would be staying. She suspected that Sarah would very much prefer her unexpected guests to be out of her house and to take all the emotional drama with them.

She entered the kitchen and nodded to Angela, who was sitting at the dining table and reading a newspaper. Pippa noticed it was Angela's article from the previous week and only just managed to stop herself from rolling her eyes.

"Good morning, how was the stargazing?"

"Beautiful. If only more people cared enough about it, then they'd change their ways to be able to experience it for themselves. We're a selfish species."

"We certainly are," Pippa agreed. She suspected that Angela was probably one of the more selfish of the species but remained silent on that subject. "Where's Sarah?"

"She headed to the shop to get some more milk. I thought we had enough, but she seemed to want to get out of the house." Angela picked up a mug of coffee, her newspaper, and the *Celfare Times*. "I'm going to sit in the living room and read the local paper. It's nice to see a local paper again. We've lost the sense of community in most of Britain."

Pippa itched to point out that the local paper was full of advertisements, and no one read the few articles that it contained. It was a waste of ink and paper, something Angela should have been aware of. It seemed that Angela's activism ended when it was something she enjoyed personally, the same as so many other people.

"Enjoy," Pippa said.

She grabbed a mug and made herself a cup of coffee. She looked out of the window and wondered where Sarah had really gone. It was entirely possible that she'd had another disagreement with her mother and had gone for a walk in order to cool off. But the bottom of the garden led to nowhere other than a rocky clifftop, which the council had long ago fenced off, and the empty garden shed.

Pippa worried about Sarah hopping over the fence and getting too close to the cliffs. They'd started crumbling decades ago and were known to be unsafe. Fear pricked at her. She couldn't fight the urge to go out to investigate.

She left the mug and headed out the back door as quietly as she could. She hurried down the path, past the overgrown bushes that Sarah claimed she enjoyed the look of. Pippa had wanted to take the trimmer to them and tidy them up, but Sarah had asked her to leave them overgrown.

Pieces of a puzzle were coming together, but Pippa wasn't sure what they were forming.

She looked around at the bottom of the garden and couldn't see Sarah anywhere. A familiar sense of fear started to nip at her. Surely Sarah hadn't stepped over the fence. Maybe she had turned back, and Pippa hadn't seen her. Pippa turned and bit her lip. If she'd passed Sarah, then surely she would have noticed. Something was wrong, but she couldn't put her finger on what.

She approached the shed. Now that she thought about it, it seemed odd that the shed was brand new and in excellent condition. As she got closer, she realised that she could hear the low hum of electricity coming from the small wooden structure.

"What on earth?" She pulled on the door handle but it didn't open.

Pippa frowned and looked at the shed. The area surrounding it looked newly paved. She circled the building, hoping for a window, but found none.

As she completed a full circle, the door opened, and Sarah stepped out. She saw Pippa and cried out in shock, bringing a hand to her chest and jumping back.

Pippa held up her hands. "It's just me."

"What are you doing here?" Sarah demanded. "Is Mum here?"

"No, she's in the…" Pippa looked around Sarah and into the shed. Her jaw dropped open at the sight of rows and rows of computer equipment. "What is that?"

Sarah quickly grabbed Pippa's arm and dragged her into the shed, closing and locking the door behind them.

Pippa walked around the tiny space in amazement. There was a desk with a laptop, and above them a fluorescent tube light illuminated pieces of equipment that she couldn't even begin to identify. Tiny lights flickered randomly in greens, reds, and yellows. She had no idea what any of them meant.

Words escaped her, and she simply looked at Sarah in confusion.

"You can't tell *anyone*," Sarah said.

"I wouldn't know what to tell them. What is all this?"

"You *especially* cannot tell my mum," Sarah continued. "But, really, no one can know."

"Know what?" Pippa looked up at the ceiling light. "Where is that getting power from? Where is any of this getting power from? There's no switch on the board in the house."

"It's got its own power source," Sarah explained.

"You don't work in remote technologies, do you?" Pippa asked. For a brief second, she wondered if Sarah was some kind of government spy. She only hoped that they were on the same side.

"Sort of," Sarah said. "This is Billy. Well, no, Billy is in the ocean. This is Billy's infrastructure."

"Billy?"

"Project B.1004.51, but easier to refer to as *Billy*. What do you know about data centres?"

Pippa shrugged. "Not a thing. What are they?"

Sarah's face expressed the slight frustration of someone who knew they had to explain something that was incredibly obvious to someone who wouldn't have a clue. It was the look of every child when explaining to their parents how to operate a new piece of technology. Pippa felt all of her forty-eight years in that moment.

"Every personal computer, business, shop, supermarket, hospital, bank...you name it, uses data centres. They are usually buildings, sometimes metal containers, but they contain routers and servers, switches, application delivery contro—"

Pippa held up her hands. "In English."

"They contain a lot of technical shit," Sarah summarised. "And all that equipment gets really hot, and if it gets hot, then it breaks. A lot of data centres have been moved to really cold climates, which helps a little, but they still use a lot of energy to keep them running and at the correct temperature. There's also the problem that humans need oxygen, and oxygen damages equipment. Equipment prefers dry nitrogen."

Pippa could tell Sarah was about to head into another scientific conversation that was way over her head. "So, this is a data centre? In a shed?"

Sarah laughed hard. "No, no. This is the monitoring station."

"I'm confused," Pippa admitted.

"The data centre, Billy, is in the ocean," Sarah said. "Swype sank a data centre just off the coast, and there's a cable from here to Billy. I'm here to monitor the system."

"And it's under the water…to keep the temperature down?"

"Partially, yes. Billy is a sealed unit. There's no one performing maintenance next door, the temperature remains the same, and he isn't going to be affected too much by a power outage. But data centres are full of servers. In a normal centre those servers fail a lot and need to be replaced. That's why the rooms need to have oxygen because we send people in to replace them. But when we replace them, we potentially damage other servers. It's really inefficient. Our tests show that we could reduce server failure by eighty-five percent. That means it's more stable, there are less outages, and we need to replace less servers, which means we need to build fewer." Sarah gestured to the room. "This is the future."

"Because you build fewer servers?"

"Partly. Building parts takes a lot of materials and energy. If we don't need to build as many, we're saving those resources. But the real opportunity is it being in the ocean. The cold temperature means the data centre never gets hot. We don't have to use a ton of fossil fuel to keep it cool if it never gets hot."

"And you're here to test it works?"

"Exactly. If it does, we will be able to roll it out across our network. We've even got a plan in place to share our experiment's data with other companies, so they can do the same. If we can convince people to sink their data centres, we'll save tonnes of cardon dioxide being pumped into the environment to keep data centres at an optimum temperature."

Pippa looked around at the equipment in awe. Sarah's impassioned explanation of what Billy was and what it could mean had given her goosebumps. She wondered if the unassuming shed would one day be considered a technological-historical hotspot, like Steve Jobs's garage in California.

"Why don't you want to tell your mother?" Pippa asked. "Surely she'll be ecstatic."

Sarah shook her head. "No. She wouldn't understand. She'd hear that we're putting things into the ocean and would start talking about the marine life we're disturbing and how we're raising sea temperatures."

"Does it raise the temperature of the sea?" Pippa asked.

"It is being debated," Sarah confessed. "It's hard to say precisely, but if it does, then it's miniscule in comparison to how much humans are turning up the heat in the oceans anyway. The closest we can estimate is that it is the same as the underwater power cables that are already there, so really negligible. But the fish like the data centres. Anything put in the ocean gets covered in bacteria, which means organisms grow. Food and shelter for the fish."

"Can't you explain that to her?"

Sarah chuckled and sat on the office chair. "Do you think I can explain anything to her?"

Pippa considered the question for a few seconds before she shook her head. "Probably not, no."

"She can't find out," Sarah said. "She doesn't understand the technology, and she'll just cause mayhem."

Pippa nodded. She looked at a blinking red light. "What's this mean?"

"Data uploading," Sarah said. "Could be a heart patient sending telemetry data to their doctor, could be a bank wiring money to a new business, could be an email being sent around the world. All sorts come through here."

"And you manage it all?"

"I monitor Billy to ensure he is working how we hope he will. If things fail, I switch to redundancies. I report in every day to say what the situation is."

Pippa shook her head in amazement. "And Billy is just…out there in the water?"

"About a mile away from land," Sarah said. "This location was chosen because of the proximity to the Atlantic Ocean. The undercurrents aren't too choppy here, but the floor of the ocean is deep and the right temperature. And we're close enough to be able to have a tethered line. In the future, we won't need to be tethered to the centres. We'll probably have something like an oil rig out to sea. We've not ironed out all those details yet. This is the first big step."

Realisation hit Pippa like a falling rock. "This is why you were so panicked about your mother visiting. Besides the obvious. You didn't want her to find out about this."

Sarah nodded. "Yes, that's a big part of it. I believe in this project, but no matter how I might try to explain it to her, she wouldn't get it. She'd try to destroy it."

Pippa caught up to the fact that Sarah was hiding a very big secret just metres away from her mother. No wonder she'd been so stressed. Things were starting to slot into place. She couldn't help but feel a little upset that she'd been lied to. On the other hand, she'd been involved in building projects that had required signing non-disclosure agreements and even the Official Secrets Act. Work was work.

"Please don't say anything," Sarah said at the continued silence.

"I won't."

"I know you think that Mum and me can see eye to eye on some things and have a better relationship, but this really isn't it," Sarah added. Desperation was mounting in her tone.

"I won't say anything," Pippa promised. She smiled. "You're quite incredible—do you know that?"

Sarah's cheeks reddened. "I'm not."

"You are. You did all this. Planned it, built it, monitored it. Kept it secret. I wouldn't know where to start. I don't know what most of this is, but I know it's an accomplishment."

"Kept it secret until *now*."

"Well, yes, but you managed to keep it from me, and I've been working here for weeks."

Sarah shrugged. Pippa realised that she didn't want to talk about it anymore. It was too soon after their emotionally charged conversation the previous evening to be attempting to slip back into their old relationship. She didn't know if they would ever be able to be the way they were before. She hated that she'd misread the situation so badly and put their friendship in jeopardy. Thankfully, Celfare was a small island, and she'd hopefully have time to fix things.

"We should get back," Sarah said.

"You're supposed to be getting milk," Pippa pointed out.

"Yep. She doesn't know how far the shop is, so it seemed like a good fib to tell." Sarah unlocked the shed door and peeked outside. A moment later she gestured for Pippa to follow her back into the garden.

"I so wish you and your mother had a better relationship," Pippa said. "She should be proud of what you're doing. You have the same objective at heart."

"Similar," Sarah corrected. "She'd like to see the data centres gone entirely. There's no halfway with my mother, you know that. Still, just another four months and the experiment will be over."

"Over?"

"Yes, this is a timed experiment. Six months and then we take all the data and look at what we've found. We're two months in. By November I'll be done, and then I can go home."

Pippa's thought process faltered for a moment. "Home?"

"Yes. London. Big noisy city with new builds no one should buy and anything delivered any time you want it. Home." Sarah got a padlock out of her pocket and started to fasten it to the door.

"You're going back to London?" Pippa asked. She noticed her voice rising a little.

"Yes, of course I am."

"But you're building a home here." Pippa gestured to the cottage behind them.

"No, I'm renovating a cottage here. If someone else from Swype comes to stay, then they won't have to put up with the mess I had to put up with. Or if Swype sells it, it will be worth more, I guess."

Pippa felt cold at the thought of Sarah leaving. And angry at the realisation that Sarah had always known that she would be leaving and hadn't mentioned it.

"Why did you never say anything?" Pippa asked.

"I couldn't say that I was here temporarily—you'd ask why." Sarah fiddled with the padlock, struggling to get it to close.

"But…I thought you were living here." Pippa knew she sounded desperate, but she couldn't help it. The realisation that Sarah would soon be leaving Celfare had come as a shock. She wasn't ready for things to change again. "You're just going to leave?"

Sarah spun around. "Yes. And it's probably for the best, wouldn't you say?"

Pippa blinked at the cold tone. "I thought we'd remain friends," she admitted.

Sarah laughed bitterly. "Do you really think we can do that? Come on, Pippa. It will be best for both of us for me to go back home."

Pippa hated hearing Sarah say *home* as if it wasn't where they stood. She'd assumed that they'd built a home from the shell of Hillcrest Cottage, and Pippa was only now discovering that Sarah had other ideas.

"Look, I appreciate what you told me last night," Sarah said. "And I thank you for wanting to be clear and not string me along. But I like you, Pippa. I'm not immune to you, either. I can't just snap my fingers and decide to turn it off like you can. I can't just make the decision that I'm not going to feel that way. My heart doesn't work like that. I wish I could just decide that I don't want to get hurt and make it so. But life isn't like that. Not for me."

Sarah brushed past her and hurried up the path towards the house.

"Sarah," Pippa called and jogged after her. She'd known that Sarah had started to feel something for her, but she'd hoped that she'd managed to nip it in the bud with the chat they'd had. Another miscalculation that had her wanting to kick herself.

"No," Sarah said. "We're not going to talk about this. I don't want to. You're not the only one who gets to decide the parameters of our relationship. How close we're allowed to get and when. Who gets hurt and who doesn't. I don't want to talk about this now. I'm barely holding it together as it is." Sarah paused at the corner of the cottage. "I'm going to get milk. Please don't follow me. I'll be back later."

Pippa stopped chasing after her and let her leave. She had no idea that she'd made such a mess of things. She'd been trying to protect Sarah's feelings, but it seemed she had acted far too late. And now she'd upset Sarah again, following the surprise that Sarah wouldn't remain on Celfare for much longer. That realisation had caused a flutter of panic and an emptiness she hadn't expected.

Sarah might feel that Pippa had the ability to turn off her emotions, but nothing could be further from the truth.

CHAPTER TWENTY

Sarah walked along the lane clutching a glass bottle of milk. It was one of the many things that had been a weird novelty when she first came to Celfare. Glass milk bottles were something she'd heard about but never seen. But as with many of the quirks of island life, she'd soon become comfortable with the change. She was starting to appreciate the peculiarities that made Celfare, and she wondered how she'd adjust to being back home.

Home.

She'd never told Pippa that she would soon be heading back to London. But that wasn't because of a desire to protect her secret project. It was because she hadn't quite accepted the idea herself yet.

She was adept at weaving lies, and she was pretty sure she could have come up with something that would have satisfied Pippa's endless curiosity. But she hadn't. She'd deliberately allowed Pippa to think that she was staying.

It was a decision she had made early on, back when Pippa was a slightly condescending handywoman who stirred feelings in Sarah that she had to try to ignore. She'd done it because she wanted to connect with Pippa on some level. People who knew they'd not be in each other's spheres for long didn't make an effort to be friends. And Sarah had wanted to be friends with Pippa. She'd realised that fact after only a few meetings.

Attraction had bubbled beneath the surface. It was hard to ignore when Pippa was so capable and forthright, features that sent

Sarah weak at the knees. She would have been satisfied keeping those feelings hidden. Look don't touch was fine in Sarah's mind. There was no point in messy entanglements that could very easily spill the beans of her secret project. Especially when she knew her time on Celfare was limited.

Her mother's visit had changed all that.

And now things were about to change again. She wished she hadn't admitted her feelings to Pippa, but it had seemed so damned unfair for her to suddenly act as if nothing had happened. It seemed that Pippa had woken up relieved that she'd packaged up everything with a neat little bow. She'd completely overlooked the fact that Sarah had to be allowed time to deal with her own feelings.

She entered the cottage. "I'm back!"

She put the bottle of milk in the fridge. They hadn't really needed more milk, but it had seemed like a good excuse at the time.

"Hello?" she called out again.

The post was on the dining table, and she flipped through the leaflets and flyers. Even Celfare wasn't immune from junk mail.

"Anyone home?"

The house was silent. She assumed that Pippa had gone out. She wished she'd said goodbye properly and had managed to find out her schedule for the day. Not knowing when or if she'd be back left a knot in her stomach. She trusted Pippa, but at the back of her mind gnawed a tiny voice that wondered if maybe Pippa might tell someone about Billy. Not that Sarah had any choice. Pippa had seen the inside of the shed. It wasn't as if Sarah could close the door and pretend that she hadn't seen anything.

Sarah stopped dead in her tracks.

The door.

Had she locked the shed door?

She remembered putting the padlock on, and it was stiff as usual. The sea air had quickly attacked the cheap lock she'd bought from the hardware store. But then she started talking to Pippa, and now she couldn't recall if she had actually gotten around to locking the door or not.

Worse than that, her mother wasn't in the house.

Sarah nearly took the back door off its hinges in her haste to leave the kitchen. She ran down the garden path and skidded around the corner. Time slowed down at the scene in front of her. Her worst fears had become reality. The shed door was open, and her mother was inside with her mobile phone raised as she filmed everything that she saw.

"Mum!"

Her mother ignored her. "You're seeing what I'm seeing?"

"We're getting all of it," the familiar voice of Martin said. "Great job, Angela."

"Mum! Stop!" Sarah surged forward and tried to grab the phone.

Her mother hung up the call and spun to face Sarah with fire in her eyes.

"I knew it was all lies," she said. "I knew something was up the moment I got here."

"Mum, please, let me explain."

Her mother approached a cluster of cables and grabbed hold of them to yank them out of the switches.

"No!" Sarah pulled her away. "No, you can't do that."

"It's a submerged data centre, isn't it?" her mother demanded. She spun around and tried to pick up a server, but it was screwed into the rack. "We hear about these projects, you know. We're not stupid."

"Let me explain," Sarah tried again.

Her mother started to kick at one of the switches. "I won't let you do this, Sarah. My own flesh and blood is killing the ocean. I won't allow it."

Sarah grabbed her mother in a bear hug and pulled her away from the precious equipment that she was hell-bent on destroying. They struggled for a moment before Sarah managed to manoeuvre her outside the shed.

"Do you know how much damage those data centres cause?" her mother demanded.

"Less than the ones on land," Sarah replied.

"That's not the point. We can't ask people if they would like to burn to death slowly or be incinerated." Her mother pulled away from her and paced the garden. "I should have known. Someone like you moving to a place like this. It made no sense."

"Hey!"

"Come on, you've never cared about nature. All that nonsense about the beautiful cliffs and walks on the beach. I should have known!"

"I care about nature, just not in an all-encompassing way like you."

"There's no halfway on this, Sarah." Her mother shook her head. Fury flowed from her in waves. "I wish I could explain to you."

"I wish I could explain to *you*," Sarah returned. "But you never listen."

"Because you don't know what you're talking about." She turned to look at the cottage. "So none of this is real? You didn't find love and settle down?"

The question felt like a punch to the gut.

"No," Sarah admitted in a whisper.

"I can't say I'm surprised."

Tears sprang to Sarah's eyes. "Mum," she whispered in a plea.

With one final disappointed shake of the head, her mother stalked up the garden path back towards the cottage. Sarah clutched her head in her hands and looked from her mother's retreating form to the shed.

CHAPTER TWENTY-ONE

Pippa leaned on the iron railing and watched the ferry arrive. The items she had ordered weren't urgent and would be put into the terminal ferry for her if she wasn't there to collect them. But she had little else to do as she was hiding from Sarah. She felt terrible about how she had handled everything. She wished she could turn back time and do things differently.

She'd never really stopped to consider Sarah's feelings as she was far too wrapped up in her own. So worried that she'd end up hurt that she'd never considered that Sarah could have been hurt, too.

Soon after Sarah had run off, Pippa had decided to do the same. She'd told Angela she was heading out to work and had then turned her phone off. She'd gone home and tried to bury herself in the complicated load-bearing calculations that she'd been putting to one side while she was playing happy families.

Only she couldn't focus. The equations that usually came to her with ease were out of her grasp. Her mind was clearly elsewhere, even when she had retreated to her safe haven, her cottage that she'd cultivated to be a place to be alone. Except now she pictured Sarah shivering on the sofa after a walk in the rain, or out in the garden with a glass of wine and a blanket as they chuckled long into the night.

In the end, she'd left her home in search of some peace. Burying herself in work wasn't working in the way it had before. The ferry shipment would get her out of the house and allow her to get a few breaths of fresh air.

She'd thought she was away from any reminders of her current predicament when a taxi pulled up and Angela stepped out. She looked furious, and Sarah was nowhere to be seen. The driver placed a suitcase on the kerb, and Angela walked into the terminal building.

It looked as if she was leaving, something which would have been a cause for celebration, but the fury that radiated from her spoke to something having gone seriously wrong. Pippa hurried after her. As she walked, she got her phone out of her pocket and switched it back on. Something big had clearly happened and she was out of the loop.

Angela was at the ticket booth when Pippa arrived.

"Hi," she said.

"Did she send you?" Angela asked.

"No. I've not spoken with her since this morning."

"I see." Angela inserted her credit card into the card reader. "Well, I'm going home. My daughter is a liar who cannot be reasoned with."

Pippa opened her mouth but didn't know what to say.

"She's killing this island. And if you know about it, then you're doing so as well."

If it was anyone else, Pippa would have assumed they'd found out about Billy. But this was Angela Campbell, and overreacting was in her nature. Pippa knew she had to tread lightly.

"I don't know what you're talking about," Pippa admitted. "Come back to the house—we can talk."

Angela laughed. "I don't think so. We've said all that needs to be said." She snatched a ticket and a receipt out of the hand of the assistant. "My daughter struggles with the truth. You seem like a nice person. Don't allow her to embroil you in her web of lies."

Pippa didn't say anything. She watched Angela spin her suitcase around and leave the building. She wouldn't be upset to see the back of her, but she wished the visit could have ended differently.

She'd been trying to push Angela and Sarah together the whole time without really appreciating how completely different they were. She wanted Sarah to have a relationship like the one Pippa had experienced with her own mother. It was only now that she realised that had never been possible.

She'd been so convinced that she'd be able to somehow get through to them both and help them see things from the other's perspective that she'd ignored what was happening in front of her. In fact, she'd been oblivious to a number of things.

Her phone showed no missed calls, no voicemails, no text messages. Sarah hadn't reached out to her. Whatever had happened must have been a while ago for Angela to have had time to pack and get across the island. Which meant that Sarah had chosen to not contact her, a fact that left her feeling a little cold.

Sarah's time on Celfare might have been drawing to a close, and Pippa might have messed up, but that didn't mean she wouldn't be there for her friend.

❖

Pippa let herself into Hillcrest Cottage.

"Sarah?"

Sarah walked into the hall, her mobile phone gripped to her face. Her skin was pale, and she looked a little green. But fury blazed in her eyes.

"I really don't know," Sarah said to whoever was on the other end of the call. "There's nothing I can do now. I'll keep monitoring. We'll wait and see. Keep an eye on the newsfeeds."

Pippa waited for Sarah to finish up her call. She entered the living room and noticed her belongings had been placed in a cardboard box. She hadn't brought much with her, but it was still surprising to see it all boxed up so quickly. If she needed any visual cue that she was no longer welcome, this was very much it.

"Do you need something?"

Pippa turned to look at Sarah, surprised that the question had been directed at her and not whoever she'd been on the phone with. It was a formal and cold tone that she wasn't used to.

"I'm checking to see if you're okay."

Sarah's expression was hard and her posture tense. "Mum found out about everything. She's told Project Earth, and now she's going home. Do you think I'm okay?"

Pippa's stomach clenched at the blatant hostility. Sarah was understandably upset, but it almost seemed to be directed at Pippa.

"It's hardly my fault," Pippa said.

"Isn't it?" Sarah asked. She folded her arms across her chest and stared coldly at Pippa.

Pippa mimicked the posture. "Why would it be my fault? I'm not the one with an enormous secret in the back garden, am I?"

"No, but you are the reason I didn't lock the door properly. You distracted me when you got angry that I'll be going home soon."

Pippa laughed with incredulity. "You're going to blame me for your not locking the shed door? Really?"

"Yes." Sarah nodded sharply.

Pippa held back the urge to argue with her. Sarah was clearly upset and no doubt panicking about what Angela might do. She needed to be the calm one or things could easily spiral out of control.

"I think that's a little unfair," Pippa said.

"I've been out there hundreds of times, and I've never, ever not locked up. But the one time you're there and…and…I'd admitted that I had feelings for you." Sarah shook her head and stormed away to another room.

Pippa followed. "Had?"

She didn't know why she questioned her on that point, out of everything that had been said. If Sarah's feelings had diminished, then that was surely a good thing. But the idea of Sarah so quickly turning her feelings off seemed unlikely. Pippa didn't like the thought of Sarah quite suddenly feeling nothing towards her. Probably because her own feelings were accelerating with each passing day, whether she claimed otherwise or not.

"I think we shouldn't see each other for a while," Sarah said, coming to a stop in the kitchen. "I think that might be a good idea for both of us."

Pippa didn't agree but didn't know what to say. It wasn't as if it was up for discussion. Sarah wasn't asking, she was telling, no matter how polite she was being about it.

"If that's what you really want."

"It is." Sarah wrapped her arms around her middle and looked at the kitchen floor. "Thank you for everything you did with the house. And thank you for what you tried to do with my mum. I'm sorry that I've caused mayhem in your world. And I do hope you'll change your mind one day and will find someone to be with, even though it obviously won't be me. You have a lot of love to give, Pippa." Sarah sucked in a deep breath and met Pippa's gaze. "But I think we have to not see each other any more. I think this has to be goodbye."

Pippa swallowed. She felt cold, and her legs felt like they had been bolted to the ground. She wasn't prepared to say goodbye to Sarah, didn't think she could. Things had gone dramatically wrong so very quickly, and she didn't understand why or what she could do to fix things.

Sarah had made her decision, and Pippa had no choice but to respect it.

But she didn't want to.

"Sarah..."

"Pippa, really. I'm having the worst day of my life, and it is probably going to get worse, okay? I don't want to end things with you on a worse note than they are already on."

Pippa clamped her mouth shut. She cursed her decision to leave earlier that day. If she'd been there, perhaps Angela would never have found out about the secret project. Maybe Pippa would have been able to calm her if she had. At the very least she'd have been a shoulder for Sarah to cry on, rather than being on the outside.

"There's a box in the living room," Sarah said.

With little else to say, Pippa nodded. She took what she suspected was one last look at Sarah and wondered how she'd managed to get things so wrong. She knew her attempts to save herself from hurt feelings were in tatters. But worse, she'd caused Sarah pain as well.

❖

Sarah watched Pippa leave from the living room window. Once she saw the van drive away, she allowed the tears to fall. She honestly did blame Pippa for her mother finding out about Billy, but only because Pippa had turned Sarah around so much that she'd become complacent.

It had only taken a couple of days of living together in their ridiculous attempt at a fake relationship and Sarah had completely fallen for Pippa Kent. She'd fallen so easily and without her noticing that it was only when Pippa put the brakes on things that Sarah had realised her heart was no longer her own.

Sarah knew she wasn't enough to ever match up to the love of Pippa's life. It made sense that Pippa wanted to draw a line under things, even if it hurt Sarah to admit that.

Now her mother hated her, Pippa was out of her life, and her job hung in the balance while a board meeting happened to discuss what she had allowed to happen with a multi-million-pound project. Her life had completely unravelled in a couple of days.

She wiped at her tears.

"Stop it," she told herself. "You've been through worse."

The words sounded confident, but Sarah wasn't so certain that she *had* been through worse. In fact, things looked bleaker than she could ever remember.

It came as no surprise to her that seeing Pippa leave was hurting more than the argument with her mum or the potential end of her career.

Chapter Twenty-two

It had been two days since Angela had left. Two days since Pippa had last seen Sarah. And two days when Pippa had been unable to focus on a single thing. Six years alone had been wiped away by mere days with Sarah. Suddenly, Pippa struggled to remember what her usual routine was.

Cooking dinner alone, the silence of her home, and the absence of laughter hit her with remarkable clarity. Her life was empty. It had been empty for a long time, by her own design. Now she fought an inner war between wanting to make a change and being frightened of what that would mean.

In the end, it all seemed irrelevant because she'd ruined even her friendship with Sarah.

Her mobile phone rumbled, and she jumped up to grab it. Her enthusiasm left when she noted it was Lawrence and not Sarah calling her.

"Why would she call you?" Pippa asked herself aloud as she shook her head. She answered the call. "Hello, Lawrence, what disaster do you bring me today?"

"Can I not check in with a friend without you thinking I want something?" He chuckled.

"Oh, dear, it's a big one."

"Peterson Brothers are tendering for the apartment building in York."

"Ah." She flopped into her office chair, leaned back, and closed her eyes.

Lawrence had lost a few deals to the infamous Peterson Brothers over the years, and their name had been banned from even being mentioned in the office.

"I think they'll get this one," he said solemnly.

"You think they'll get everything," Pippa reminded him.

"As my friend, you're supposed to tell me that they won't get it and that my proposal is stronger," Lawrence said.

"I can't just tell you whatever you want to hear, Lawrence," she said.

"I can't lose another project to them—it's soul destroying," he complained.

"It's only one project. You'll be fine."

"You sound depressed. Is everything okay?"

Pippa sighed. She hated how easily he could read her. She supposed it wasn't a big surprise—they'd shared a lot of time together at one point. But she wasn't used to anyone being able to question her. Another reason she lived such a solitary life. It was only now that *she* was questioning if that was for better or for worse.

"It's nothing."

"When do you think your internet will be up and running again?" He changed the subject, understanding that she didn't want to talk about what was bothering her. Sadly he'd walked straight into another topic that she didn't want to discuss.

The consistently flaky internet connection was a thorn in her side, but Sarah's technical wizardry had alleviated some of the issues. Sarah had given her instructions to access her router and to add some commands. Pippa didn't know what any of it meant except that it had fixed her problems for a while.

But in the spirit of terrible timing, her connection had fizzled to a crawl on the same day that her relationship with Sarah had done the same.

"Who knows?" She sighed.

"You're sighing a lot."

He wasn't pushing, but Pippa knew that he was reaching out a small olive branch in case she was ready to catch hold of it.

"I had a disagreement with a client." She paused. "A friend."

"Sorry to hear that. Did you apologise?"

Pippa laughed. "Why do you assume I was at fault?"

He laughed. "Were you?"

"It was a complicated situation," Pippa admitted. "Maybe I could have handled some things better. But so could she."

"Someone has to make the first move if it's a client or a friend that you want back."

Silence hung in the air.

"Or not," he said. "What's going on on Celfare anyway?"

Pippa frowned. "What do you mean?"

Lawrence laughed heartily. "Trust you not to notice. You're under siege."

"Under siege?"

"There's a flotilla of Project Earth boats off the coast—it's all over the news. Well, I say boats, but I mean anything they can get their hands on that will float. A couple of fishing boats, a dinghy with an engine. Lots of flag waving and megaphones. It's quite the spectacle. Turn on the news once in a while. Or look out a window."

Pippa felt suddenly cold. She rushed into the living room to turn on the television.

"Not sure what they're doing, but they've been there for about an hour. I think the coastguard was trying to get them to turn back, but they refused. I thought they were more for chaining themselves to the gates of oil refineries and gluing themselves to airplanes. Do you have a nuclear power station up there that I didn't know about? I know you don't have an airport. An oil rig? I bet it's an oil rig!"

Lawrence continued his bad jokes while Pippa stared at the live newsfeed in horror. At least twenty boats of various shapes and sizes were just off the coast of Celfare. Project Earth flags were being waved alongside other banners with environmental messages written on them. The images were grainy, coming from a camera at the main terminal and pointing out to sea. Pippa knew where they were heading.

"Lawrence, I have to go." She hung up the call and immediately called Sarah. The call redirected straight to voicemail, and Pippa hung up. She grabbed her van keys, pulled on her coat, and left the house.

⁖

Sarah leaned all her weight on the back on the old wooden fishing boat to try to get it to move.

"Come on!" she shouted at the inanimate object. "Move!"

She took a deep breath and then pushed again with all her strength. The boat moved a bit but nothing that was going to get it actually into the water. She stood up and tried to push aside the thoughts of panic that swam through her brain and clogged up her common sense. She felt as if she was drunk and unable to focus on anything.

"Think," she told herself. "You're smart, figure it out."

She'd been enjoying an afternoon of wallowing on the sofa and feeling sorry for herself. When the movie had ended, she'd started to flip through television channels before coming to a news article about Project Earth. Before she even read the news ticker, she knew exactly where they were and what their goal was. Her half-eaten bag of popcorn had fallen to the floor, and she'd run around the cottage with no idea of what she was going to do but understanding that she needed to do something and fast.

Project Earth had an armada, and they were coming for Billy. All Sarah could think was that she needed to get out to sea to protect him.

She recalled the old wooden fishing boat that had long ago been abandoned on the beach and decided to launch it. She'd rushed down to the beach without a second thought. In her mind, she was going to row out to meet the boats and tell them to turn around. In reality, she couldn't even get her rescue boat into the water.

"Rollers!" she declared to herself.

She needed to lift the boat up and roll it down to the shore. She looked around the pebble beach and realised that there was nothing much to work with. She walked to the front of the boat, knelt, and dug at the sand with her fingers.

Behind her she could hear the shouts from the boats. Music was blaring, and someone on a loudspeaker was chanting something, but it was so mumbled that she couldn't make out the words.

She wished she'd had the forethought to bring a shovel as she scooped out handfuls of sand. Once she found the underside of the boat, she placed some smooth rocks to hopefully guide it out of the ditch and onto the sand.

She raced to the back of the boat and pushed again. It held fast for a second before it moved so quickly that she fell to the ground behind it. She scrambled to her feet and pushed it again. The tide was coming in, and the water was now a few inches closer than it had been when she started. It wasn't much, but she'd take anything.

With a vow that she would join a gym when she got back to London, she pushed and pushed until the boat was finally at the water. She paused and took a few deep breaths before she climbed into the boat and picked the oars up from under the seat.

"Sarah!"

She looked up. Pippa was running down the beach towards her. "Don't do it!"

Sarah pointed to the activists in the distance. "I have to!"

"It's not safe." Pippa grabbed hold of the boat and started to drag it back from the water's edge.

"Don't do that—it took me ages to get it to the water." Sarah dug an oar into the wet sand and held on tight.

"What are you going to do when you get out there?" Pippa asked. She tugged at the back of the boat. "Assuming that you don't drown on the way."

"I'll figure that out when I get there. Let go." Sarah pulled on the oar to try to pivot the boat to the water. She knew that once she was in the water properly, Pippa's ability to fight the tide would be limited. She just had to hold on and wait for the tide to take hold of her vessel.

"I'm not going to let you go and get yourself killed." Pippa held on tight to the edge of the boat, her knuckles white. "Have you even stopped to think about what you're doing?"

She hadn't, but the last thing she needed right now was a lecture from Pippa.

"Have you even stopped to think that I didn't ask for your opinion?" Sarah retorted.

"I don't give a damn if you want my opinion or not. I'm not going to let you float away in a boat that probably isn't seaworthy, with no coat on, with no lifejacket, with no plan...with no, no...no hope of surviving."

Sarah squinted at Pippa and realised that tears were streaming down her face. Thoughts of arguing further drifted away. She let go of the oar and stepped over the wooden seat, placing her hand on Pippa's shoulder.

"Hey, I'm okay. It's okay."

"It isn't." Pippa shook her head and continued to try to drag the boat backwards. "I got to the house, and the door was open. Your phone was on the floor, popcorn scattered everywhere. I had no idea what had happened to you. And now you're here, about to sail away in this ridiculous boat that has been rotting on this beach for a year. For what? For what?"

The sounds of the Project Earth activists drifted to nothing for Sarah as she realised how distraught Pippa had become. She stepped out of the boat, put her hands on Pippa's shoulders, and turned her to face her.

"Hey, look at me."

Pippa's eyes were wild but eventually settled on Sarah. Pippa sniffed and wiped away some tears with the back of her hand. "You're all bloodied."

Sarah frowned and looked down at herself. Her trousers were torn at one knee, and a trickle of blood dribbled from a wound, which she assumed happened when she was kneeling in the sand. She felt fingers on her temple.

"Here," Pippa said. Fingers moved lightly to her cheek. "And here."

Sarah hadn't realised that she'd injured herself, but she wasn't surprised, considering her panic.

"I'm fine," Sarah said softly. It felt good to feel Pippa's fingers on her skin again. She hated seeing Pippa in such an emotional state, and she wondered if old and painful memories were bubbling to the surface. Her concern turned away from Billy and towards Pippa.

"I thought I'd lost you," Pippa said. She shook her head a little. "Sounds silly, I know."

"It doesn't," Sarah admitted. "I felt the same way. I'm sorry."

"I'm sorry." Pippa took Sarah's hand in hers and softly ran her thumb over the back of it. She looked miles away and deep in thought. "I did say I was bad with people."

Air horns started to blare from the direction of the armada, and they both jumped back. They looked out to sea. People were shouting, their tone celebratory, between the honks of air horns.

"What's happening?" Pippa asked.

"I think they've found Billy," Sarah said.

"What will they do?"

"Cut the cables. There's not a lot else they can do. It's as big as a train carriage. They'll never get it out of the water without the right equipment." Sarah watched as the boats started to gather at one spot.

They were too far away to see anything, but Sarah's heart sank at the knowledge of what they were trying to do. She tried to comfort herself that this would be an excellent test for the redundancies she'd built in if Billy ever went offline.

She'd always thought those systems would be tested manually by shutting Billy off under controlled conditions. Now she knew that wouldn't be the case. Project Earth had diving teams who would go down and cause as much damage as they could.

"Have you managed to gather much useful data?" Pippa asked.

Sarah nodded. "Yes. Not as much as I'd like but enough to create a case for moving to the next stage of development."

She shivered a little. The sun was setting, and the evening was creeping in, but that wasn't the cause of her chills. The adrenaline was wearing off, and the reality that there was nothing that she could do to help Billy was crystalising in her mind.

The tide had come in a little further and started to claw the fishing boat out to sea. Pippa took hold of her hand again as if frightened that Sarah might change her mind and make a last-ditch effort to get into the boat.

"Please, don't," Pippa whispered.

Sarah clutched Pippa's hand tight and leaned her head on her shoulder.

"I won't," she whispered. "Bye, Billy."

CHAPTER TWENTY-THREE

Pippa opened the front door to Hillcrest Cottage and helped to guide Sarah in.

"I'm okay, really," Sarah said.

She'd been saying that since they left the beach and walked home. But Pippa wouldn't be convinced of it until she got Sarah home and warm, and she'd seen to her wounds. Deep down she knew they were superficial, but she couldn't help but worry.

Pippa had draped her coat over Sarah's shoulders as they'd walked back from the beach hand in hand. The shock of not being able to find Sarah and then seeing her on the beach about to go into the water in a boat that was surely going to sink had hit her like a lightning bolt. All she could focus on was ensuring that Sarah was safe.

Sarah knelt down and started to clear up pieces of popcorn that had been sent flying when she'd left earlier. Pippa went to the downstairs shower room and found the first aid kit that she knew was in the medicine cabinet.

When she returned to the living room, Sarah had cleaned up and was sitting on the sofa looking at her mobile phone.

"My boss wants to talk to me," Sarah said.

Pippa sat next to her. "I'd like to talk to you, too."

Sarah placed her phone on the coffee table, screen down. "Can I start?"

Pippa swallowed. She'd only just managed to find the nerve to say what she wanted to say. She didn't want to lose the courage to tell Sarah how she felt, to explain that she was starting to realise she needed a change in her life. But if Sarah was about to reassert her decision that they couldn't see each other, it wouldn't matter what Pippa said.

She nodded. "Go ahead."

"Thank you for coming to get me," Sarah said. "I would have gone out in that boat, and who knows what trouble I could have gotten into. The boat probably wouldn't have held out. And if I did manage to get out there, I didn't have a plan. I was just reacting without thinking, so thank you."

"I—"

"I'm not done," Sarah continued. She turned to face Pippa and then looked down at her hands, fidgeting in her lap. "I'm sorry that I overreacted. Of course it wasn't your fault that I didn't padlock the shed."

"It was a little," Pippa admitted.

"I'm still not done," Sarah said.

"Sorry."

"I was hurting because—wow, this will sound so cold, but I have to say it—I was kind of thinking that we were coming together, you know? Maybe on the way to being more than friends. And then you said that you wanted to stay friends, and it hurt. Because I realised that I wasn't enough."

Pippa's heart clenched. "Sarah…"

"No, I mean, it's not your fault. Of course, it isn't. I'm so glad you had Kim and you both lived a happy life. I'm really glad you experienced that. But it just hurt to think that I could never match up. Not that I expected to, but it was hard to hear. Does that make sense?"

Pippa remained silent, waiting for her chance to speak.

Sarah looked up. "It's your turn now."

She smiled. "Thank you. I'm sorry I made you feel as if you weren't enough. That wasn't my intention at all. And it wasn't the case. It isn't the case. I was frightened. And the reason I was frightened was because you are enough. More than enough. You make me remember feelings that I've tried to bury."

Sarah frowned. "I'm sorry?"

"Don't be sorry. I think it was good for me to remember those feelings, even if I didn't think so at the time, and I'm more scared than I can ever remember being right now."

The frown on Sarah's face deepened, and confusion painted her features. "What are you saying?"

Pippa chuckled. "I don't know. I've not done this kind of thing for a long time."

"What kind of thing?"

"Been honest about my feelings."

Sarah jumped to her feet and walked over to the window. Pippa bit her lip. Her chest felt tight as she wondered if she'd done something wrong again.

Sarah looked out of the window. She had her arms folded across her chest and her gaze was pensive. Pippa didn't know whether to speak or wait. Having a lack of words to choose from, the decision was made for her.

"I've been trying to get over you," Sarah whispered. "I know it's only been a couple of days, but I'm in my moving-on period. I watched *Four Weddings and a Funeral*. Ice cream has been consumed. A lot of ice cream."

Pippa couldn't help but smile. It was little details like this that had woken her from her six-year silence and reminded her that being with other people could be exciting and preferable to her own company day after day.

Pippa's life made sense. She'd created it to do so. Sarah was at times chaotic, and Pippa found she adored that. The randomness that Sarah sometimes brought to a day was adorable and fascinating.

Sarah turned around. "What are you actually trying to say?"

Pippa's words were swept away as she saw the angry scratch on Sarah's forehead. She plucked an antiseptic wipe from the first aid kit and walked over to Sarah.

"I don't really know what I'm saying," Pippa confessed. She tore open the packaging and removed the wipe. "You're leaving. I was hurt when I realised you wouldn't be here for much longer."

She smoothed Sarah's hair out of the way and carefully cleaned the wound. It was nothing more than a scratch, but that wasn't going to stop her from fixing it up as best as she could.

"I'm sorry I didn't tell you that I was leaving," Sarah said.

"You couldn't—it might have alerted me to the train-carriage-sized secret you have off the coast."

"I could have told you something," Sarah said. "I didn't tell you because I didn't want to drive a wedge between us. I didn't want you to know I was leaving and then to keep your distance."

Pippa hummed her understanding. She'd cleaned the scratch on Sarah's forehead and moved to the mark on her cheekbone. It was a smudge of blood and dirt that came away easily, but that didn't stop Pippa from continuing to tend to the non-existent wound.

It was soothing to be so close to Sarah, to be able to touch her once again. It was also frightening to be having such a real discussion so soon after her realisation that she'd missed the boat on avoiding falling in love with Sarah. Pain would come now either way. It was just a matter of whether it would be because she had lost Sarah already or because she might lose her in the future.

"I don't have all the answers," Pippa admitted. "In fact I think I have more questions than answers. But I'm starting to realise that burying my head in the sand in the hope that I don't get hurt again is just hurting me in a different way. Being away from you was… hard."

"I felt the same way." Sarah took the wipe from Pippa's hand. "You don't need an excuse to touch me, Pippa."

Pippa hesitated for a second before cupping the side of Sarah's face. The connection instantly calmed her. Sarah leaned into the touch.

"Where do we go from here?" Pippa asked, her practical side not able to be silent.

"I don't know," Sarah said.

"I don't think I want to go back to the mainland," Pippa admitted. She was nervous to confess that the thought had crossed her mind. Nothing was tying her to Celfare. And yet the thought of leaving her quiet life and throwing herself into the big city was maybe a step too far. Maybe one day, but she wasn't ready yet.

"I'm not sure if I do either," Sarah said.

Pippa laughed. "What about your twenty-four-hour supermarkets and next-day deliveries?" Her heart started to beat a little faster at the suggestion that Sarah might stay.

"I've gotten used to going to the farm shop for fresh eggs and waiting for the ferry. Sometimes things are better when you have to wait. Instant satisfaction is sometimes not all it's cracked up to be, wouldn't you say? Sometimes things are sweeter when you've had to wait for them. Had to work for them."

Pippa didn't need to be told twice. She closed the distance between them and placed her lips on Sarah's, grateful that this time it was real and not some performance for Angela. Sarah's arms wrapped around Pippa's neck to hold on tight. Sarah's eager tongue entered Pippa's mouth, and she realised then that the kisses they'd shared before had been innocently chaste.

She wrapped her arms around Sarah and held her in a way she'd been eager to do each time they'd been close. At the back of her mind a warning bell sounded. She tried to ignore it, but it persistently rang and rang.

Sarah pulled back. "Let me go and turn that off."

Pippa realised it was a real sound and not just in her mind. "What is it?"

"It means Billy is offline." Sarah went to the laptop set up at the dining table and started to type.

"I'm sorry."

"It's okay." It was clear Sarah wasn't okay. "He did well. And hopefully the data we gathered will help to create Billy Two. It's just hard to see him gone. I know it sounds weird, but I feel like I've lost a pet or something."

With a final keystroke, she silenced the alarm. She closed the laptop lid and looked at Pippa again. This time there was warmth in her expression, and Pippa knew they were on their way to repairing the damage that had been done.

"I'm sorry your mother sold you out." Pippa took a seat at the dining table. "And I'm sorry for pushing you two together. I realise now that you were just too different to come together in the way I thought you would. I think I just assumed that mothers and daughters could have a relationship like the one I had with my mother."

"I take some responsibility for the way we are," Sarah said. "I've spent a lifetime lying to her. I can't expect us to have a good relationship if I've never once told her the truth about me."

Pippa nodded. "Agreed. But I can see how it's the path of least resistance."

"It is." Sarah sighed and rubbed at her eyes. "But I need to fix that. If she wants to know me for who I am, then that's great, and if she doesn't, then I need to accept that. Living in a fantasy land in the middle and never telling her the truth isn't helping anyone."

"I'm glad you're seeing things that way now."

Sarah grimaced. "Yeah, I know it's for the best. I'll leave it awhile before I talk to her, though. She's just enlisted a mob to kill my puppy."

"As sad as I am at Billy's demise, I'd rather that than see you injured. Or worse." Pippa swallowed. "I can't imagine a world without you in it."

Sarah reached her hand across the dining table for Pippa to take hold of.

"I know you're scared," Sarah said once Pippa took hold of her hand. "And I understand why. But we'll work it out. Just...don't lock me out, okay?"

"What if Swype ask you to go back to London immediately?" Pippa asked.

Sarah squeezed her hand. "I'll tell them that I want to stay."

A hundred questions whizzed around Pippa's mind, but at the forefront was one thing—she wanted to be with Sarah even though she knew that she had very little idea what that meant yet. It felt right. It also felt impossible to argue with. As if they had always been destined to come together.

"One step at a time," Sarah said, as if able to read Pippa's mind. "Starting with helping me choose a new tap for the kitchen sink."

Pippa laughed. "I thought you'd decided."

"You didn't like it," Sarah said. "And if I'm to encourage you to maybe live here one day, I need to make sure you like the fixtures and fittings."

Pippa grinned and bit her lip. "Oh, and what's wrong with my place?"

"You don't have a generator buried in the garden that can sustain a base of operations for a covert undersea data centre."

Pippa laughed. "You're right." She looked around the room. "I always said that this place had a lot of potential and could be lovely."

"You did." Sarah grinned. She stood up and sat in Pippa's lap, draping her arms around Pippa's neck. "Stay for dinner?"

Pippa nodded. Sarah leaned in to kiss her again. Pippa realised that her fears, which had been so present for so many years, were silent. She wrapped her arms around Sarah and held her close. She didn't know what the future would bring, but for the first time in a long time she was excited to find out.

CHAPTER TWENTY-FOUR

Pippa woke up to the sound of distant murmuring. She opened one eye and ascertained that she was in Sarah's bed, it was late in the morning, and Sarah was walking around the house on a phone call.

She sat up and rubbed her face. The previous day came back to her in a burst. Panic that Sarah was injured, the fishing boat, admitting her feelings, Billy going offline. And then Sarah had sent a text to her boss, saying she was signing off for the night before turning her phone off.

They'd cooked dinner side by side, discussing anything but what had happened over the last few days. The conversation was safe, and the tone was soft as they attempted to heal the rifts and avoid anything that might lead them back to being at odds.

They'd eaten dinner by candlelight, shared a bottle of wine, and then Sarah had looked at Pippa and asked, "Take me to bed?"

She'd looked so relaxed, leaning back on the dining chair with a glass of wine in her hand and a neutral expression on her face. Pippa had known in that moment that Sarah would have understood if it was too much too soon. There was no pressure, just a suggestion. An offer. One that Pippa didn't refuse.

She smiled to herself at the memory of finally being intimate with someone again. It hadn't been as daunting as she'd worried it might be. Sarah was unhurried and relaxed, which made Pippa feel the same.

The only problem was that she still didn't know what it meant for them. Would Sarah go back to London? Were they a couple?

"Stop," she whispered to herself. "Not now."

She knew deep down that she had to get her worries under control. A relationship wasn't like an instruction manual. There were no easy answers, and they'd have to work together if they wanted to overcome the obstacles.

And Pippa did want to overcome them. Not just because she was in the morning glow of the night before, but because she was starting to realise that it was time. And, more than that, Sarah was the one.

The bedroom door opened, and Sarah entered with a mug in one hand and holding her mobile phone to her ear with the other. She wore a dishevelled tank top and the shortest shorts Pippa had ever seen.

Sarah placed the mug on the bedside table next to Pippa and gestured towards it. Pippa leaned over and smelt the black coffee. Sarah started to walk away, but Pippa reached out and hooked a finger in the elasticated waist of the shorts. Sarah smiled and allowed herself to be pulled back towards the bed. She sat on the edge of the bed. Pippa sat up and gratefully took a tentative sip of the coffee.

It was scorching hot. The best way Pippa knew to drink coffee.

"I think we need to get Professor Cassidy to write up an article about the fish," Sarah said to whoever was on the other end of the call. "There's no point in pulling Billy up early—it will just disrupt the fish habitat, and it's the mating season for Atlantic Cod at the moment."

Pippa raised an eyebrow. If she'd had fifty guesses at what Sarah might say on her call, she'd never have thought the mating season of fish would come up.

"Thanks, Abbie. Just tell him we need something we can reference. Usual rate. Okay, team, is there anything else?"

Pippa leaned against the headboard and looked at the rumpled sheets. Flashes of memories of the night before were slowly returning to her. She itched to hang up Sarah's call and pull her back into bed but knew she was too tired to make good on any promises of that nature. The emotional turmoil was starting to take its toll. She'd already slept in far longer than was usual, and she still felt as if she could sleep the whole day away. Some of that was the worry about what was to come. No matter how she tried to push it out of her mind, it lingered.

"Great. I'll check in again this afternoon, and then we can check off the rest of those agenda items. Good job, everyone, and remember, this isn't a failure. We expected and planned for these issues."

Pippa heard a flurry of goodbyes and watched Sarah hang up the phone with a sigh.

"Of course," Sarah said to her, "we hadn't planned for my mother."

"You can't blame yourself for that," Pippa said. She shuffled over to make a little more room for Sarah and held up her arm.

Sarah tossed the phone onto the bed and immediately curled up beside Pippa. Pippa wrapped her arm around Sarah and sipped at her coffee.

"I do right now. I should have tried harder to keep her away. Anyway, we're not talking about her."

"Good," Pippa said.

"I had fun last night."

"So did I."

"Good. I wasn't sure if it was too soon," Sarah admitted, her tone suddenly unsure.

Pippa didn't reply. She didn't think she was the best judge of what was too soon. She'd spent years with her life on hold. If she'd had her way, she'd never have been intimate with anyone ever again. Which she was now realising was the opposite of what she needed. And the opposite of what Kim would have wanted.

"I spoke with Gail before the team meeting," Sarah continued. "I've asked to take my work-life balance days."

Pippa felt her brow furrow. "Your what?"

"Swype gives every member of staff five work-life balance days a year. You can use them if you're feeling overwhelmed or if you just want some time off."

"How very modern," Pippa said.

She felt Sarah's elbow poke her ribs playfully.

"So what does that mean?" Pippa held her breath. She wanted Sarah to stay, a feeling that was growing more pressing with every moment they spent together.

"It means, if you're in agreement, that we get to spend some time together." Sarah plucked the mug out of Pippa's hand and placed it back on the bedside table. She then swung her leg over Pippa's to straddle her. "If you'd like that?"

Pippa placed her hands on Sarah's hips. She licked her lips and nodded. "I'd like that a lot. Five days together sounds very nice."

"Twenty-five," Sarah corrected. "Of course, you don't have to spend all twenty-five days with me. I'm just saying that I have that many days off work. I'd like to spend them with you, but I get it if you need some space. I mean I—"

"You said five," Pippa said, cutting off Sarah's adorable rambling.

"Five a year."

"You haven't taken your work-life balance days for five years?" Pippa chuckled. "That's not very balanced of you."

Sarah rolled her eyes. "Maybe just five days with you. I'll spend the other twenty on my own."

Pippa leaned forward and captured Sarah's lips in a short and sweet kiss of apology.

"Okay, fine. Maybe six days with you," Sarah said.

Pippa laughed. "Oh, I'm going to have to earn each day, am I?"

Sarah cupped Pippa's face in her hands and leaned in to deliver a ghost of a kiss. "I want to spend every day with you," she said softly. "But I know you need time and space. So I'm here if you want to be here. And if you need time alone, then that's fine, too."

"How did I get so lucky?" Pippa whispered.

"Robin broke my light," Sarah said.

Pippa lifted her hand a few centimetres to Sarah's sides and started to tickle her.

CHAPTER TWENTY-FIVE

Pippa turned off the chainsaw and lifted her face shield to examine the apple tree. The tree was very old and had weathered many a storm on Celfare. It grew almost sideways from struggling to reach the sun during the few weeks of summer. She'd been trying to straighten it for the last four years, worried that the unbalanced weight would send it crashing to the ground.

"Well, now, that looks much better."

Pippa turned to Rowena Findlay. "I wonder if I should take a little more off."

Rowena dug her hands into the pockets of her apron and took a few steps closer. She squinted at the tree. She looked thoughtful for a long couple of minutes before finally shrugging. "Looks fine to me."

Pippa blew out a breath. Rowena wasn't an expert on garden maintenance. That had always been Mr. Findlay's area of expertise. Pippa suspected that Rowena would be just as happy with the whole garden concreted over and a few plastic plants in some pots.

"What's on your mind?" Rowena asked. She'd turned away from the tree and was now fully focused on Pippa.

Pippa shrank a little under the scrutiny. "Nothing."

"You don't lie well."

Pippa sighed. "It's private."

Rowena stared at her in a manner that indicated she'd not take that as an answer.

Pippa didn't know how to start on what was wrong. She didn't even know if something was wrong. She'd spent eight days at Hillcrest Cottage with Sarah, and they had been wonderful. They'd spoken for hours about anything and everything, they'd cooked meals together, walked the island together, made love more times than Pippa could count. And then Sarah had suggested that Pippa might want some time alone.

And for some reason, Pippa had agreed.

"I…" Pippa didn't know how to summarise her confusion.

Rowena squinted and stared at her for a moment before pronouncing, "This is a tea and cake discussion. Come inside."

Rowena walked back towards the house, leaving no room for discussion. Pippa shut down the chainsaw and engaged the safety mechanism. She took off the protective helmet and gloves and placed them in the plastic box she used for safety equipment. She toed off her work boots and shrugged out of overalls covered in tree sap and sawdust.

By the time she got to the kitchen, the kettle was nearly boiled, and a full tea tray with cups, saucers, side plates, and Dundee cake was prepared. Pippa wondered if Rowena always had one on standby just in case or was practising for some kind of afternoon-tea-preparing Olympic event that she didn't know about.

"It's the girl at Hillcrest, isn't it?" Rowena asked.

"Yes," Pippa admitted. She didn't see any reason to lie. She needed a second opinion on the situation, even if Rowena was probably the last person whose advice she should listen to.

"You asked her to marry you," Rowena guessed.

Pippa balked. "No. It's only been a little while."

"My Robert proposed the day we met, and I said yes. Never regretted it a day in my life."

Pippa thought back to the countless times she'd seen the couple arguing.

"Now, was he perfect? No. But I loved him all the same. My only regret was that I didn't meet him sooner. When you get to my age, you think about wasted time a lot."

The tea tray was thrust into Pippa's hand, and a finger pointed the direction she should take. She placed the tray on the table in the living room. Rowena followed shortly after, and tea and cake were quickly served.

"So, what's the problem? What did you do?" Rowena asked with an accusatory tone that did nothing to help settle Pippa's fears.

"I...went home. I was staying there, and then she suggested I might want some time alone. And I said yes. And I went home."

"Did you want time alone?" Rowena asked.

"No."

"Then why did you say yes?"

"I don't know." Pippa stabbed at a slice of cake. "I think I thought she wanted me to leave. So I did."

Pippa chewed on a piece of cake and thought about the conversation. It had been like a runaway train. One moment Sarah was suggesting Pippa might want some space, and the next Pippa was agreeing. It had been to save face. She'd been enjoying herself in the little bubble they had created at Celfare and the whole conversation had come out of the blue.

"Why don't you just ask her?"

"I..."

"You'll not know until you ask her."

Pippa knew that, but that didn't mean she had to like it.

"Off you pop."

Pippa swallowed another piece of cake and looked up to see of Rowena was serious.

"Go on. Time waits for no one."

"You're kicking me out?" Pippa chuckled.

"You've been skulking around my garden like someone who lost a ten-pound note and found a penny. You're depressed. Do you know why you're depressed?"

"Because I told Sa—"

"No. Why are you depressed?"

Pippa frowned. "We said that we'd—"

"Nope. That's not it. Why?" Rowena stared at her.

Pippa opened and closed her mouth a few times as she tried to think of another way to explain the situation.

"Good heavens, are you thick?" Rowena shook her head. "You're in love with her."

Pippa blinked. "I...No. It's too soon. I—"

"Love doesn't wear a watch, Pippa. It's your heart that falls in love. If it's decided, then it's decided. And I can tell on your face that you're in love with this woman. Now, go and fix it." Rowena flicked her wrist. She picked up the television remote.

Pippa stood and walked through the kitchen. She felt numb with shock.

Love. Was that what she was feeling? Had it been so long that she'd not been able to identify it?

She entered the garden, got her phone out of her pocket, and dialled Sarah before her nerve left her.

"Hey!" Sarah said, seemingly happy to hear from her.

"Hi." Pippa swallowed. "Um. Can I come over?"

"Of course. Now?"

"I...didn't want to leave," Pippa said. "I mean, if you want space, then that's fine. But I don't. But if you want me to go—"

"What? No. Of course not. I'm giving you space. You've been a hermit for years. I thought you might be sick of all my noise and mess."

"I love your noise and mess." Pippa picked up a box with her free hand and started to load up her van.

"Did you think I wanted you to leave?" Sarah asked.

Pippa hesitated a moment. She leaned against the side of the van. "Yes."

"Oh, sweetheart," Sarah whispered. "I just wanted you to know that you didn't have to stay if you wanted some time alone. I was trying to consider your feelings in all this. This has been a lot."

"I don't want to be alone any more," Pippa whispered, suddenly feeling very small.

"Then don't be. Forget I said anything about letting you have space. I want you here. I was just trying to give you what you might need. Come over. I'll put the kettle on."

"Okay. I'll be there in ten minutes." Pippa hung up the call and realised her hand was shaking. She quickly packed away her things and started the short drive back to Hillcrest Cottage.

Falling in love with Kim had been instant. The moment Pippa had seen Kim, she'd known that she'd wanted to be with her. It was only now that Pippa realised that a lightning strike of infatuation was unlikely to ever happen again. She'd been younger, a different person in many ways. She'd now experienced loss, and that changed a person. Falling in love in an instantaneous head over heels explosion of emotion wasn't going to happen to her again.

But that didn't mean that her feelings for Sarah were any less real. She had previously wondered if she was incapable of loving someone again. It was becoming clear that she absolutely was capable of love. Just maybe a different kind of love.

Infatuation was unlikely to come to her, but that didn't mean the depth of her feelings was any less real. From Sarah's cheeky little giggle, to the way strands of her hair would fall in front of her face as she concentrated on her work, Pippa could see it all. Every little action was permanently recorded in her mind's eye.

Pippa understood entirely why Sarah had given her the option of some space. Because, if she was honest with herself, Pippa had spent the last few days wedged between being blissfully happy and worrying that she was about to lose everything all over again.

For the first time in many years, being happy and running the risk of losing that happiness felt like the better option than being alone. And with that realisation, it felt as if a weight had been lifted from her shoulders. She had always known that Kim would have wanted her to find someone and live a happy life. Pippa wondered if she was on the brink of that now.

If only she would allow herself to fall in love. To reclaim the pieces of her broken heart, pull them back together, and offer them to Sarah.

❖

Sarah saw Pippa's van pull up outside the cottage. She'd been a little nervous since the phone call just a few moments ago. Pippa had sounded so lost and alone. Sarah had never meant to send her away, just give her space. But suddenly the conversation had gotten out of control and the offer of time away had taken on a different tone. Sarah didn't know how she had managed to allow being respectful of Pippa's feelings to turn into something quite different.

When Pippa had agreed to go back home, Sarah had felt cold. But she tried her best to sound chipper and okay with the plan. After all, if Pippa needed space, then Sarah had to be willing to give it.

The front door flew open, and Pippa rushed inside. Sarah was swept into a hug before she knew what was happening.

"I missed you," Pippa said into Sarah's hair.

It had only been a day, but Sarah felt the same. She wrapped her arms around Pippa and held on tight.

"I need to tell you something," Pippa said.

Suddenly, the hug ended. Pippa took a step back and regarded Sarah with a concerned look. She chewed her lip and worried her hands together. Sarah's heartbeat faltered.

"I love you," Pippa blurted out.

Sarah smiled.

"I know we don't really know each other," Pippa continued. "Or maybe we do? We have spent so long talking, getting to know one another. I feel like I know you inside out. And I do, I do love you."

"I love you, too," Sarah said without hesitation.

Pippa stared at her in shock for a moment. "You do?"

Sarah reached out to take Pippa's hand in hers. Pippa stared down at their connected hands.

"I do. I think I've loved you for a while. And I think that love is something that grows and grows. It starts as a little feeling, and as it grows you start to become aware of it. And then it fills you and somehow still manages to grow even more."

Sarah could practically see the cogs turning in Pippa's mind. She knew that Pippa worried about the future. Sarah had deliberately avoided the topic, not wanting to get ahead of herself. But now that they were both on the same page, she could say what had been on her mind for a while.

"I have asked Swype if I can stay here and work remotely, and they have agreed. We're going to sink another Billy. We've found a charity who have reviewed our research, and they want to work with us, so they can examine our data from the inside. Which is really exciting. Hopefully that means no more disruption techniques from people like Project Earth."

"You're staying?" Pippa's face lit up.

Sarah held up one hand. "I have to go back for one week every two months to report to head office and have meetings and stuff."

She'd been working on the plan for a couple of days, already knowing that Celfare had started to feel like home for her. The woman in front of her held a place in her heart and was too important to leave behind. She needed to have both. But that didn't mean she wouldn't miss the city.

Pippa's expression turned serious, and she slowly nodded as she took in the information.

"A week in every eight," Pippa said. "That sounds reasonable."

"I know you don't want to go back to the mainland. And while I miss my twenty-four-hour delivery and all the convenience that comes with living in the city, I would trade it all for you." Sarah had been wanting to say those words for a while but hadn't wanted to scare Pippa away.

"Maybe," Pippa mused, "I could come with you now and then."

Sarah's heart swelled with joy. Pippa was meeting her halfway.

"I'd like that." Sarah pulled Pippa closer and pressed a kiss to her lips.

"Maybe a trip to Bournemouth?" Pippa suggested. "Lawrence would love to meet you."

Sarah knew that an invitation to meet Lawrence was not dissimilar to an invite to meet the family, and she felt warmed by the offer.

"Sounds like a good plan," Sarah said.

Pippa was beaming from ear to ear. Something had clearly changed her outlook. Sarah didn't know what it was, but whatever invisible wall Pippa had kept up was finally starting to crumble. Sarah knew that the journey wasn't over yet. There would be a long way to go with peaks and troughs, but she knew that Pippa was worth the effort.

Sarah had come to Celfare with the hope that she would heal the world. And while she hadn't quite managed that, she was satisfied that she was healing one very special woman's heart.

About the Author

Amanda Radley had no desire to be a writer but accidentally turned into an award-winning, best-selling author. Residing in the UK with her wife and pets, she loves to travel. She gave up her marketing career in order to make stuff up for a living instead. She claims the similarities are startling.

Books Available From Bold Strokes Books

A Fox in Shadow by Jane Fletcher. Cassie's mission is to add new territory to the Kavillian empire—murder, betrayal, war, and the clash of cultures ensue. (978-1-63679-142-5)

Embracing the Moon by Jeannie Levig. Just as Gwen and Taylor are exploring the new love they've found, the present and past collide, threatening the future they long to share. (978-1-63555-462-5)

Forever Comes in Threes by D. Jackson Leigh. Efficiency expert Perry Chandler's ordered life is upended when she inherits three busy terriers, and the woman she's referred to for help turns out to be her bitter podcast rival, the very sexy Dr. Ming Lee. (978-1-63679-169-2)

Heckin' Lewd: Trans and Nonbinary Erotica, edited by Mx. Nillin Lore. If you want smutty, fearless, gender diverse erotica written by affirming own-voices folks who get it, then this is the book you've been looking for! (978-1-63679-240-8)

Missed Conception by Joy Argento. Maggie Walsh wants a relationship with Cassidy, the daughter she's only just discovered she has due to an in vitro mix-up. Heat kindles between Maggie and Cassidy's mother in a way neither expects. (978-1-63679-146-3)

Private Equity by Elle Spencer. Cassidy Bennett spends an unexpected evening at a lesbian nightclub with her notoriously reserved and demanding boss, Julia. After seeing a different side of Julia, Cassidy can't seem to shake her desire to know more. (978-1-63679-180-7)

Racing the Dawn by Sandra Barrett. After narrowly escaping a house fire, vampire Jade Murphy is unexpectedly intrigued by gorgeous firefighter Beth Jenssen, and her undead existence might just be perking up a bit. (978-1-63679-271-2)

Reclaiming Love by Amanda Radley. Sarah's tiny white lie means somehow convincing Pippa to pretend to be her girlfriend. Only the more time they spend faking it, the more real it feels. (978-1-63679-144-9)

Sol Cycle by Kimberly Cooper Griffin. An encounter in a park brings Ang and Krista together, but when Ang's attempts to help Krista go spectacularly wrong, their passion for each other might not be enough. (978-1-63679-137-1)

Trial and Error by Carsen Taite. Attorney Franco Rossi and Judge Nina Aguilar's reunion is fraught with courtroom conflict, undeniable chemistry, and danger. (978-1-63555-863-0)

A Long Way to Fall by Elle Spencer. A ski lodge, two strong-willed women, and a family feud that brings them together, but will it also tear them apart? (978-1-63679-005-3)

Forever by Kris Bryant. When Savannah Edwards is invited to be the next bachelorette on the dating show *When Sparks Fly*, she'll show the world that finding true love on television can happen. (978-1-63679-029-9)

Ice on Wheels by Aurora Rey. All's fair in love and roller derby. That's Riley Fauchet's motto, until a new job lands her at the same company—and on the same team—as her rival Brooke Landry, the frosty jammer for the Big Easy Bruisers. (978-1-63679-179-1)

Perfect Rivalry by Radclyffe. Two women set out to win the same career-making goal, but it's love that may turn out to be the final prize. (978-1-63679-216-3)

Something to Talk About by Ronica Black. Can quiet ranch owner Corey Durand give up her peaceful life and allow her feisty new neighbor into her heart? Or will past loss, present suitors, and town gossip ruin a long-awaited chance at love? (978-1-63679-114-2)

With a Minor in Murder by Karis Walsh. In the world of academia, police officer Clare Sawyer and professor Libby Hart team up to solve a murder. (978-1-63679-186-9)

Writer's Block by Ali Vali. Wyatt and Hayley might be made for each other if only they can get through nosy neighbors, the historic society, at-odds future plans, and all the secrets hidden in Wyatt's walls. (978-1-63679-021-3)